Hymn of Life

JENNIFER WILLCOCK

Hymn of Life

Copyright ©2025 by Jennifer Willcock

Author photos by Kendra Foerster of Portraits by Kendra (portraitsbykendra.ca)

Cover Design by Yummy Book Covers

All rights reserved.

No portion of this book may be reproduced in any form without written permission from the publisher or author, except as permitted by U.S. copyright law.

Print ISBN: 978-1-7386703-6-9

ebook ISBN: 978-1-7386703-7-6

To all the Pastors' Wives who have felt invisible and unloved. You are seen. You are loved.

Contents

Prologue		IX
1.	Chapter One	1
2.	Chapter Two	13
3.	Chapter Three	17
4.	Chapter Four	25
5.	Chapter Five	34
6.	Chapter Six	43
7.	Chapter Seven	54
8.	Chapter Eight	61
9.	Chapter Nine	67
10.	Chapter Ten	77
11.	Chapter Eleven	85
12.	Chapter Twelve	90
13.	Chapter Thirteen	98
14.	Chapter Fourteen	107
15.	Chapter Fifteen	113

16.	Chapter Sixteen	127
17.	Chapter Seventeen	133
18.	Chapter Eighteen	136
19.	Chapter Nineteen	145
20.	Chapter Twenty	151
21.	Chapter Twenty-One	159
22.	Chapter Twenty-Two	166
23.	Chapter Twenty-Three	173
24.	Chapter Twenty-Four	179
25.	Chapter Twenty-Five	184
26.	Chapter Twenty-Six	189
27.	Chapter Twenty-Seven	195
28.	Chapter Twenty-Eight	203
29.	Chapter Twenty-Nine	210
30.	Chapter Thirty	212
31.	Chapter Thirty-One	222
32.	Chapter Thirty-Two	227
33.	Chapter Thirty-Three	230
34.	Chapter Thirty-Four	233
35.	Chapter Thirty-Five	239
36.	Chapter Thirty-Six	245

37.	Chapter Thirty-Seven	260
38.	Chapter Thirty-Eight	265
39.	Chapter Thirty-Nine	268
40.	Chapter Forty	274
41.	Chapter Forty-One	277
42.	Chapter Forty-Two	281
43.	Chapter Forty-Three	286
44.	Chapter Forty-Four	290
45.	Chapter Forty-Five	295
Acknowledgements		302
About the Author		304
Also By Jennifer		306

Prologue

Toronto, Canada

THE SCREAMS OF THE girls in the audience were deafening as the band took the stage. Lauren Cooper covered her ears, but it did little to block out the roar. Lights flashed and smoke from liquid nitrogen created a screen across the front of the stage. As it faded, five silhouettes appeared, silent, as the fans went crazy for the hottest Christian boy band, The Light.

"Oooh, there's Tye!" Val Johnson shouted in Lauren's ear. Even at that, Lauren had to lean closer to hear her friend. Squinting at the stage, she could just make out the drummer behind his drum kit. Val was crazy about the guy. Lauren nodded, giving her best friend a thumbs-up.

"How are you not freaking out right now? This is *The Light*!" Val's eyes widened to the size of dessert plates.

"If it were Weezer or Green Day, I'd be freaking," Lauren admitted. She'd only bought a ticket because Val was insistent Lauren come with her. Christian bands weren't really her thing. Although this didn't seem like a Christian concert, not with all the hysteria. Girls were actually crying. How pathetic.

The frontman, Aaron Miles Scott, strummed his guitar a couple of times before he began to sing acapella, and like magic, the females in the audience stopped their antics, transfixed by the guy's voice. It was rich and smooth, like fancy hot chocolate. Despite herself, Lauren got lost in his voice and the thrill of hearing live music. For the next two hours, she sang and danced with her friend, forgetting she'd come under protest.

After the final encore (there were three!) the two girls made their way to the exit. A couple of teen boys raced by, knocking into Lauren. Stumbling, she grabbed at anything to steady herself but grasped only air when two large hands landed on her biceps, keeping her from knocking out her two front teeth on the cement.

"Whoa. You, okay?" Tall, dark, and handsome eyed her.

She gasped. "Yeah..." Lauren found her footing as well as her tongue. "I'm good. Thanks to you." She smiled.

The guy grinned, showing off his dimples and perfectly straight teeth. The room spun. Was this how it felt to swoon? The guy had the looks of a Calvin Klein model. He stuck his hand out. "I'm Solomon Grace, but my friends call me Sol."

Lauren slid her hand into his warm one. "Lauren Cooper. Thanks for saving me from eating the cement." Her smile matched his as his touch sent tingles zinging up her arm.

"That's what I'm here for." He winked, which normally she would have found cheesy, but this guy could say or do anything and make it look sexy.

Lauren forgot about the concert, the music, and everything else except the guy in front of her.

Chapter One

Ten Years Later – Toronto

*P*LEASE BE OVER SOON.

The mantra cycled through Lauren Grace's thoughts as the sun streamed through the stained-glass windows, spraying the carpet with flecks of bright colour. Resisting the urge to blow out a huff of air, Lauren shifted her weight slightly, hoping her serene expression hid the battle waging within her. Her stomach growled, and she pressed her arms into her traitorous belly. The mint container in her bag was empty since she'd eaten the last candy twenty minutes earlier, and she didn't dare root around in the hopes of finding another one.

Lauren flicked her gaze to her husband, Sol, standing at the pulpit. His handsome face was flushed, and he gestured with his hands. Sneaking a glance at her Fitbit, she calculated how long he'd been speaking. She twisted her wedding ring around her finger until it pinched her skin. After five more minutes, Lauren crossed her legs. Uncrossed them. She locked eyes with Sol. She forced her lips up in the smile she'd had eight years as a pastor's wife to perfect. His attention moved beyond her, and her shoulders eased.

Pastor's Wife Rule Number One: Never Fidget.

She'd learned that lesson the hard way after she'd been restless during one of his sermons early on in their marriage and earned his ire.

Finally, Sol began his closing illustration. When the final prayer was prayed, Lauren popped up from the pew and beelined for the door of the sanctuary. Several people waved to her as she passed them. She smiled but didn't stop to chat. Her head throbbed, and she wanted to get home. Mrs. Krauss, a kind, elderly woman, stumbled as she exited the pew. Lauren reached out, grabbing the frail lady's elbow.

The woman smiled. "Thank you, dear. I'm a little unsteady this morning."

"My pleasure. Do you need further help?"

"No, no. My husband is just over there. I'll wait for him." The woman eased herself back into the pew. "You run on."

"Have a good day, Mrs. Krauss." Lauren turned to head out the door, but several people pushed by her. She glanced to the front of the sanctuary. Sol caught her eye, motioning her to come to him. Averting her gaze, Lauren squeezed through the crowd, walking as quickly as she could in her four-inch heels, to Sol's office.

A buzzing sound caught her attention, and she tugged her vibrating phone from her purse. Her sister's smiling face filled the screen.

"Lily!"

"Hey, baby sister, how's life in the Holy Land?"

Lauren snorted at her sister's nickname for her life. "Fine. Aren't you on a plane to Calgary right now?" Lily often travelled for work.

"I'm on my way to the airport. Are you sure you can't come with?"

Lauren gripped her phone tighter. After their parents were killed in a car crash three years earlier, Lily was the only family Lauren had, and she hated saying no. She wanted to go with her sister, but that would cause more trouble with Solomon.

"I can't, Lil. I'm sorry. It won't work. Besides you'll be too busy with work to have time to sightsee. Isn't that always your complaint?"

"Maybe I'd find time if you came with me."

Sol entered his office. The door clicked as he shut it.

"I gotta run. Church just got out. Safe travels." She hit the end button.

"Didn't you see me waving you over?" Sol's eyes narrowed.

"What?" Lauren played dumb.

"I wanted you to meet a new couple." His tone was low.

Lauren dropped onto the sofa in the spacious office, easing her feet out of the torture devices, and rubbed her toes. A sigh escaped her lips. So. Much. Better.

Sol shrugged out of his suit jacket and tugged at the knot of his coordinating tie. It wasn't one Lauren had seen before.

"When did you buy that tie?"

Sol flipped it up and studied it before tugging on the knot. Lauren noticed the red flush on his neck. Weird.

Sol flung the tie over the back of an overstuffed grey armchair. "It would have been nice for you to meet them."

Lauren rubbed her temples. "I'll meet them next week."

Sol grabbed a water bottle from the mini fridge and uncapped it. "I think this morning rated an eight. The worship team could have been tighter." He drank down the bottle in one go.

In Lauren's opinion, the worship team had been incredible. Perhaps the problem was the long sermon, although she'd keep that thought to herself. It wasn't worth the argument that was sure to follow.

Pastor's Wife Rule Number Two: Don't criticize the sermon.

Lauren stood, hoping Sol would take the cue that it was time to go home.

"Timothy was off key." Sol tossed the plastic into the recycle bin. "His head's so big it's a wonder it hasn't popped off. He doesn't listen to a word I say."

Lauren breathed out a silent sigh. "Timothy doesn't have an ego nor was he out of tune. He has a fantastic voice." She eyed her husband, who was picking up his files and Bible. "Jealousy doesn't become you." She couldn't resist the dig.

Sol dropped his armload onto the desk with a thud. Lauren jumped.

"He's faking." Sol grabbed the keys off his mahogany desk, scraping them against the wood.

She stood, the shoes hanging like weights from her hands. "He's a good kid. Leave him alone."

"You attracted to him? He's a little young for you." He sneered.

The shoes thudded on the thick carpet. "Don't be ridiculous." She wasn't even thirty yet. Nor was she romantically inclined toward the young music pastor. She bent and grabbed her shoes before heading out of the office.

"You can't leave with bare feet. Put your shoes on."

She shoved them at his chest, as she passed by. "You wear them."

Pastor's Wife Rule Number Three: Appearances are everything.

Sol grasped her arm and held out the shoes. She locked eyes with him before grabbing the offending things and shoved her feet into them. On the way to their car, they walked down the long hall, smiling at other staff and church members. Lauren hugged her bag close to her chest.

She settled into the passenger seat as Sol turned the key in the ignition. When he didn't back out of his space, she faced him. "What?"

"You like Timothy." He stared out the windshield and waved at one of the board members walking by. It drove Lauren crazy when he pretended things were all rosy.

"He's a good worship leader. That's it." She turned the radio on, hoping to diffuse the tense moment.

He leaned closer and cupped her chin. His face was only inches from hers. In another reality, this would be foreplay to a kiss. Sadly, it wasn't that kind of intimacy.

"If I catch you anywhere near him..." Each puff of air hit her face like a slap.

Sweat trickled down her arms. He'd fire Timothy without a thought because he imagined something existed between her and the young man. She blinked her burning eyes, refusing to let him see her cry. She yanked her face away from him.

"Let's go home. Do you want people to talk?"

Sol glanced out at the emptying lot, smiling at a young family who were staring at them. He backed out and headed out of the church's parking lot.

Lauren bit her lip. Cars passed on her side of the car. She hated fighting.

"I'm sorry. I was out of line."

He didn't sound sorry. Lauren forced her mouth into a smile. "It's fine." Maybe he'd put his words into action this time. A girl could hope.

The DJ's voice from the radio filled the car. "And now a hit from a few years ago by The Light. We all wish they hadn't broken up, don't we?"

When the dream fades
And the emptiness calls,
I will abide with you
Forever and always.

Lauren ground her teeth. Ugh. "I hate this song." She flicked the knob. The lyrics made her feel things, and she didn't have the capacity to deal with feelings. If only turning a knob could solve all her problems.

A screech of tires jolted Lauren's attention to the driver's window, which exploded as the grille of a pickup truck smashed into it.

Lauren screamed before the world flipped over and over and black descended.

One Week Later

Lauren shivered in the cold air conditioning of the church's multipurpose room. Rain pelted the roof, the sound soothing her. How did one say goodbye to one's husband? Surely a eulogy and several hymns weren't enough to bring closure to a decade-long relationship. One fraught with many conflicting feelings that didn't dissolve upon the death of the other person.

"You need to eat." Lily set a plate of food in front of Lauren. "You may not have been seriously injured in the accident, but you need to take care of yourself. Your body was traumatized too."

Lauren put up her hand, forcing the plate away. "No, Lily. I'm fine. Please stop fussing over me." Lily had been there for her the past week, flying home from the west as soon as Lauren was able to call her.

The aroma of egg salad wafted under her nose, and she held her breath. Her stomach was pitching like she was on a catamaran. When was it socially acceptable for her to leave her husband's funeral reception? She snuck a glance at Solomon's parents, brother, and the rest of his family. They had briefly spoken before the service and the previous night at the visitation. Lauren had never been close to them. She'd always had the feeling she didn't measure up to their expectations for their golden son.

Her temple throbbed. She had walked away from the car accident with minor cuts and bruises. Sol had died at the scene. The image of his broken body and the seatbelt keeping him hanging upside down haunted her. How many times had she wished she'd never awakened? Instead, she'd hung there beside her dead spouse, the seatbelt firmly keeping her captive in her own private hell. She blinked the memory away. Shuddered as she pulled the sweater tighter around her frame.

Val Johnson, her best friend, hurried over to their table. "Here's a cup of hot tea. My grandmother always said a cuppa did wonders." Val held out an ornate teacup to Lauren. "Not sure that holds at a funeral, but the warmth might be good."

"Thank you for coming. You didn't have to drive all the way from Ottawa." The city was a four-hour drive from Toronto, and Val ran a very busy hair salon. Lauren was grateful her best friend was there. The warmth of the tea took the cold edge off her fingers.

"I'm not sure what you're going to do next. So, I'm just going to put this out here." Val pulled apart a tuna sandwich. "Come stay with me in Ottawa. I've got room, or rather, a pull-out couch. It could give you a fresh start or space to figure out...stuff."

Lauren glanced around the large room filled with congregation members and big wigs in the church world. All the conversations over the last week made her dizzy. However, foremost on her mind was the question: *What am I going to do?*

At Lauren's hesitation, Val grabbed her hand. "You don't have to decide now. It's a standing invitation."

Lauren squeezed her friend's hand. "I appreciate it, Val. I'm not sure what the next five minutes are going to bring, but I'll keep it in mind." She stood. "I need to use the restroom. Excuse me." Weaving her way through the crowd, head lowered, Lauren hurried to the washrooms. *I just need a minute.*

Once the metal door of the stall clanked shut behind her, Lauren's breath whooshed out. She leaned her cheek against the metal of the door, relishing its cooling effect.

Her solitude didn't last long, as the door to the restroom opened, voices spilling into the silence.

"What a wonderful service for a great pastor."

"Beautiful. Such a loss. He was a man of the people."

A sniff. "Be nice if his wife was more people-orientated," the first voice responded.

"Now, now, Shirley. Can't have everything."

Lauren peeked through the slits between the door and the stall. Two middle-aged ladies, Shirley Crowe and Mimi Leades, stood at the sinks, re-applying lipstick.

"No, I guess you can't. It makes me wonder..." Shirley smacked her red lips together. The wife of a successful businessman, she'd been one of the women Sol wanted Lauren to befriend at the country club. Lauren had resisted, not wanting to join the gossipy group. Most people thought she had inside info on people in the church, and Lauren figured that's why Shirley had wanted Lauren to join them for their biweekly luncheons. Maybe Lauren was wrong.

"What?" Mimi voice hitched.

Lauren quietly stepped away from the doors to the opposite side of the stall and pressed her spine against the wall.

"Don't repeat this, okay?"

Or maybe Lauren wasn't far off the mark.

Shirley lowered her voice. "I thought I saw Pastor Solomon and Brittany Clarkson at Clyde's Steak House together. My brother and I were there for lunch."

Mimi gasped.

Lauren's head jerked. *What?*

"It could have been nothing or maybe church business."

"Isn't Clyde's rather far away?" Mimi questioned.

"Up Highway 401. About forty minutes. Not sure what kind of church business it could have been, although they seemed awfully cozy. And the way Brittney's been carrying on today, you'd think she was the widow."

Lauren had noticed Brittany had been "overcome." Surely it wasn't because... She covered her mouth, not sure she was going to keep her tea down.

"Brittany's a drama queen. You don't think...?"

"No! Pastor Sol would never do such a thing." Shirley didn't sound like she believed the words coming out of her mouth.

Lauren pressed her fingers tighter over her lips. Sheer willpower kept her from vomiting. No way were these women going to witness that. She wouldn't give them the satisfaction. Lauren sucked in a breath.

With shaking hands, Lauren turned the lock and opened the door. The ladies' eyes widened as she exited the small space. "Good afternoon, ladies. Sol would have loved that you were here." Drawing on every ounce of acting skill she had, Lauren turned on the faucet and washed her hands while the women stood by silently, casting their gazes anywhere except on the widow of their pastor. Only the sound of the running water echoed through the room.

Lauren dried her hands before striding from the bathroom. Bypassing the door to the reception, she marched out the side exit to the parking lot. Clicking her fob, she raced to the blinking lights. Jumping into the driver's seat, she turned the key in the ignition. The radio blared.

I am with you
Always and forever.

"Shut up!" She jammed her hand on the dial, turning off The Light's lyrics before she wheeled out of the parking spot.

The words she'd overhead in the bathroom echoed in her mind as she sat at a red light, her hand shaking on the wheel. The light turned green. It wasn't until a car behind her honked, that Lauren thought to drive through the intersection. A sob caught in her thickening throat. An affair? How could she have been so stupid?

The SUV jolted to a stop in front of the house she and Sol had lived in for the past five years. Running inside, Lauren shot straight to Sol's home office. Flinging aside folders and research notes for his sermons, her fingers landed on his calendar. She flipped it open and scanned each page. Her breath caught. Several meetings were noted with the initials BC. Brittany Clarkson? A weight dropped on her chest as the four walls closed in on her. Lauren threw the calendar across the room. Before she could lay her hands on anything else, her phone buzzed.

> Lily: WHERE ARE YOU?

Lauren ignored the text. She frantically peered around the room. What was she looking for? Sol's Bible sat on a side cabinet. A humourless laugh bubbled out. "Is this your idea of a joke, God? Because it's not funny."

Vision blurry, she held the book in her trembling hands. Silence filled the room. It had been that way for months. *It's not just Sol who has betrayed me.*

Heat rushed through her veins. She strode over to the garbage and held up the Bible. Before she could rethink it, she pitched it into the can. "We're done, too." She walked out of the room, shutting the door firmly behind her. She pulled her phone out of her pocket, thumbing through her contacts.

"Val, is your invitation still open?"

Chapter Two

Seven Months Later – Ottawa, Canada

THE BELL TINKLED OVERHEAD as Lauren strode into Val's hair salon. She was a woman on a mission.

"Lauren." Val's voice boomed over the hair dryers and chatter of the salon. "What are you doing here?" Her best friend walked over to her.

"I was wondering if you had time to cut my hair?"

Lauren ran her hand over the long braid that fell past her shoulder blades. Sol had liked it long. A part of her hadn't wanted to change her style because it connected her to him. That was warped, considering how he'd treated her the previous year or so. Grief was weird that way. As was love. She wasn't sure why, but Lauren still loved Sol. The Sol who had stolen her breath away the first time he'd smiled at her.

"You want it trimmed up? Maybe a few highlights?" Val's questions brought Lauren back to the present.

Lauren inhaled deeply. She could do this. "Cut it off. I need a new me. It's time to move on."

Val lifted Lauren's braid. "You sure, sweetie? I can't put it back if you aren't. I don't want you to have any regrets."

Lauren nodded, her smile wobbly as she wiped away a tear. "No regrets. Do it."

Val pulled her into a hug. "I think you're brave."

Lauren pulled away, afraid she'd lose it right in front of all Val's customers. She sniffled. "No, I'm not. I'm just tired of being mad and sad. It's been seven months since Sol died, and I know we all grieve differently, but I want to move beyond the lies of the past. I want a fresh start." Lauren forced the corners of her lips up, hoping if she appeared confident, she'd feel it.

Her friend loosened Lauren's hair from its tie and undid the braid. Val grinned as she cupped Lauren's face, sizing up angles. "Let the makeover begin."

LAUREN RAN HER HAND through her shoulder-length hair for the hundredth time as she sat in the lawyer's swanky waiting room later that afternoon. Val had cut and thinned it out and then conditioned "the crap out of it," as she so eloquently put it. Whatever she'd done, Lauren was infatuated with it, especially the pink tips which added a fun twist to her style and lifted her spirits. She no longer looked like a pastor's wife. Or the widow of a pastor. Her throat thickened and she cleared it.

"Lauren Grace?"

Lauren glanced at her lawyer's administrative assistant, who stood behind her desk. "Mr. Jones will see you now."

After greeting Teddy Jones, Lauren settled into a large leather chair opposite the man.

"Lauren, I've reviewed Sol's will as well as the other documents from the church. I'm sorry to say you don't have grounds to fight this. Signing the housing agreement with York Community Church when Sol took the position gave away any rights you had to the money from the sale of the house. I'm sorry."

Lauren clenched her fingers around her purse strap. "What you're saying is I have nothing."

The lawyer's poker face didn't budge. "All the proceeds from the house will stay with the church. The little that was left in your account paid the funeral costs." He shut the file in front of him. "Do you have any idea why Pastor Grace stopped the life insurance payments?"

Lauren shook her head. "No, I don't." She didn't understand many of Sol's decisions over the previous year.

He nodded. "I'm sorry I don't have better news."

Lauren thanked the man. Quickly she made her way to the elevator. Jabbing the button, she stood, pushing down the panic that was threatening to overwhelm her. Her phone rang.

"How did it go?" Val's voice was hard to hear amid the noise of the foyer.

"I have nothing." Her voice caught. "Not only did he cheat, he left me with no security. Our whole life was a lie." Finding the texts between him and Brittany on his phone after the hospital gave her his personal belongings still made all the oxygen leave her lungs. The ladies' gossip in the bathroom had been true.

"I'm so sorry. Let me pray for you."

Lauren squared her shoulders. "Don't bother. It's not going to change anything. God has been silent for months."

"He hasn't left you."

"Sure feels like it. Anyhow, this is supposed to be a new beginning, right? I can now put the past behind me for good. I have my job at the community centre. I have a new haircut. I'm all set for a fresh start. Forget the past. That's my new motto."

"You go, girl." Val's voice lacked conviction.

Lauren didn't care because that's exactly what she planned to do—go. She was going to embrace what the world had to offer her with one exception. No, two. No men. And she was done with God.

Chapter Three

Ottawa, Canada

"You're talking crazy." Aaron Miles Scott hung the guitar back on the rack in the music store.

His best friend, Will Patton, picked up an electric guitar and ran his fingers across the strings. The store was empty except for the two of them. "You'd be perfect for the job."

"I do not have time for a full-time job as a worship pastor. I'm going on tour for eight months starting in September. Besides that, I'm not a pastor. I don't have a degree in ministry or music." Aaron counted the reasons on his fingers. He'd known Will since he was a kid, living on the same street in this very neighbourhood.

"How long are you going to hide on your uncle's farm? I mean, the Ottawa Valley is beautiful, but you're taking it too far."

"I'm not hiding. I'm working the land. Once this album is out and the tour is over, I'm retiring from music." Will's words hit close to the truth. However, Aaron wasn't going to admit it. No reporters stalked him while he mucked out stalls. He didn't have to answer questions that he didn't have the answers to—not from the media or his fans. He pulled a banjo from the hook and played a bluegrass melody.

Will leaned against the wall. "You're giving up music, eh?" He glanced around. "Since we got here, you've played at least five instruments."

"Not the same thing. Sure, I can play fine. What matters is that I can't write songs anymore. You could be threatening me with liver and onions, and I still couldn't write a note." Aaron faked a gag.

Will was undeterred. "Don't be ridiculous. Everyone has slumps."

"It's more than a slump. I haven't written anything new in three years, not since before..." Aaron let the sentence trail off.

"You've had a lot going on. Give it time. Music is as much a part of you as the dust you were made from."

"You're a poet now? Maybe *you* should take up songwriting." Aaron shoved his finger into Will's chest.

Will held up his hands in surrender. "I'm a youth pastor. I know and *accept* it because I love teenagers. Although, at times, it's challenging to like them. And other times, I see how rough it is for them." He frowned, but just as quickly, it was gone. He nodded to Aaron. "You're a musician because God created you that way."

"I've been reduced to a cover artist. This new solo album is covers of old hymns and worship songs." Aaron ran a hand through his hair. He hadn't wanted to release it except he'd committed to it, and he didn't go back on his commitments. Besides succumbing to the pressure from his agent, Aaron hadn't wanted to let the musicians down, many of them friends or acquaintances who had been hired to make the recording. Everyone had to eat, and things were lean all over. He didn't want to be that divo rockstar who bailed and let everyone down. He'd already disappointed enough people in his life.

Aaron ran a hand over his mouth. "This living out of a suitcase is getting old." Maybe if he settled down and found a woman to share his life with, he'd be inspired to write again. Retirement? Who was he kidding? The only way it was going to happen was if he couldn't write again. He scrubbed his face. Whatever it took, he'd find his muse again.

"What makes you think I'm a good fit for this job at the church? I bring a lot of baggage, as well as publicity—not all of it positive. I wouldn't think a church would want that."

"At your concerts with The Light, there were times it was more of a worship service than a show. And now that you're solo, the few times I've seen you live, it's the same. Only more intimate. Less performance. Your new album is a worship album. I think you can translate that into a service for a church." Will deadpanned. "Besides Cartwright is so large that you'll be just another face. Pastor Ed speaks all over the globe. We have at least two retired NHL players, one of whom sits on the board of directors. A few MPs. Want me to go on?"

Aaron stared at his chucks, his friend's words bouncing around his brain. "No, you've made your point. I get it that I'm just another Joe Schmoe, which is fine by me. It's just... I don't know what I want. I made a lot of mistakes when I was in the band. I don't want to repeat that. From what I've seen, worship directors can get a little big-headed at these large churches." He rubbed his temples as news headlines of worship leaders and pastors falling from grace scrolled through his mind.

"You're not one of those guys. I believe you've learned from your past. You just told me you don't want that rockstar status."

"It's a slippery slope. Accolades, approval, and fame are like eating potato chips; one is never enough."

"We're accountable to each other, right?"

Aaron nodded.

"You've got me." Will held up a finger. "And Ed, the lead pastor, won't put up with an ego or any other crap. You have a good heart and a good head. You need to trust God to lead you and stop listening to all the lies the enemy wants you to believe."

Aaron glanced around the store. "What kind of guitar are you looking for?" He hoped Will would go with the change of subject because Aaron would need more than a good head and heart if he applied for this job. He'd need a miracle.

Will frowned. "I'll let you off the hook for now, but we aren't done talking about this."

"We're done." Aaron's tone indicated he was finished with the conversation.

For once, Will let it go. "A beginner guitar. The kid has talent, and I hate to see it wasted because he can't afford an instrument. The church is going to help out."

Aaron pointed at his friend. "You mean the Will Patton Fund is helping him out."

Will ran his hand over his jaw. "Whatever."

"You're one of the best youth pastors around. I hope they appreciate you."

"They do. You would know that if you applied for the job and came and worked for Cartwright." Will paused. "This is about more than losing your muse or getting a big head. When are you going to let go of the past? Wade would want you to."

Aaron picked up a guitar, running his hands over its smooth exterior. "This isn't about Wade. I'm just tired. And applying for this job, or any job, isn't an option. I'm going on tour. And the last time I checked, touring and promoting a new album weren't considered running away." He pointed to the other side of the store. "Beginner stuff is over here."

"THE TOUR IS OFF. I'm sorry."

Aaron stared at the man who had been his agent since he'd signed with the boy band at age seventeen. Jeremy Tait had done well having Aaron as a client and vice versa. "What are you talking about?"

"There weren't enough ticket presales."

"The album's only been out for a couple of weeks. What do they expect?"

"You've lost ground being out of the limelight over the last couple of years."

"I took a break and then I was recording the album." And keeping a low profile.

"It's all about the bottom line. The sponsors are jittery, and the churches in Toronto and Vancouver backing out didn't help."

"That had nothing to do with me. Can I help it if a church gets damaged by high winds or has a scandal with the associate pastor? How am I going to promote the new album if there's no tour?"

"I'm working on it. However, I do have an option in the interim."

Aaron leaned forward, resting his elbows on his thighs. Maybe all wasn't lost.

"There's a teen talent competition being held at the Glebe Community Centre. I'm friends with the director there. They need judges." He studied Aaron. "I think you'd be perfect for a judge since you are a local boy who used to hang out there as a kid—before your big break. Besides showcasing your musical talent, it would boost your album sales and help them sell tickets to raise money for the centre. It makes you look good. Promoters and marketers love that stuff."

"You want me to judge a local teen talent show?" Aaron blinked. Sure, he'd been a regular at the community centre growing up, but that didn't mean he wanted to revisit the past.

"Yes. It's a win-win for everyone. There's also the opportunity to gain press coverage. So, I'm asking if you can be a part of that. It's a natural fit." Jeremy sat on the edge of his large glass and wood desk. "Two words: free promotion."

Aaron groaned. "I hate local press. They always have something to prove." A chill ran up his spine. In his experience, the reporters were looking for the next scoop that would help them climb the journalistic ladder. He understood to a point.

"Between your new album and the teen competition, there won't be time for them to focus on anything else." Jeremy's phone buzzed. He silenced it without even glancing at it.

Aaron rubbed his temples. "What exactly do I have to do?" He couldn't believe he was agreeing to this. This wasn't part of the plan he and Jeremy had concocted when he'd agreed to do the album. Aaron was no amateur musician trying to make it big. How bad was it going to look for him to do a local gig? Aaron didn't want to know the answer to that question.

"I'll get the details from Tony, the youth director who is running the show, and get back to you."

"What if I open for a band on tour? Is that a possibility?" Aaron was grasping at straws.

"Maybe. Depends who it is. It also looks like a demotion."

"And this doesn't?" It would look worse if he didn't sell any albums.

"It's for a good cause. People can get behind that. Plus, I'm going to hook you up with a social media wizard. You need to step up your online presence."

"I hate social media."

"And it shows. Audra will contact you. Make sure you connect with her." Jeremy rubbed his clean shaven jaw. "Look, you gotta work with me. I'm doing what I can. Just trust me. Haven't I gotten you through the last decade?"

Jeremy had a point. Aaron never would have had the success he'd had if it weren't for his agent, who had heard him play as a teen and signed him. He was the one who had sent Aaron to the audition for the band, changing both their lives.

"Call me when you have news." He strode out of the office to the elevators. After jabbing the Down arrow, Aaron pulled out his phone and noticed a text from Will with a link to the job posting for the position at Cartwright Church. Thumb hovering, Aaron hesitated only a second before clicking the link. Maybe leading worship at one of the largest churches in the province would help promote his music. And give him time to get his head into the writing game again.

Chapter Four

"Lauren."

Lauren stopped short before the glass doors of the Glebe Community Centre. Turning, she saw Phil, the director and her boss, huffing down the hall and waving. "I need a favour."

She nodded absently, her mind ruminating on the meeting with the lawyer earlier that day.

"Tony has laryngitis, and he was supposed to be on the morning show with Charlie Most on CRYM tomorrow about the teen talent contest. I have a breakfast meeting with the Chambers of Commerce, which I'm presenting at. So, I can't do it. Will you fill in for Tony?"

Lauren blinked, coming out of her daze. "I've never done a radio talk show before."

"You'll be fine. You're working with Tony on this project. So, you know as much as he does. We really need to get the word out." He shoved a paper at her. "These are the talking points Charlie's going to ask about. As for Aaron Miles Scott, we got the okay from his agent to mention we snagged the former boy band member for one of the judges. No other details are to be given."

Lauren frowned, as she took the sheet. "Why do we have to mention him at all? This is about the kids."

"Exactly. If we fundraise enough money, we'll be able to run the programs you and Tony have dreamed about. Aaron Miles Scott will help bring attention to the contest, and hopefully more tickets will be sold." Phil knew what buttons to press.

"For the kids." Lauren muttered.

"You'll be great." Giving her the thumbs-up, Phil hurried back to his office.

Lauren strode down the block to her bus stop, getting there just as the bus pulled up to the curb. It was easier to take transit rather than find parking in the Glebe. Once she was settled in her seat, Lauren read over the questions. She could recite the answers half-awake without caffeine. Phil was right. They needed to raise the money. Charlie Most's morning talk radio show was number one in the region. She could do this. She ran her finger over the judges' names. Aaron Miles Scott—former frontman for the Christian boy band The Light. He'd disappeared for a bit after the band broke up a few years earlier, but had re-appeared recently with a new solo album. Tony knew his agent and had approached him about Aaron being a judge. Apparently, the former lead singer lived in Ottawa and was home for a bit before going on tour.

Lauren's fingers crumpled the paper slightly. She had no desire to rub shoulders with the rich and famous. Sol's celebrity status within the church world had been enough for a lifetime. Lauren suspected all that adoration had led Sol down a path she would have never imagined when they married. Sol had thought himself untouchable.

The bus stopped and more people got on. As Lauren made room for a woman and her stroller, she forced her mind in a different direction. Forget the past. And as far as the celebrity, all she had to do was mention he was a judge. The radio show was all about the kids and the centre. *Raise the money. Run the programs to help the kids.* Not only was she giving these kids a chance, but it was going to help her start afresh too.

THE NEXT MORNING, LAUREN walked up to the receptionist desk of CRYM. "Hello, I'm Lauren Grace. I'm here for an interview with Charlie Most about the teen talent competition."

The young man, whose name tag said Peter, sipped his coffee while glancing at his computer. "Right. Josie, the producer, will be out shortly. Have a seat."

Lauren sat on a faux leather chair, stifling a yawn. Six-thirty in the morning was too early for an interview.

"Hi, Lauren. I'm Josie." A woman about Lauren's age with large green-framed glasses stood in front of her. "Come this way and I'll explain the process." She turned to the young man. "Any sign of Mr. Scott?"

Peter shook his head.

Lauren raised her eyebrow. "I didn't realize Mr. Scott was part of the interview."

"Sorry, my fault. I forgot to call the centre when it got hectic around here. His agent thought it would be good for him to be included in the interview, and your director agreed. Raises the profile of the event with a star like Mr. Scott on board." She hugged her clipboard to her chest. "That's okay, isn't it?"

"Sure, I guess." The guy had a reputation that was a mix of both good and bad press. It wasn't her call though, and Phil and Tony obviously wanted him involved.

Lauren followed Josie into the On Air room. Charlie Most was a young up-and-comer who had taken a sinking morning show and turned it on its head.

Josie introduced Lauren to Charlie. As Lauren glanced around the booth, Josie whispered in Charlie's ear while he glanced at the clock. What was that about?

"Lauren, we'll get you situated and explain what you need to know. Mr. Scott has probably done this a million times. So, he'll be fine."

The next few minutes flew by as Lauren learned about speaking into the mic. Five minutes to air time and the seat beside her remained empty. Before she had a chance to ask Charlie what would happen if the celebrity didn't show, the door opened.

A tall, well-built man strode in, his hand outstretched to Charlie. "Sorry I'm late. I got held up at another interview. My day started at 4:00 AM."

"Good to see you again, Aaron." They shook hands. "This is Lauren. She's representing the community centre and is going to speak about the competition."

Lauren glanced up and was immediately lost in the bluest eyes she'd ever seen. They reminded her of summer days and beaches. Long lashes framed them. Sheesh.

Aaron Miles Scott had matured from the teen heartthrob that Lauren remembered into a handsome man. Women probably threw themselves at him. *You are not one of those fangirls. Or homewreckers.* She pulled her shoulders back and refocused on the notes in front of her as Aaron sat beside her, tugging on his earphones.

"We're on in one minute. I'll try and indicate which one of you I want to answer since we didn't have time to go over it."

Aaron winced. Maybe he wasn't as arrogant as his lateness implied. But she doubted it.

"And we're back. Today I'm interviewing Lauren Grace, from the Glebe Community Centre, and Aaron Miles Scott, who doesn't need any introduction, but I will give one all the same."

Oh brother. Lauren covered her nose to silence her snort. Could the guy gush any more?

Charlie continued, "Lead singer for the Dove award-winning boy band, The Light, who has just launched a solo album. Welcome to both of you. You've got exciting news to share with our viewers. Go ahead, Lauren."

Lauren locked eyes with the host, who gave an encouraging nod. "We certainly do. The Glebe Community Centre is holding a teen talent competition for youth ages 15-19. Much like the American Idol format, there will be auditions followed by three nights of performances. Twenty-five will be chosen from the auditions, then the top ten, ending with the final three. The audience will vote after the first and second nights to see who moves forward. The judges will pick the winner. Those three nights of performances are open to the public. Tickets will go on sale after auditions. All the funds raised go to the community centre to run programs."

"And I hear you have a special judge as well?"

"Yes, we are lucky enough to have Aaron Miles Scott as one of our judges." Lauren forced her features into a smile and injected enthusiasm into her tone. A skill she'd honed.

"Aaron, it's amazing you're willing to give your time." Charlie nodded to Aaron.

"Always love to give back to the community I was raised in. I grew up hanging out at the Glebe Centre. So, this feels like coming full circle." Aaron didn't seem too enthused with that circle if his clenched jaw indicated anything. His very strong jaw that had a nice layer of scruff on it.

She focused on Charlie, who was directing his next question to her. "What is the purpose of this competition, Lauren?"

Right—the interview. *Stay focused*. "Government funding didn't come through for the centre, and with the rising cost of everything, we need to fundraise so we can run our after-school programs. We thought a competition focused on the teens who will directly benefit from the proceeds was a great way to ask for help."

"Where can kids sign up for the auditions?"

"Two places. Online at our website or in-person at the centre. We have a sign-up sheet at the front desk."

"Aaron, will you be performing at the competition? You have a new solo album out."

"We're in the process of working out the details for the competition." Aaron spoke into the mic.

What? This was news to her.

"I would think it would help sell tickets." Charlie motioned to his producer. "Who out there wants to hear Aaron sing? Call or text us." He recited the number.

Lauren clamped her mouth shut as a bunch of lights lit up the board. "What do you think, Lauren? By the looks of the response, people want to hear Aaron."

Lauren clenched her fists. "Absolutely. We'd love," she swallowed, "for Aaron to sing. At the same time, we want to keep the focus on the kids."

Aaron leaned forward slightly. "I wouldn't want it any other way." He raised his brows at Lauren.

"We can't wait to see how this all works out. And, Aaron, we are definitely going to have you back to play from your new album." Charlie asked a few more questions about the contest and then gave them a thumbs up, signalling the interview was over.

Lauren breathed a sigh of relief as she pulled the headphones off and tiptoed out of the sound booth.

"Hey. Lauren, right?"

Lauren halted mid-race to the foyer. "Yes?" She faced the rockstar—if you could call him that. His star had faded over the previous few years.

He smiled, a dazzling display of teeth and charm that didn't extend to his eyes. Lauren wondered how long it had taken him to perfect it.

"Correct me if I'm wrong, but aren't we trying to promote the event and sell tickets?"

"Absolutely. I wasn't aware you'd be here this morning, and my boss told me not to give out details. In fact…" She pointed between them. "Your people told my people that we weren't to speak about you performing." Her tone was snarky even to her own ears.

"Okay, I get that. However, I was sitting right there. I can speak for myself and give details. If me performing helps raise more money, I don't get what your problem is." The fake smile was gone. His blue eyes flashed and his face had a reddish hue.

"I don't want to promise something only to disappoint a lot of fans. Aren't you going on tour? Are you even going to be here for the competition? Besides, this isn't about you, Mr. Rockstar. It's about the kids. You're here only to help. We want the attention solidly on the teens competing—not on you or your album."

A nerved twitched over Aaron's eyebrow. "I'll be here. I'm not trying to steal their thunder."

"Aren't you? Tell me this isn't about free publicity and the press that comes along with judging this contest. A chance to appeal to your fans to buy your album as you help the kids." Lauren finger quoted the last words. Aaron's eyes widened. She ground her teeth so she wouldn't say more. The last thing she needed was to get into trouble with Tony for scaring away the talent. They had been lucky to score Aaron as a judge. And whether she wanted to admit it or not, they needed his profile to sell more tickets. The deficit in funds was going to cripple the centre if they couldn't find the money.

She glanced at her watch. "I need to get to work. I'm sure you have an important photo shoot or interview to get to." She whirled around and strode out of the studio. "Argh." she growled as she stepped into the cool spring air.

After storming down the block to the bus stop, Lauren's temper cooled. Regret for her harsh words made her doubt herself. She'd projected her feelings about Sol onto Aaron. Not every guy was a schmuck. Although the idea he'd use the kids to promote his album made her want to scream. Raindrops fell, hitting her in the eye. She swiped away the moisture. After the competition, she'd never see Aaron Miles Scott again. Which was good because the last thing she needed was another celebrity in her life. Instead, Lauren was going to run into her fresh start, arms open wide, alone.

Chapter Five

At the Glebe Community Centre later that evening, Lauren sat next to Tony at a large table with other volunteers who were helping with the competition. They had exactly a month left to pull this thing together. Val sat on the other side of Lauren. She'd volunteered to do hair and makeup for the kids during the event.

Next to Val sat Marisa, one of the three judges. Active in the local theatre, Marisa brought experience in both stage presence and performance to the competition. She was a single mom. Her ten-year-old son spent two or three afternoons a week at the centre, while Marisa worked. Lauren often saw him hanging with Tony as she left work. Lauren thought Marisa would do a great job.

Next to Marisa sat two empty chairs for the other two judges. Of course, the rockstar was late. It seemed to be a pattern with him.

Will Patton, the emcee for the talent contest, slipped into the third empty seat. Lauren leaned back in her chair, eyeing the guy. Will's dark hair was that messy style that looked good. Lauren couldn't figure out if he styled it that way or just didn't care. She went with the latter since Will seemed pretty easygoing from what she had seen so far. He was the youth pastor at nearby Cartwright

Community Church. Val, who attended there, told her he was married with two adorable kids.

Even so, Lauren hadn't wanted Will or the church involved in the competition. Since Sol had died, Lauren had avoided any contact with religious organizations. However, it was a losing battle, as Tony had insisted. As youth director at the centre, Tony worked closely with Will, and they often did events together.

Will rubbed a hand across his five o'clock shadow. "Sorry I'm late. Carolyn called me. She's flying out to Winnipeg as we speak. Her mother fell. She won't be able to judge."

Lauren sighed. Before anyone could respond to Will's announcement, the door opened and Aaron strode into the room. She glanced at her watch, then at the latecomer.

Their eyes locked. Raising his own watch, Aaron tapped the lit numerals on it. "Seven PM. On the dot," he mouthed. Grinning, he took one of the empty seats.

She rolled her eyes. This guy was a piece of work. In her books, being on time meant arriving at least five minutes early. The room had quieted at Aaron's entrance, but now everyone was speaking at once. Val grabbed Lauren's hand under the table and squeezed.

"It's Aaron Miles Scott," Val gushed in her ear.

"Calm down. He's just a man," Lauren whispered back.

Tony raised his hand and the room quieted. "Thanks for coming everyone. Excuse my voice. I'm getting over laryngitis. I'm excited about this competition. I hope you are too. I think everyone except Aaron knows the others here. If he looks familiar, that's because he was the frontman for the boy band, The Light, which won a Dove award and was nominated for a Grammy. He's just released a solo album. He's also an alumni of the Glebe Centre. It's a coup for us to have him. Thanks, Aaron, for participating in this remarkable event and worthwhile cause."

Will clapped Aaron on the back while the others woo hooed. Lauren crossed her arms over her chest.

"Our immediate attention needs to focus on finding a third judge. Does anyone have any ideas?" Tony grabbed a pen.

Silence. Lauren racked her brain for anyone she knew who might be able to do the job.

Aaron raised his hand, staring at Lauren. No. He wou—

"I nominate, Lauren. On the radio show this morning, it was apparent she knows the ins and outs of the competition, and I also understand she's one of the music teachers here at the centre. To me, it makes perfect sense to have her as a judge."

Val raised her hand like a school child. "I agree. Lauren would be perfect."

Lauren pinched her friend under the table while directing her scowl at the latecomer. "No, that's a terrible idea. People might think I'm prejudiced since potential competitors may be students of mine."

"Everyone will know kids in the competition. Marisa works within the community at the playhouse." Lauren didn't like the look on Tony's face. "I agree with Aaron. You'd be perfect."

"Isn't it all about the kids?" Aaron smirked.

The words she'd thrown at him earlier smacked her right between the eyes. She squeezed the pen between her fingers.

"Please, Lauren." Tony smiled and nodded.

How could she resist those big brown eyes of Tony's? Raise the funds. Run the programs. Programs to invest in these kids, give them opportunities not afforded to them due to economics or their family situation. She could do this. Maybe if she did help out, God would smile down on her and she'd get her own happy ending. Not likely, since he'd remained silent these last months. Still, it wouldn't hurt to help.

"Okay. I'll do it."

Cheers erupted. Aaron's smirk grew as he sat across from her. Unfortunately, it made him sexier rather than obnoxious. That wasn't fair at all. *Ignore his good looks and blue eyes.* That was her plan going forward. The competition would be over in a month, and he'd be gone to wherever rockstars toddled off to when they wanted to re-light their star status.

ARON SLOUCHED IN HIS chair as he waited for the judges' meeting to finish. The three of them had to stay after the general meeting ended so Tony could go over a few things. Aaron drew his phone closer, checking to see if Jeremy had texted. All that stared back at him was a blank screen. The man had been silent since their last meeting. *Guess I'm on my own.*

"Always consider the performer's feelings. I know you guys know this. We want to give constructive criticism." Tony referred to his tablet, where he'd obviously plugged in notes.

Aaron clasped his hands over his stomach. Nothing coming out of Tony's mouth was news to him. He'd been critiqued enough in his career that this was a waste of his time.

"Are we boring you?" Lauren's low growl got his attention. He raised his head, locking eyes with the feisty woman. Her narrowed eyes accentuated her long lashes. Her frowning lips were full and pouty, which probably wasn't the look she was going for. He covered his mouth with his hand to cover his smile.

He'd stirred a hornets' nest by volunteering her. The satisfaction of poking her with the suggestion had been too great to resist. It made perfect sense for her to judge, especially when they were in a bind. What would be nice was if she'd turn down the intensity. The woman was high strung. And now he had to work with her. *Way to go, idiot.*

"Not boring me at all." That wasn't exactly true. However, he wasn't about to give her the satisfaction. "I was remembering all the critiques I've had over the years. Which ones hurt and which ones helped." *Take that.*

"Oh." The intensity dulled. Her face softened, and her cheeks turned pink. She glanced at the table.

Great. Now he felt like an A-class jerk. "I mean...we all know what it's like receiving a critical review. That's all."

Tony's gaze flicked between Aaron and Lauren. "You're right. Let's move on to the last item I wanted to discuss before I lose my voice totally. What would you say to performing a number the night of the finale?"

"Absolutely, Aaron should perform." Marisa smiled at him. "We all want to hear him sing."

"Yes, Aaron is going to perform a solo." Tony hesitated. Aaron sensed a *but* coming.

"But I thought it would be great if all three of you did a number together. And before you say no..." He motioned to Lauren. "Hear me out. It would be inspiring for the kids to see you all perform."

Lauren shook her head. "No, just let Aaron perform. That was part of the deal, wasn't it?" Her tone was flat.

As Aaron opened his mouth to object, Tony interjected, "Lauren, you've got a great voice too. I've heard you with the kids. And Marisa is a wonderful dancer."

Said dancer held up her hand. "I'm not a singer. Seriously, I'm tone deaf. I could do choreography for you two. Plus, I'm working on the number with all the kids."

Tony pursed his lips. "You've got a lot on your plate." He turned to Lauren and Aaron.

"I can sing whatever you want." Aaron forced the words out. The last thing he wanted was to sing with this irritating woman. However, he wasn't going to give her anything else to complain about. He didn't need her going to the press or saying in an interview that Aaron Miles Scott was a diva. Jeremy would have a fit.

Tony steepled his hands in front of his chest. "Please, Lauren. You'll be great." The guy was laying on the charm. Was Lauren so ornery that buttering her up was a condition to get her to do anything or was it something more? If Aaron's instincts were right, he'd bet Tony was interested in the woman.

"If I agree to do it, we keep it simple. We don't have a lot of time to rehearse." She looked like she'd rather eat dirt.

"Awesome. It's going to be amazing. I'll leave you two to work it out. We've only got a month until the competition. So, we have a lot of work to do." He smiled. "Thank you all for giving up your time to do this." He gestured to Lauren. "And especially to Lauren, for filling in the gap. You're the best."

Oh brother. Aaron stood, but he wasn't fast enough.

"Did your agent force you to sign up for this competition?" Lauren stood with her hands on her hips. Aaron grabbed his keys off the table. He wasn't in the mood to deal with her anymore.

"We can find another judge. We wouldn't want to intrude upon your lifestyle." Her mocking tone raised his hackles.

"Hey, wait a minute." Aaron's chest burned. "You don't get to make assumptions about me." His tone was sharp. He inhaled, then exhaled. "You don't know me. I've got a lot on my mind. I'm sorry I zoned out. I do know what I'm doing. I've been critiqued, judged, you name it—more times than I can count. I think I've got this." Why was he trying to prove himself to her? He didn't really want to judge this stupid competition.

"Fine. Make sure you give it 100 percent because those kids deserve your absolute best." She stalked away, leaving Aaron gaping after her. He didn't know what he'd done to earn her ire.

He turned and hurried out of the community centre, his body humming. The woman was insufferable. A real pain in the— Her flashing green eyes came to mind. Green with gold flecks in them. He shoved the thought away, not liking that he'd noticed.

"Aaron."

Aaron pulled up short and glanced around the parking lot. A tall man strode toward him, his hand out.

"I'm Ed Weiss. I'm lead pastor at Cartwright Community Church."

"Hello." Aaron raised an eyebrow. "What can I do for you?"

"Will Patton spoke to me about you. Said you'd be a great person for our director of worship position. He mentioned you might be interested. When I saw you leave the centre a moment ago, I thought I'd introduce myself. I agree with Will. Is there any chance you might want to try something new?"

First Will, now Ed. God wasn't being very subtle. "I did check out the job description," Aaron admitted. It had several appealing perks, such as three weeks of holidays and sabbaticals—time for writing, if he ever got his muse back.

Ed leaned his forearm against the back of Aaron's truck. "Would you have time for a coffee? I could answer any questions."

The man had a quality about him that drew Aaron. He didn't seem like the preachers Aaron had run into on tour with The Light. This guy seemed authentic, not phony like so many in the music industry. "I'd like that. Do you have time now? I know it's getting late." He glanced at his watch, remembering Lauren doing the same when he'd arrived *on time*.

Ed nodded. "It's 8:30 now. Let me just take care of some business with Phil. It will only take a few minutes. How 'bout I meet you in fifteen minutes at the Starbucks on the corner? I think they're open until 10:00."

"Sounds good."

Ed strode into the building. Aaron stared after him. For a reason he couldn't explain, he felt excited. He must be burned out or desperate. Maybe both. His mind wandered as Aaron walked to the coffee shop. He'd been on the road more than at home over the last decade. Boxes still lined a few walls in his apartment. He'd lived in limbo for a decade. The thought of being in one place permanently eased his anxiety. A stillness and warmth filled his body. At the very least, Aaron would see what the man had to say. He'd deal with the fit his agent would pitch when and if the time came. And it provided a nice distraction from the competition and the most irritating woman he'd ever met.

Chapter Six

ED HAD BEEN PERSUASIVE, while Jeremy's silence had been a death nell. Within two days of submitting his resume and video, Aaron received a call from Ed to set up an interview. Surprising himself, Aaron agreed to it.

Now, here he sat, a week later, his palms sweaty and a smile pasted on his lips for the three people sitting across the table from him in a boardroom at Cartwright Community Church.

"Thank you for joining us today. We enjoyed the video you submitted," the head of the hiring committee, Paul, said. "You've had quite the musical career for a young man. I think most of us listened to The Light's hits over the years. One article called you a prodigy. Another the Boy Wonder. Why come here to Cartwright, especially as you launch a solo album?"

"I'm at a point where I'm re-evaluating my life. The fame and the tours are gruelling. I'm not as young as I used to be," he joked. The others in the room chuckled. Turning thirty in a year wasn't old; yet some days Aaron felt ancient.

"I'm growing weary of living in the spotlight. It can be a lot." *A lot.* That's how he'd describe being famous? It had gotten way out of hand.

"Describe *a lot*." Ed spoke for the first time. Aaron had done his homework on the man after they'd met for coffee. He had the reputation of being a no-nonsense guy who dealt quickly with conflict rather than sweeping it under the rug. Both staff and congregation spoke well of him.

Upon Ed's arrival to the interview, he'd made sure Aaron had water, as well as doing so for the other committee members. Aaron had witnessed many leaders as he'd sung at churches across the country and in the United States. The leadership had ranged from self-serving jerks to true shepherds who wanted only what was best for their flocks. This man was one of the good ones; yet he was no pushover. He'd drawn Aaron in with his vision for the church. With his own doubts about where his future was headed, Aaron hadn't expected to be intrigued with this job.

"The touring keeps me living out of a suitcase. I don't get to see my friends or family much. And it's been that way since I was seventeen." He glanced at all three of the people in front of him, forcing himself not to look down. "In The Light's heyday of popularity, I made poor choices." *Choices I'll regret for the rest of my life.*

Ed nodded. "Would you mind telling us about those choices? It won't go any further than this table."

Aaron cleared his throat. "I was a dumb kid who was on his own for the first time. I experimented with weed and alcohol because I was curious and wanted to be cool. We were compared to the secular boy bands. I wanted to be as popular as them. Later, I partied as a way of dealing with the loneliness. Travelling from city to city, never stopping long enough to visit beyond the venue, was rough." Anything to numb the emptiness. His therapist had helped him understand that.

Ed nodded, encouraging Aaron to continue.

"I did weed for a bit. I didn't like the high it gave me." He'd take the high that came from performing any day over drugs. "I stuck mostly to alcohol later on."

"Are you an alcoholic?"

"No. I was able to stop when I wanted to. I wasn't drinking outside of parties. Not that that's any better."

"Girls?" Ed wrote on a pad of yellow paper.

Aaron blew out a breath. "Publicly our handlers made sure nothing happened. We had chaperones for formal events, especially if it included females. The guys with girlfriends couldn't have them up to their hotel rooms, and they weren't allowed to sleep on our bus. We were discreetly escorted on our dates. At least until we turned twenty-one." At the time, the guys had complained loudly about their "babysitters." Now, Aaron saw the wisdom in it and was grateful. It had saved him a ton of headaches.

Ed studied him. "Stuff happens. And if anything did, we need to know now. Anyone in the public limelight has groupies and a rockstar, even a Christian one, isn't immune."

"We were never alone with a strange girl—for any reason. For me, I had a girlfriend who I was faithful to until we broke up, two years before the band split." It hadn't worked because he never saw her. Her parents had frowned upon her travelling on the bus.

A wise choice by her parents, who had protected not only their daughter but also Aaron, with that decision.

"And she's not going to come out of the woodwork with accusations?"

"No, sir. We're friends and have a good relationship. She's happily married." Aaron was glad for her.

"I'm confused as to how you got weed and alcohol if you had chaperones," asked Paul.

Aaron nodded. "Early on the guys and I figured out how to sneak out without alerting our managers and babysitters. We'd pad our beds to make it look like we were sleeping and then escape out the emergency window. We went to parties after hours, and the people there gave us whatever we wanted. And before you ask, yes, there were women there. I didn't engage with them. I was too busy schmoozing with the higher ups. However, I can't speak for the rest of the band." He clasped his hands in front of him. "Since I've been solo, I've led a quiet life. When I haven't been recording, I've been working on my uncle's farm in the Valley. When I have done small tours, I perform, then go back to the hotel and sleep. I have an accountability partner." The life of a rockstar. Not anymore.

Ed set his pen on his pad of paper. "Thank you for being honest with us, Aaron. I wanted to hear your side. Several of these things made headlines at the time and later, when the band broke up. It couldn't have been easy being so young, living on a tour bus, and having the world handed to you." Ed drummed his fingers on the wooden table. "It's important to me that if you're hired, you will not shy away from your past if asked. Because people are going to ask.

"It's imperative you're honest and approachable. I believe in second chances because I serve a God who specializes in those." He locked eyes with Aaron. "We don't hide from our past here. We learn from it and move on." His words echoed Will's from the other week.

"How have you dealt with your issues?" The woman, Carol, spoke up.

"Counselling has helped. My therapist taught me coping techniques that I use daily. I haven't had a drink since just before the band broke up. If I'm honest, I'd have to say I've struggled more spiritually. I have many questions and few answers. I am sorry if my actions caused others to stumble." Aaron's voice cracked over the last word. He swallowed. It was the perfect opportunity to tell them about his cousin Wade. He opened his mouth only to clamp his lips together, the words stuck in his throat. If he told them, would he lose this opportunity? Suddenly he wanted this job very much.

Ed smiled. "Well, Aaron, you're in good company. I wrestle with God many days, and if you asked anyone else around this table, I think they'd say the same." He gestured to the people around them and they nodded. "None of us are perfect. Anyone have any other questions?"

"I'm concerned that you quit the band." Paul spoke up. He reminded Aaron of a college professor with his wire-rimmed glasses and button-down shirt and tweed jacket. "You've explained why.

How do we know you aren't going to quit if a better offer comes along professionally? What happens if you get overwhelmed? The director of worship position can be intense. There's a lot of responsibility involved as well as expectations and conflict to manage. Music is personal and people take it to heart. If they don't like something, you're going to hear their opinions." The man's lips formed a thin line, a slight furrow to his brows.

The moment to open up about Wade was gone. It didn't matter. Didn't Ed just say he believed in second chances? And hadn't Aaron already bared enough of his soul?

Aaron sipped from his water glass before answering. "I've matured since my band days. Even in the band, we had to deal with issues and complaints from the Christian community. I learned a lot from our PR people. Often the band members were in on discussions." He paused. "With all due respect, quitting doesn't always mean you're running away, sir. Sometimes it's choosing to run to something else."

"What are you running to now?" Paul leaned forward slightly.

"I'm figuring that out."

Carol, who sang on worship, asked, "Tell us what you envision for worship in services, special events, and holidays."

Aaron's shoulders eased a couple of inches. He picked up the pen in front of him and twirled it between his fingers. This he could answer no problem. Aaron smiled as he launched into his ideas for Sunday services and a whole lot more. Maybe his past was just that—in his past.

L AUREN SLOWLY TURNED IN a circle, appraising the gym of the community centre. "What if we brought in a small stage? It will elevate the performers so the audience can see them better."

Tony checked his clipboard. "I agree. And we have it in the budget to rent one."

"Perfect. I think if it's close enough to the wall, we can drape black fabric and make it look nice. Val is great at decor, and I think she would help me. Maybe a balloon arch or another decoration, either in the centre or off to the side." She framed the stage area with her hands, imaging where the decoration would work best.

The door burst open and Phil strode in. "Just the two people I need to speak with."

The man's face was red and his normally neat hair was dishevelled. Lauren side-eyed Tony, who raised his eyebrows.

"The board chair just called and said he saw the advertisement for the auditions. He said he booked the space here at the community centre several months back for that date. It's his mother's 90th birthday. We're gonna have to change the location for the auditions."

"I do the bookings, Phil, and that date was free on the calendar." Lauren was already heading to her office, her heart racing. "When did he make the arrangements?" she called over her shoulder.

Once in her office, Lauren moved her mouse, and the computer screen came to life. Phil and Tony crowded around the small desk. The calendar was empty except for the auditions.

Phil glanced up from his phone. "He says he spoke with Vivian and she confirmed it. He's paid already."

Lauren frowned. "Vivian was the temp who filled in before I was hired, right?" Lauren hit the Notes button. A message popped up from Vivian about the event for the birthday party. "I'm so sorry. I don't know how I missed that." Except no one used the Notes of the calendar ever. "Why wouldn't she have just scheduled it?"

"It doesn't matter. We need a Plan B. We've already publicized the dates. Where can we hold the auditions?" Tony ran his hand through his dark hair.

Will Patton knocked on the doorframe. "Here you are. Why the gloomy faces?"

Tony explained the problem.

"What's the date?" Will scrolled on his phone.

"Three weeks from now," Tony answered.

"The church is free. Do you want the sanctuary, the chapel, or another room?" Will glanced up.

"Are you serious?" Phil stared at Will.

Uh oh. Her boss looked hopeful. Not good. "How much do you charge for rent?" Lauren pictured her decorating budget going down the toilet.

"Pretty sure it won't be much, if anything at all. I can check for you."

"For the auditions, I guess the chapel. We weren't opening them to the public." Lauren didn't like where this was heading.

Tony tapped his chin. "Would it be possible to hold the whole event at Cartwright?"

Will pointed at Tony. "Brilliant. If we held it in the sanctuary, we could sell more tickets and raise more money. We seat 500 people in the sanctuary."

No. No. No. Lauren balled her fingers into a fist. She was not going to set foot in a church. "Can we even sell that many tickets? It will look silly if the place is only half-filled."

"With Aaron Scott performing? Absolutely." Tony and Will nodded.

"Let's do it. Work out the arrangements with the church." Phil waved his hand at Lauren and Tony, before leaving the office. Will was already on the phone.

"We have the space available when you need it. Rental fee is fifty bucks. Sorry, but it's policy to charge a nominal fee. Let me know what you need in terms of lights, soundboard, etc." Will smiled. "This is gonna be great." He headed out.

Tony studied her. "You got awfully quiet. It's not your fault about the double-booking. Don't feel bad."

"It's not that. I, uh, haven't stepped foot in a church in a while." She clicked out of the calendar program.

"Ah. Well, I'm not a big fan of organized religion either. Cartwright is okay. And it's not like it'll be a church service. We're only using their space, youth pastor, and equipment." He laid his hand over his heart. "No sermons will be preached, I promise."

Lauren chuckled. "Well, when you put it that way..." It was her issue. So, she kept the rest of her thoughts to herself and instead, focused on her to-do list. "It's just about time to go home. We'll have to visit the church to get an idea of what we'll need. That's a job for tomorrow."

"Call the church and arrange a walk-through. We need to know what we're working with. It will be so much better than what we have here. Marisa is creating scoresheets for the auditions. That way, there's a standard."

"Good. I'm going to need all the help I can get." Lauren sank into her chair.

"You'll be fabulous. Don't sell yourself short." Tony crossed his arms, his biceps filling out his T-shirt. Obviously, the guy worked out. Lauren glanced up, her gaze catching Tony's, which was more intense than usual. His dark eyes were framed by long, dark lashes. The man was good-looking. He reminded her of Erik Estrada from an old seventies' cop show.

He stepped closer. "You do that a lot, don't give yourself enough credit. I don't think you realize what an amazing person you are. You've made working on this project so much more fun. You have great ideas and you're creative. Plus, you are a wonderful musician."

Lauren rubbed her palms along her thighs. The vibe coming from Tony wasn't one of an appreciative co-worker, not that he'd done anything wrong.

He backed up a step. "You do a lot for all of us here at the centre. Frankly I'm not sure how we functioned without you."

"Thank you, Tony. I appreciate that." She gathered up her bag, hoping Tony would take the hint. "I'll see you tomorrow."

Tony headed down the hall to his office. It had been a long day and she was going home. However, Tony stuck around in her thoughts as she walked to the bus stop. Although he was a nice guy and single, Lauren had no romantic feelings toward him. Nor did she want to get involved in a relationship. *With Aaron Miles Scott?* The thought from left field blindsided her. She didn't need any man to make her happy. Even gorgeous musicians with a swagger. The bus pulled up and she stepped on. Her pep talk didn't work because Aaron hijacked her brain for the ride home. It was crucial for her to exorcise him from her thoughts or else she was in a heap of trouble.

Chapter Seven

THE NEXT DAY, LAUREN stood outside the front doors of Cartwright Community Church. She licked her dry lips. She wanted to murder Tony for bailing on her today. They were to have a tour to see what they needed for the competition. It was a beautiful, sunny day, despite her murderous thoughts.

Her feet refused to listen to her brain and move. *Breathe.* She could do that. That's what normal humans did—inhale and exhale. Clutching her phone to her chest with one hand, she pulled the foyer door open with the other, holding her breath.

Lauren rolled her head from side to side, stretching her neck and loosening her shoulders. When no lightning struck her, she exhaled the breath she'd been holding. She was losing her mind. It was a building, an inanimate object. It didn't hold anything over her. It wasn't the bogey man made of bricks and mortar.

A middle-aged man who was starting to grey at the temples strolled across the foyer toward her. "Hi, I'm Pastor Ed Weiss. Welcome. You must be from the community centre. We're thrilled you'll be holding the competition here. Not sure why we didn't think of it sooner." He held his hand out to Lauren.

"Lauren Grace." She shook his hand, which was warm and firm.

"Nice to meet you, Lauren." He turned to the tall woman who had come up beside him. She was nicely dressed in navy pants and a white ruffled blouse, with her blonde hair pulled into a low bun with a few tendrils framing her face. If the look on Pastor Ed's face didn't give it away, then the light kiss did. This was the pastor's wife.

Lauren wiped her sweaty palms on the back of her pants. Seriously, she needed to calm down. What was going on with her?

"This is my wife, Isobel." Ed smiled at the woman while his hand slid around her waist.

"Lauren, I'm glad to meet you." Isobel's grin was wide and welcoming.

"Nice to meet you." Lauren forced up the corners of her lips, already zeroing in on the office where she was supposed to meet the facilities person. She did not want to talk to this pastoral couple despite the fact they seemed nice.

"Did you say your last name was Grace?" Isobel's warm hand held Lauren's, which was the main reason she still stood with the couple. The warmth of the other woman lessened the blow of the question.

"You're Solomon's widow?" Isobel's blue eyes held hers.

"Yes." Out of the corner of her eye, Lauren saw Ed raise his eyebrows.

"I was sorry to hear about your husband. How are you doing?"

"I'm fine. Thank you." Lauren pasted on the fake pastor's wife smile she had perfected years ago. Only she was out of practice, and it felt more like a grimace.

"I'd love to visit with you sometime. We pastors' wives have to stick together."

"I'm not a pastor's wife anymore," Lauren blurted.

Isobel waved her hand. "It doesn't matter. Once you're initiated, you're a lifer." She winked. "We've earned it."

Lauren opened her mouth to protest that she wasn't a lifer. In fact, she was done with that life and never wanted to go back and revisit it. Except the glint of mischief in the woman's eyes silenced any objection.

"Are you free this week, say Friday night? Why don't you come for dinner?"

Lauren racked her brain for an excuse. Isobel's gaze met hers, understanding crossing her face. The woman backtracked, giving Lauren an out. "Check your calendar and let me know."

Relief washed over Lauren. "Thank you. I'll do that."

Ed inclined his head to the doors. "We should move along since we have an appointment. Our offices are to the right. Gwen, our office and facilities administrator, is going to give you the tour."

"Thank you. It's very generous of you to offer us the building practically for free." Lauren finally found her manners.

"Anything for the kids. What's the point of having a building like this if we can't share it? We believe in being engaged in the community here at Cartwright. Speaking of which, here's our new director of worship and one of the judges, Aaron. I believe you two already know each other."

Lauren stared at her co-judge. "You work here?"

"Aaron was just hired actually." Ed waved at a woman in the office area. "And there's Gwen. She'll be right out." He glanced at his watch. "I'm so sorry to run. It was a pleasure to meet you. We really appreciate all that the community centre does." He nodded at Aaron. "I'll be in touch."

Ed and Isobel walked out the front doors hand in hand. Lauren stared after them, twirling a strand of hair around her finger.

"Here on business?" Aaron stared at her.

She dropped her hand. "Yes, for the competition. We're holding it here." She'd sent him an email; so, he obviously knew that. "You're a pastor?" Lauren's tone was snide. She couldn't help herself. Both a celebrity and a pastor—awesome. This guy's ego was going to take up the whole building.

"I applied for the job and got it. I start next week. I was filling out the paperwork." He eyed her. "Look, I think we got off on the wrong foot." His face held no guile.

"Oh? Because now you're a pastor, you're trying to look good?"

Aaron's eyes narrowed as he crossed his arms over his broad chest. Lauren stared at the wall behind the man.

"What's your problem?"

"I don't have a problem. I just don't like..." She motioned around her. "All this."

"What are you talking about?" He gestured at the space around them.

"Religion. God stuff," she muttered.

Aaron raised his brows. "Does that make me a leper?"

"It makes you untrustworthy." She glared at Aaron.

"Huh? Shouldn't it be the reverse? Shouldn't I be more trustworthy?"

Lauren scoffed. "You *would* think that." *Arrogant man that you are.*

A middle-aged woman approached, halting all conversation.

"You must be Lauren. I'm Gwen. So glad you're here. And Aaron, we'll talk later." She pushed her dark-framed glasses up her nose. "We're all looking forward to working with you."

Gwen faced Lauren. "I'll give you the tour, and you can tell me what you need for the competition." The woman pointed down a hall, and Lauren followed, glad to leave Aaron behind. She glanced over her shoulder. He stood there, watching them. Quickly she faced forward. No point in boosting his ego. She couldn't deny the guy was very good-looking, but she wasn't going near him with a ten-foot pole. Nope. As soon as this competition was over, she never had to see him again. She'd hang on to that thought to get her through the next few weeks. At least he'd made her forget her trepidation at being in a church.

Aaron tossed the takeout bag on the kitchen counter, re-evaluating how hungry he was. His apartment was quiet, and he didn't want to spend any more time lost in thought. After speaking with Lauren, he'd talked to Will for a bit, then grabbed takeout for lunch. He had been looking forward to starting his new job the following week, but Lauren's reaction had stolen his appetite—and excitement. What did it matter what she thought? Although the spark that lit her up when she was mad was rather irresistible, he wondered what would happen if she laughed. He didn't think she did much laughing, not that he'd see that, as he couldn't seem to catch a break with her. *Stop right there.* He needed to stop thinking about Lauren Gra—Wait. Lauren Grace. He tipped his head back. How had he not put two and two together?

She was Solomon Grace's widow. The guy had been the lead pastor of a mega church in Toronto. So, what was her problem with churches? That made no sense, but neither did anything else about the woman.

Aaron unwrapped his chicken pita wrap and took a large bite. He barely registered the creamy garlic sauce and spiced meat. Would her reaction be indicative of the church members and even a few fans? He chewed his food while his mind pondered that unwelcome thought. No, Lauren's reaction was personal.

Her negativity had stirred up his own doubts. Pastor Ed's words came to him *Anyone in the public limelight has groupies and a rockstar, even a Christian one, can't be immune.* Aaron wasn't naïve to the fact that the director of worship at Cartwright could take on a rock and roll image and fanbase. Much like Solomon Grace. Perhaps that was why Lauren didn't want anything to do with Aaron. There were rumours about Pastor Grace, how he treated his church like his personal kingdom. Yikes. No, that wasn't the kind of leader Aaron aspired to be. People came to worship God, not the pastor. Aaron had enough of the idol worship as a member of The Light.

Finished with his lunch, Aaron wandered to his bedroom and picked up a picture of his old band. It was taken at a mega church in Sydney, Australia. Hands held high, eyes closed, guitar hanging across his body, Aaron appeared the epitome of wholesomeness. Josh rocked out on the bass beside him, and Drew was on keys. Only Tye's drumsticks were visible above the kit. The crowd had gone wild, girls' screams drowning out the monitors. Who had they been worshipping? It wasn't hard to figure out the answer. They had come to see the band and their frontman, Aaron Miles Scott. They'd chanted his name, not God's. And he hadn't cared. Instead, he'd lapped up the attention. Turning the picture face-down, Aaron ran his hand through his mussed hair.

Please God, don't let this be about me. Less of me. More of you.

Aaron picked up the other picture on the dresser, a picture of him and his cousin Wade. Aaron wasn't going to repeat the past. He'd promised himself and he'd promised Wade the day they'd laid his cousin in the ground. Aaron had kept himself squeaky clean since, and he'd make sure God got all the glory for the worship at Cartwright.

He picked up the guitar that sat by his bed and strummed it softly. He missed it, the music pouring out of him like breath. His mind, however, remained blank. Not a hint of creativity in sight. He sighed and placed his guitar back on its stand. He hoped the changes he was making would bring back the music.

Chapter Eight

Aaron held the door of the local cable TV station as Lauren slipped by him, out into the parking lot. A large raindrop splashed on her forehead. They raced to his truck and jumped inside. Lauren pulled her hair away from her face.

"It's been raining for two days. The ground is like a soggy sponge," Aaron muttered. He looked as miserable as she felt.

Despite her resolve to stay away from her co-judge, Phil and Tony had other ideas. They had insisted Aaron join her in as many promo events and interviews as he was able.

"Ahh." Lauren watched a bird drink from a nearby puddle. The truck didn't move. "Are you waiting for something? I should get to work."

"Um, do you mind if we take a detour? Jeremy, my agent, suggested I stop in at the sick kids' hospital and bring them a little joy." He chewed his lip as he stared out the front windshield. "I know you're probably busy at work, but I've had a few requests from both staff and patients. It always helps to have another friendly face with me."

"You're my ride unless I want to get soaked," she joked.

"So, you don't mind?" He waited.

"I'm kidding. Of course I don't mind. I'll let Phil know I'll be in later. It won't be a problem." Did Aaron think that badly of her? Not that she could blame him since she'd practically bitten his head off about his job and his motives for judging.

She pulled out her phone and sent a text, releasing a soft sigh. So far, the morning had been awkward between them. Aaron shifted his weight while he waited for her to finish.

Lauren dropped her phone into her tote. "I'm sorry for my negative attitude the other day. I have issues with church."

"I appreciate the apology." He rubbed the scruff on his chin. "Maybe we can call a truce since we have to work together?"

Could she do it? Anything was better than the stilted conversation of that morning. "Sure." She held out her hand. "Truce."

His warm hand shook hers. A tingle ran up her arm. Lauren quickly pulled her hand away.

"Let's go." Aaron pulled out of the lot. "This is one thing I love about my fame."

"What do you mean?"

"Wait and see." He grinned. She smiled back, looking forward to the next couple of hours.

"W<small>E'RE SO GRATEFUL FOR</small> your time."

The nurse blushed as she led Lauren and Aaron down the hallway of the children's hospital. The walls throughout the ward were brightly decorated with murals of fairies, puppies, and trucks.

Aaron walked into the first room, Lauren right behind him. The 'tween boy played checkers with his dad. The look on the boy's face when he noticed Aaron was priceless. Lauren grinned. Aaron walked up to the bed.

"Hi, Lucas. I'm Aaron and this is my friend Lauren."

The boy's smile lit up his face. "I know who you are. I listen to your music all the time." Aaron shook the dad's hand. Lauren nodded to the man as she stepped back and watched Aaron with the boy. They played several games of checkers, and then the boy asked if Aaron would sing something.

Lauren handed him the guitar he'd left at the door to the room.

"What do you want to hear?"

"Your first hit song. I forget the song title." The boy closed his eyes.

"He has some short-term memory issues from the car accident," his dad explained.

"No problem. I know the song." Aaron strummed the guitar. The boy opened his eyes, watching Aaron.

Lauren couldn't keep her eyes off the musician either. She doubted her first instincts about the man, a feeling that didn't go away as they visited room after room. An hour later, the emotional roller coaster of not only visiting sick children but also witnessing joy and laughter on their faces as they sang and chatted with Aaron had Lauren ready to drop in exhaustion.

She stared at the man's back as she followed him to the last visit of the day. He had been anything but an egotistical rockstar. While a few of the nurses had fangirled, he'd gone red in the face. He'd been friendly, taking selfies with them and signing autographs. However, it was his interaction with the kids that left her in awe. He'd treated each child with compassion, kindness, and sensitivity. If they wanted to hear a song, he'd play his guitar and sing for them—not half-heartedly either. Each song was heartfelt and meant just for that one kid. The smiles on the kids' faces were priceless. Once he let a little girl strum his guitar when she'd asked.

If a child appeared too sick or tired, Aaron left his guitar untouched at his feet and visited with them or held their hand. He read a story to a little boy, who had broken both his legs and was restless. None of these things were reflective of a spoiled celebrity.

As they entered the room of a teen girl, Lauren swallowed the lump burgeoning in her throat. The girl lying on her side, listless, glanced up when they entered.

"What?" she rasped as she rolled onto her back. Her sunken eyes widened as she saw Aaron. "You came." Colour flooded her cheeks, which had been a pasty white.

"Hi, Amy. It's so good to meet you. I received your letter. Thanks for that." Aaron introduced Lauren.

She waved, staying off to the side while Aaron chatted with the young girl, asking about what kinds of music she liked and what her favourite hobbies and school subjects were. When she stated music was her best subject, Aaron high-fived her. The difference in the girl from when they first walked in to that point was incredible.

The nurse who was escorting them to each room stood beside Lauren. The young woman said, "This brightens everyone's day. Although most of the kids' families come by, they don't always get other visitors."

"I can't even imagine what the kids and their families are going through." Sniffing, Lauren fumbled for a tissue in her pocket.

"Would you like me to play you a song before I leave?" Aaron asked Amy.

Amy clapped her hands. "Would you? I'd love that. Can you play 'Hero'?"

"Great choice. I wrote that song about a man who saved a family from their burning home where I grew up. His actions reminded me of God's love for us and how he saved us."

The simple notes on the acoustic guitar filled the room. As Aaron's voice blended with the chords, Lauren had goosebumps pop out on her arms. Amy closed her eyes and settled into her pillows. A look of peace crossed the young girl's face. Lauren wiped her nose again before slipping out of the room.

She pressed her fingers into her eyes, trying to stem the flow of tears. Memories of being in the hospital after the accident, combined with the sadness of seeing sick children, overwhelmed her. How did a teen girl look so at peace when she was that sick?

How did Aaron do it? Maybe she had made a few wrong assumptions about the guy. She slid down the wall and cradled her head in her hands. Hadn't Sol fooled her for years? *It makes you untrustworthy.* Her words to Aaron came back to her.

Sol had lied and cheated. He'd been all about appearances. How could she know if this was an act for Aaron? It certainly made him look good. She pressed the palms of her hands into her eyes. Only time would tell, but Lauren couldn't take that kind of risk again. And Aaron would be gone after the competition, promoting his album or onto the next gig. She'd honour their truce while guarding her heart. She would not be a fool again. And that was the only thing Lauren could control.

Chapter Nine

THE TEXT THAT CAME in right after lunch had been cryptic, increasing Lauren's curiosity. She hadn't seen Aaron since the TV interview and hospital visit two days earlier. The memory of that morning spent at the hospital and Aaron with the kids brought a smile to her lips. A small fissure had streaked across her hardened heart. *Danger.* Despite the word blinking bright neon pink in her mind, Lauren couldn't make herself care today.

As she strode into the restaurant, shortly after 5:00 PM, she spotted Aaron and Marisa seated at a table. A small stage was to the left, and the place was surprisingly empty for it being the dinner hour. Lauren hurried over to them.

She read from her phone, "'We're practicing for the show.' Is this a joke? We're in a bar." Lauren gestured to their surroundings.

"Really? I thought we were in a recording studio," Aaron deadpanned before dragging a chair out beside him. "Have a seat. We're doing karaoke to practice and see what we'd like to perform."

Lauren hugged her purse to her body. She stepped back. Aaron stared at her, gestured at the chair. If she sat, then she was committed.

His tone soothing, he said, "We've got to figure out our act. We only have a few weeks to pull it together. It's a tryout. We can see how we sing together and maybe..." He winked. "Maybe have a little fun. Marisa is going to take notes." He pulled the ball cap lower on his forehead.

"Do you really think that hat..." She ducked a little to peer under the cap which made him look cuter than necessary. "Do you think that ball cap and those glasses are going to disguise you?" Blue eyes stared back at her. A zing went through her, and she hastily straightened. She sank down on the wooden chair. Guess she was committing to this. "As soon as you open your mouth, people will recognize you."

"So be it. It's early enough that there may not be many people here." He shoved the song list at her. "Tell me what you like to sing."

Lauren ran her finger over the songs, focusing on the duets. "Islands in the Stream."

"Yeah, no. Pick another."

"Cruisin'."

"Huey Lewis and Gwyneth Paltrow?" Aaron rubbed his chin. "Good choice." He stood and walked to the DJ, who was coordinating the songs.

Lauren turned to Marisa with wide eyes. "Does he really think he can do this anonymously?"

Marisa leaned back in her chair. "Won't hurt to get a little publicity for the competition and for his album should someone recognize him."

Right. It was all about *his* music. Lauren clenched her jaw. How annoying he could cast a spell on her with those eyes while, at the same time, she was irritated about his ulterior motives.

Aaron returned to the table. "Do you want anything to eat?"

Lauren eyed Marisa's wings and suppressed a gag. "No, I'll throw up if I eat anything."

Aaron eyed her. "You're a barfer?"

She swallowed as she held up her hand. Just the word alone could make her gag.

Marisa pulled her food closer to her. "You don't look so hot."

"Let me get you a soda." Aaron strode to the bar, returning quickly with a glass of ginger ale. "Sip this, and if you have an antacid, take it. One of the guys in the band struggled with nerves. That was his go-to cure. The last thing we need is you fainting up there or worse. How are you going to perform at the finale?" His brows knit together.

"Don't get your feathers in a ruffle. I'll be fine." Lauren forced the words out. *Do not faint in front of Aaron Miles Scott.* Her dignity wouldn't allow it. She sipped her ginger ale. After slowly drinking half the glass, she felt better. Or at least like she wouldn't throw up her lunch.

"Next is L and A singing 'Cruisin.'" The host called their song.

Already?

"That's us." Aaron held out his hand to her. Lauren stared at it, not moving. He knelt down and gently placed his hands over hers, which clutched the armrests. "If you don't think you can do this, I can do it myself. But I'd love to sing with you."

Oh. His unexpected kindness wrapped around her, boosting her courage. She blinked, becoming more present. His body heat warmed her legs as he kneeled in front of her. Clearing her throat, she nodded.

His bright smile shot another dose of adrenaline through her. He tugged her up, holding her hand as he led her to the stage. Her legs were weak and she took a fortifying breath. It was just nerves at singing in front of a crowd. That's all it was.

Before she could think about it, Lauren stood next to Aaron, a mic in her hand. The tables near the stage had filled with people. Breath catching in her throat, she made a strangled sound. A gentle squeeze on her fingers brought her back from the brink of panic.

Aaron tugged her so she faced him. "Stay with me." He leaned in close. "Look only at me." It was hard to focus on both those blue eyes and her nerves. She gave into the eyes. The people faded, and it was just her and Aaron in the room.

He sang the first verse, his gaze never leaving her face. Confidence radiated off his body, boosting Lauren's as well. When it was her turn to sing, he moved a half step closer, forming their own intimate cocoon. His presence along with his confidence in her calmed her nerves. Aaron made performing look easy and fun. She wanted to join him.

At first, she sang softly. As her confidence grew, her voice gained volume. Her grin matched his as they belted out the chorus. As he swayed to the music, she mimicked him, having more fun than she'd had in a long time.

Too soon the song ended, and Lauren stared at Aaron, dazed. Heart hammering in her chest, Lauren giggled. A warmth crashed over her as he squeezed her hand, which he'd never let go of since he'd led her from the table. He nodded to the audience which had grown even larger during their song. The people whooped and whistled.

"Your audience is cheering for you. Take a bow," Aaron whispered. He turned her to face them and held her hand high. A victory pump.

Of course it was him the audience loved. She didn't mind as she clumsily curtsied. They hurried off the stage together, Aaron's hand on her lower back. Her whole body tingled. Probably from the buzz of performing.

Marisa mimed a mic drop while Val and Tony stood beside her. Val was cheering and waving her arms. Lauren chuckled at her friend's antics.

Tony clapped loudly, shouting over the noise, "Amazing. I'm so glad Marisa texted us earlier. We got here just in time. I knew you'd be outstanding." He stepped closer to Lauren, giving her elbow a squeeze.

Lauren hadn't even noticed them come in. "Thanks for coming."

Val pulled her in for a hug and whispered, "You and Aaron make beautiful music together."

"Shh." Lauren stole a glance in Aaron's direction. Thankfully, the man was engrossed in conversation with Tony. "We were practicing. That's it."

"Practicing what? The sizzle between the two of you was louder than a whole pan of bacon frying."

Val wasn't wrong. Besides the chemistry, she had felt a connection on a deeper level as they sang. How bananas was that? Obviously, the thrill of performing and her nerves had gotten the best of her.

Lauren shook her head, changing the subject. "Did you come with Tony?"

Val shook her head. "No, we arrived at the same time." Her friend sounded wistful.

If Lauren had to guess, she would bet Val liked Tony. She studied the pair. They would make a striking couple with their good looks.

A group of women approached their table, interrupting Lauren's internal matchmaking. A brunette with hair halfway down her back stepped forward. "Are you Aaron Miles Scott?" Her breathy voice made Lauren want to roll her eyes.

Aaron stopped mid-sentence. "Yes, I am." The thousand-watt smile made its appearance. So different from the one at the hospital.

A collective sigh went through the group of women. "Can we get a picture with you?"

"Sure. Do you want me to take it?" Aaron stepped closer to them.

"I'll do it for you," Tony held out his hand.

The woman dropped the phone into his hand and cozied up next to Aaron. The other two leaned in too close in Lauren's opinion. She cut off that thought.

"If you post it, be sure to tag the Glebe Community Centre and our teen talent competition," Tony said.

The women agreed to do so. Aaron frowned slightly but then seemed to wipe it from his face. He smiled and thanked them as more people came up to him. Surrounded by fans and curious bystanders, Aaron signed autographs and took selfies.

Lauren picked up her soda and chugged it. *Stupid.* She didn't have a connection with Aaron. It was all in her imagination. He was a consummate performer. The carbonated drink burned her stomach. Inhaling deeply, Lauren held her breath then blew it out. She picked up her bag.

"Well, if we're done here, I need to go." She cast one last look at Aaron, who laughed with several women and a couple of men. Guess he'd get the free promo he wanted, after all. This was a good reminder of who Aaron Miles Scott was and the kind of life he led. The version of Aaron who she'd seen at the hospital was an anomaly. Lauren would be wise to remember that. She wasn't about to repeat the mistake she'd made falling for Sol's charm and charisma. No, this was her second chance, and she wasn't about to ruin it.

LAUREN IGNORED THE LITTLE voice questioning her sanity as she tapped the words "The Light" into the search engine on her laptop. Despite the inner voice shouting *danger* in her ear, Lauren was curious to see Aaron in his glory days as the frontman for The Light. She'd only been to one concert with Val, which is where she'd met Sol. Huh. Maybe that was why she felt irritated with Aaron. He was responsible, in a backhanded way, for her meeting Sol. She didn't know how to feel about that. She sighed. She didn't want to think about her late husband. Her finger hit Search.

Images popped up with a long list of articles about the band. They had certainly had their share of press in their heyday. Lauren opened the first photo. The band consisted of Aaron, the lead guitarist, a bass player, the drummer, and the keyboardist. The Light had risen to stardom in the Christian world a decade earlier. The church's answer to the secular boy bands that were "swaying teens away from God," Lauren rolled her eyes at that particular comment, which she'd heard several of the parents at her father's church declare when she was a teen. Perhaps it had more to do with people who talked up God yet failed to model him in their daily lives that made kids leave their faith and church.

She tapped the Images button. The Light morphed before her eyes, playing in concert at the biggest churches and venues in the country and around the world. An arrow indicated a video clip, and she pressed Play before she could stop herself. A younger Aaron Miles Scott with his messy hair, tight T-shirt, and black jeans strutted around the stage. A tattoo peeked out from his shirt sleeve. She zoomed in, but it was too small to decipher. Leaning in, her breath fogged the screen. His sleeve hid most of it. Shoot.

Sweat trickled down the sides of his face as his smooth voice spilled out of her computer speakers. The guy had pipes that could rival any singer out there. His guitar playing wasn't too shabby either. She paused as she listened to the music. Each member of the band was a talented musician.

She finished the video and scrolled through a few more articles. Most praised the band for their talent, while a few later pieces questioned why they broke up at the height of their popularity. The only reason given was that the members wanted to pursue their own projects. As far as she could figure, Aaron hadn't pursued much of a career after that. The only thing he'd released was this new worship album made up of old worship songs and hymns. Nor had there been a tour, although there had been rumours of one. Now, he'd taken a job at a church. None of it made sense.

"What are you looking at?"

Lauren jerked, slamming down the top of the computer. "You scared the daylights out of me."

Val sat on the edge of the couch. "Checking out Aaron?"

Lauren scowled at her friend's smug smile. "No."

"Could have fooled me—and Google."

"I was searching for music."

"Pictures help you listen better?" Val's eyes widened.

Lauren whacked her with a throw pillow. Val cackled.

"It's research. If I know where he's coming from musically, it will help me judge better. I can take a different approach from him."

"You keep telling yourself that." Val leaned down and opened the laptop. She typed in the password, which Lauren regretted giving her previously. "Ah hah." She pointed at the image of The

Light staring back at them. "He was super cute back when he was in the boy band. Now he's just gorgeous."

Lauren snorted. "It goes beyond looks."

"Just stating the facts. And to your point, he seems like a really nice guy. You guys had serious chemistry singing together tonight."

"You've lost your mind." Although the tingle from that chemistry continued to hum through her, Lauren wasn't going to admit it to Val because that would be confessing something was there.

"You deserve happiness. Sol's betrayal isn't on you. You need to open your heart again. The world needs you, Lauren. Stop hiding."

Lauren said nothing. Val squeezed her shoulder before heading to the kitchen.

Lauren stared at the photo of The Light. Val's words hit deep. Maybe she had been hiding. However, her friend was wrong about Aaron. She could not trust him even if he was good-looking and nice.

Been there, done that. She closed the window, removing the pictures of the boy band that had hit super stardom. Maybe Aaron had matured, changed, but it was risky. She didn't need that kind of drama in her life.

Chapter Ten

THE FOLLOWING WEEK, AARON stared at the whiteboard with all the worship team members' names written on it. Since Aaron had only started, Ed had tasked Will to help Aaron put together the worship teams for the summer and fall.

There were at least fifty names on the list. This job was a bigger responsibility than he'd realized. His heart stuttered. Aaron sucked in a breath, releasing it slowly.

Will hesitated at a name. Ryan Walters.

"What's up?" Aaron tapped his marker on the name. His friend was usually laidback, but his lips were puckered and his brow drawn together. Will's expression did nothing to ease the panic swirling in Aaron's chest, threatening to cut off his breath.

"Nothing." Will wrote Worship Leader beside Ryan's name.

Aaron tapped the name again with more force.

Will sighed. "Word to the wise. Ryan's a bit prejudiced against you. He wanted the job and was a shoe-in until you submitted your application."

"Should I be worried?" Aaron set his marker down.

"Just a heads-up. He's a good kid but a little lost at the moment." Will checked his list. If he was trying to convince Aaron, he was doing a terrible job.

"Explain."

"His mom has cancer. Ryan graduated from Wilfred Laurier University with a music degree. He thought he'd get the job and be able to help at home."

"That's terrible about his mom." He'd go easy on the kid.

"Yeah." Will pointed to two more names. "Put these women in his group. Just beware. Ryan can get a little pigheaded when he doesn't get what he wants. I ran into a few issues with him when he was in youth group." Will paused. "I'm sure he's grown up and matured since his teens."

As Aaron wrote the names beside Ryan's on the whiteboard, the door opened and two teen boys entered.

"Hey, Jordan." Will fist-bumped one of the guys, who must have been at least six-foot-two.

Jordan motioned to his friend, who was much scrawnier and a few inches shorter. "This is Mike. Can we talk to you for a minute, Pastor W?"

"Sure." Will directed them across the room, where the three spoke in low voices. Aaron kept adding names to the dates.

After a few minutes, Will and the two guys headed to the door. "Go see Gwen in the office, and she'll help you with the pantry." Although they spoke in low voices, Aaron could hear them, even though he tried hard not to eavesdrop.

The smaller guy muttered something. Will clapped his hand on the kid's shoulder. "Don't give it a second thought. We're here to help you. It's not your fault your dad lost his job."

Jordan fist-bumped Will again. "Thanks, Pastor W."

"Anytime." Will shut the door behind the boys. "Man, it's tough out there." He sighed.

"I couldn't help overhearing when you were at the door. Do you get a lot of requests for help from the youth?" It hadn't really occurred to Aaron that kids would be asking for food for their families.

"Occasionally, especially if they aren't associated with the church but have friends who are. They're embarrassed to come, but hunger and worry for their families bring them here. I try not to make it a big deal. It's hard though. You wonder what's going on in their homes."

"That's a lot for kids to carry."

"You know it. I can't imagine Matty or Ella ever having to do that. It makes me shudder." Aaron didn't even want to think of Will's kids suffering in any way.

The memory of the snack tables on tour popped into his mind. They had been laden with every sort of food you could want: fruit, sweets, junk food. All for the band and crew. Half of it wasn't eaten. He'd never bothered to wonder what happened to the leftovers. Did they all get thrown out? What a waste. The kid today, Mike, was too thin, and he seemed too burdened for a teenager. What else could they do to help him and others?

Aaron tapped the board. "What if we asked people to bring a nonperishable food item for the pantry when they come to the competition? Have big boxes at the entrances for people to leave their donation?"

"That's a great idea." Will pointed at Aaron. "Now you're thinking like a pastor."

"Whatever." Aaron turned back to the board, grinning. It felt good to help others and not just think about how it would help album sales or his image. Perhaps this could be the start of giving back to those who needed help.

Later that evening, the buzz of chatter faded as Aaron entered the worship rehearsal space in the church. Forty-five people who comprised the four or five worship bands and sound crews sat on couches and chairs scattered around the room. Most tried to pretend they weren't staring but were failing miserably. Pulling up a plastic chair, he laid his jacket on it before addressing the small group.

"Hey, everyone. For those who don't know me, I'm Aaron, the new director of worship. I'll address the elephant in the room. Yes, I was the frontman for the band The Light." A few people smiled while others scrolled on their phones. Probably looking him up.

One kid who didn't look much older than twelve held up his screen. "You're famous."

"In the world's eyes, we had success. However, the only one who should be famous in this room is God."

"What are you doing here?" The challenge came from a twenty-something guy in the corner. His scowl wasn't welcoming. Was this Ryan?

"It's a new chapter for the church and me." He'd leave it at that. "I thought it would be good to get together and let you know what you can expect from me. I also want to hear what your expectations are. I thought we'd start with a short study on serving before we discuss schedules for Christmas. For those of you not counting, it's only three months away. So, I've hit the pavement running."

Most of the group had their eyes on him, not their phones. He hadn't lost them yet. The weight on his chest eased. Maybe this wouldn't be bad except for the guy in the corner, who glared at him. Aaron's shoulders tensed. Yup, it had to be Ryan, or else Aaron was in bigger trouble than he'd imagined.

"Great. Let's look up Mark 9." He picked a middle-aged woman to read.

"Whoever wants to be first must take last place and be the servant of everyone else." She finished the passage.

"Thank you. These are hard verses to listen to, aren't they? This isn't what the world is telling us. Me, how I feel, what's right for me, my rights—that's what they say matters, isn't it?" Aaron glanced around the group. Everyone was focused on their Bible or him except the young man in the corner. He stared at his phone, his thumbs moving quickly over the screen. Aaron returned his attention to the group.

"Shouldn't we look out for ourselves? Because if we don't, we get lost in the shuffle. Or we'll get left out," Katelyn, a young girl who played guitar, asked.

"I understand that it's a risk. However, I don't think that's Jesus's main concern—our happiness or that we may have a fear of missing out. In fact, I'd say you probably will miss out if your main goal in life is to follow Jesus."

"Then why should I bother to follow him?" Corner Guy glanced up from his phone, his thumbs resting for the moment.

"Ryan." A girl sitting beside him nudged her elbow into the young man's side.

This *was* Ryan. Aaron held up a hand. "No, it's a legit question. If Jesus isn't going to make us happy or famous or give us what we want, why bother? I doubt this idea is new to any of you. It's a good reminder, however, that Jesus is more concerned about the state of our heart than anything else. If we're too inward-focused, how can we lead others?"

"I want to know my leader isn't going to lead me down a wrong path," James, one of the regular worship leaders said.

"I want a leader who's going to take me on an adventure. Who cares if it's a wrong path?" Ryan said. "No one is guaranteed safety. I choose adventure."

Aaron rubbed his jaw. "You're right, Ryan. Jesus never guaranteed safety. If you choose to follow his will for your life, you will experience trouble. Yet there's a difference between the trouble that comes from following him and the heartache from making unwise choices." Aaron knew that all too well. He focused on the group in front of him, not wanting to go there in his thoughts. "Leadership is asking 'How can I serve this person? How can I help them become the best person, worship leader, worshipper they can be?' That's servanthood. That's leadership."

"What you're saying is that in our role as leaders of worship, you want us to consider the congregation first? How we can help them be the best worshippers." Sheila ran her hand over her open Bible. Aaron could picture the lightbulb going on.

"Exactly. As you plan the service, think about them first, before your own personal preferences." Ouch. Wasn't he keeping his past out of the conversation because it was his personal preference? No, he wasn't going to open old wounds. He didn't want the focus on himself.

"Don't we need to challenge them by bringing in new music and ways of worship? I think we could do a cool rap version of a few of the songs. We younger people want a change. We don't want a funeral every week." Ryan spit out the last sentence, bringing Aaron back to the conversation.

All eyes focused on Aaron. "Our preferences should not be number one. It's what's best for everyone, not a select group. While we want to try new ideas and music, perhaps it's better to wait for the right moment if the church isn't ready for it. If it's what God wants, he'll help us prepare the people. Rap might be a possibility in the future. Today, it's a no."

Ryan scowled as the nodding heads outnumbered him. Aaron answered a few more questions before he closed their time in prayer. As people scattered, Ryan waited for Aaron.

"I want to talk to you about trying something new."

Aaron ground his teeth. Had the kid not been listening the past half hour? The night loomed long before him.

Chapter Eleven

AARON RAN HIS FINGER down the order of service one last time, but his mind wasn't on his work. It was Friday of his first week and he was suffering information overload. So, what did he do instead? He thought about his co-judge and singing with her at karaoke last week. She'd kept it together, although at one point, Aaron had been afraid she'd pass out. Instead, once he got her focus away from the audience and on singing, she blew him away. Those eyes had mesmerized him. He'd forgotten what he was doing for a couple of seconds. Where he was.

Jeremy's ringtone sounded. Maybe he had news.

"Hey, man, what's up?"

"Aaron, just wanted to let you know that there might be a possibility for you to tour in the fair circuit this fall."

"Really? That would be awesome...as long as it's not on Sundays."

"Shouldn't interfere with your new job, which, by the way, interferes with me trying to do *my* job. You're killing me. Try scheduling anything when you can't work half the weekend."

"Are there that many opportunities?" Was Jeremy turning down offers?

Jeremy's silence was all the answer Aaron needed. Oddly, he didn't feel as disappointed as he thought he would. Maybe he was getting used to the rejection. Or maybe it didn't matter as much anymore.

"I gotta go. Let me know what works out. I'd be happy to perform in the fall fairs circuit. We did that early on in The Light's career."

"It won't be the lead act FYI."

Oh. "Doesn't matter. I'll do it." Aaron said goodbye and hung up.

A light rap sounded before Pastor Ed appeared in his office doorway. "Do you have a minute? Ryan dropped in to see me yesterday."

Aaron motioned for Ed to sit in the chair by his desk. "What did he say?"

Ed sat, clasping his hands in his lap. "He has concerns."

"Why didn't he come to me first?"

"He said he did."

"We spoke after the worship meeting regarding issues he had about leadership. I thought we were on the same page by the end, other than a disagreement about music he wanted to incorporate."

"What was the music?"

"Rap. He's arranged an old hymn to rap." It had been a great arrangement but wasn't suitable for Sunday's service—or the first month of Aaron's tenure.

Ed didn't blink. "Well, I can see why you'd put a hold on that."

"I didn't say never. It's a good arrangement. It's just with being new and not knowing the congregation, I thought it best to wait for now."

"Wise choice. I told him he needs to work it out with you." Ed tapped his finger on the desk. "Can I give you a little advice? Deal with this before it becomes a bigger problem."

Aaron nodded. "Sure. I'll talk to him."

Ed left. Aaron checked his watch. It was time for worship practice, and he was in no mood to deal with egos today. Good thing Ryan wasn't on his team. He drew in a deep breath, let it out, and bowed his head. He was going to need all the help he could get.

Aaron plugged in his amp and played a brief riff. He'd scheduled an extra worship practice with his team since it was their first time playing together. A couple of the worship members made their way down the aisle whistling and whooping. The drummer jumped on stage. "Do it again."

"I was just fooling around."

"Can you show me how to do that?" The other guitarist motioned to his own guitar.

"Sure, after worship practice."

The rest of the team arrived except for one of the singers.

"Does anyone know where Christa is?"

No one did. Aaron pulled out his phone. No text. He sent a reminder. It was already ten minutes past the scheduled start of rehearsal. He turned to the group. "We'll begin practice. Christa will have to catch up."

An hour later, practice was done, and Christa was a no-show. And still, no text.

He called her number.

"Hello." The voice was breathless and giggling.

"Christa, it's Aaron."

Muffled sounds came over the line before Christa said anything else. "Hi." Her voice was noticeably lower and softer.

"You missed practice. I was just calling to ask if everything was okay."

"Sorry. I'm...sick." She coughed.

Aaron pursed his lips. She hadn't sounded sick when she'd answered the phone. "Sorry to hear that. Next time I need a text to let me know."

"It came on suddenly."

"Will you need to find a replacement for Sunday?"

"Maybe."

"Make sure you ask in plenty of time."

"Sure."

Aaron signed off, mentally preparing to be a singer short. She wasn't going to show or find someone to fill in. At least that was his gut feeling.

He'd noticed Christa was quite chummy with Ryan at the worship meeting. This kid was going to give him an ulcer. Ed seemed to believe the young man would come around. Aaron wasn't sure.

Guess he'd find out in the coming weeks. However, the evidence was pointing to the fact that this was going sideways.

Chapter Twelve

L AUREN WIPED THE PERSPIRATION from her brow with a towel supplied by the gym.

"Great class, Lauren." The Pilates instructor smiled as she passed by. She didn't even look sweaty.

Lauren rolled her mat up and headed to the door. The end-of-week workout energized her. At least that's what she told herself. As she fumbled in her bag for her car keys, a voice called her name. Isobel waved as she walked toward her. Lauren resisted the urge to turn around and head out the back way. Instead, she greeted the woman.

"I'm so glad I ran into you." Isobel, looking sporty in her yoga pants and tank top, said, "I didn't know you went to this gym."

"I just joined a month or so ago."

"Excellent. How are you doing?"

"Good. I'm sorry I haven't been able to meet. It's been busy with the competition."

"I've heard good things about it. Listen, I need to get to my class, but I was hoping you'd come over for coffee one evening. If you have time. I was going to invite Janey, Will's wife. She's nice and about your age. What do you think?"

Lauren studied the woman. She probably won't give up until Lauren gave in. Might as well get it over with. "Sure. Why not?"

"Excellent. Since it's the weekend, what about Monday? Let me get your number and I'll text you."

Lauren punched her number into Isobel's phone. "Thank you. I've got to get going as well."

"Take care, Lauren." Isobel jogged down the hall to one of the smaller studios. Lauren didn't want to revisit her life as a pastor's wife. Why had she agreed to the date? Maybe they'd talk about jobs or the competition. Anything besides ministry. Ha. Lauren doubted it. She trudged out to her car, already dreading the meeting.

SHE DIDN'T WANT TO be there. Monday evening, Lauren stood inside the woman's house. Lauren wiped her sweaty palms along her jeans. *Why did I agree to this?* She amazed herself at her inability to say no.

"Please have a seat, Lauren." Isobel carried a tray of steaming mugs, the scent of apples, vanilla, and cinnamon wafting from them.

Lauren sat on the edge of a pale yellow chair, ready to bolt if the opportunity presented itself. Will's wife, Janey, sat across from her on the matching couch. Sunlight streamed through the floor-to-ceiling windows on the far side of the room. Two tall maples shaded the yard. Isobel set the tray on the coffee table before she situated herself beside Janey.

"I'm glad you had time to meet me." Isobel passed them each a mug. She pointed to a plate of oatmeal raisin cookies. "Please help yourself to the cookies or else I'll eat them all." Isobel chuckled.

"Why bake them then?" Janey laughed.

"Oh, I didn't. Ed did." Isobel broke a cookie in half and popped it in her mouth. "Ed loves baking. He discovered his culinary side during a burnout early on in ministry. It's wonderful for me, but not so great for my hips." She stirred her tea, glancing at Lauren. "I hear you're a musician."

"I teach piano at the community centre. I wouldn't call myself a musician." Not like Aaron was.

Surprise crossed Janey's face. "That's not what Will said."

"Several of the parents were pleased with the work you, Aaron, and Marisa are doing with the kids. They can't stop talking about the competition." Isobel sipped her tea, made a face, and added more milk.

Lauren had received similar comments from parents whose kids she taught. Her students were already planning to audition next year.

"How are you settling in? You live with Val. Is that right?" Isobel set her mug on the coffee table.

Lauren sipped her drink. She'd gotten good at this kind of questioning as a pastor's wife. Everyone wanted to know you when you were the new couple. "Good. Val has been very generous, and I was fortunate to get the job at the community centre." Lauren wiped her mouth with a paper napkin.

As Isobel and Janey compared notes about Ottawa, Lauren studied the two women. Pastors' wives could win Oscars for their acting skills, which she knew from experience. However, both Isobel's and Janey's smiles reached their eyes, and they had no trouble meeting her gaze. Maybe they did want to make her feel welcome. Janey's stained sweatshirt made Lauren like her more.

"I'm sorry. You must feel like you're on the hot seat. I didn't mean to grill you." Isobel grinned sheepishly.

"Oh no. It's fine."

"I thought it might be fun to meet since you're new, and I wanted to introduce you to Janey. It's nice to meet people outside your circle, you know?"

Lauren did know. She had isolated herself in Toronto, and it had been suffocating. Moving to Ottawa and meeting new people was reviving her soul—little by little.

"And can I address the elephant in the room?" Isobel leaned forward.

Lauren raised her eyebrows. "Sure."

"We aren't perfect. You know that as a former pastor's wife. Your husband wasn't perfect and neither is Ed."

"Or Will." Janey rolled her eyes while her smile tempered it.

"You don't need to put on any airs for us. And we won't either. Deal?" Isobel popped a bite of cookie in her mouth.

"I'd like that." Lauren's words squeezed past the lump in her throat. She had not expected this kindness.

"Good." Isobel lifted her hands and motioned to the air around her. "Because what you see today is the result of a lot of hard work and growth. Five years into our marriage, I was on my way out the door because Ed and I were a mess. I'd had enough of being the last person he thought of in any situation. Tired of competing with God and board members for his attention, I gave him an ultimatum, get his priorities straight or I was leaving."

Lauren's jaw dropped. Never had she heard another pastor's wife be this honest and open.

Pastor's Wife Rule Number Four: Never admit your weaknesses.

Isobel's lips lifted slightly. "Thankfully, Ed listened to me and we spent the next three years in marriage counselling. It wasn't only Ed who had to work through issues. I did too. I had become resentful and angry with both my husband and God."

Lauren balled the paper napkin. This woman had been angry with God?

"I prayed daily, a lot of days it was hourly, for a daily dose of the Holy Spirit, and it was hard work, but we—Ed, God, and I—forged a new future. I wasn't going back to what we'd had because it was unhealthy." She stood and motioned for Lauren to follow.

Confused, Lauren followed Isobel to a door, Janey bringing up the rear. They descended stairs to the basement. The room had a desk and chair in the far corner and shelves overflowing with books. Next to it sat a stack of rubber storage tubs. At least five cardboard boxes were stacked beside it. A dusty exercise bicycle sat forlornly in the opposite corner. A heap of unfolded clean laundry sat in a laundry basket on the floor.

"See this mess? I keep the upstairs tidy because it's important to have a place for friends to visit and not feel smothered." She spread her hands. "This is me. The grey areas in my life are untidy. I'm organized in my own way. I know where everything is. But to anyone else, it's a disaster."

Janey chuckled. "Our whole house is one giant playroom. With two kids under five, I don't even bother trying to keep it spotless."

Isobel laughed. "What we're trying to say is that neither of us is perfect. People sometimes expect the pastor's wife to have it all together, but I don't."

"Neither do I," Janey piped up. "I just want people to accept me for who I am."

Lauren understood. It was what she'd wanted, too, when she was married to Sol, but people had expectations of what she should be like. Even Sol had wanted her to play a role.

Heat flooded Lauren's face. Hadn't she had expectation coming here? Even before meeting them, Lauren had put them in a box. Automatically, the little scoresheet had been adding up in the back of Lauren's mind, comparing them to what she had been like as a pastor's wife. A hand gently squeezed her elbow, and Lauren lifted her face to Isobel's.

"I don't know you, Lauren. But I do know being a pastor's wife is never easy. We do the best we can with what we have. Don't believe the lies that you don't matter or won't measure up. God loves you more than you can fathom, and he created you exactly how he wanted."

Lauren stared at the bookcase across the room, moisture blurring her vision. She clenched her jaw to keep her emotions at bay. If she let her guard down, she'd be a puddle on the floor.

Janey pressed a tissue into Lauren's hand. Lauren dabbed her eye. These women were kind and offered friendship. Lauren was surprised to find she craved a relationship like that. She was tired of running. Isn't that what she'd been doing all along? Despite her new appearance, new job, and living in a new city, Lauren was the same person inside. She couldn't outrun herself. It was time to stop. Lauren cleared her throat. "I'm struggling right now. I don't understand why Sol did what he did. Maybe part of it was my fault."

Isobel cocked her head. "I don't know the details of your life. However, people are responsible for the choices they make. Own your decisions and don't take on Sol's. Learn what you can from your past and move on. It doesn't help anyone to stay stuck there. The only thing God desires is a relationship with you. Be open and available to him. That's all you have to do."

"Why does everything go wrong no matter what I do?"

Isobel sat on the corner of a rubber tote. "Maybe God's trying to get your attention. Unfortunately, life isn't fair. Suffering is a part of life, as you know. It's what we do with our suffering that's important. Are you going to believe what you know is true, that God is good, or go with how you feel?"

"I don't like how he operates."

Isobel huffed out a laugh. "No kidding. I don't always either. But in the long run, it's worth the challenges and the hard work."

Janey mumbled her agreement around the cookie she was chewing.

"We girls need to stick together. It's a tough world, made more challenging by the roles we're placed in because of our husbands' job."

Lauren pulled on the hem of her shirt." I'm not a pastor's wife anymore."

"Doesn't matter. You understand. I'd like to be your friend, Lauren—if you'll let me."

"Me, too." Janey smiled.

The two women stood there, representing everything Lauren had run from. Yet their faces were open and kind. Could she trust them? Only one way to find out.

"I'd...I'd like that." Lauren smiled as a warmth filled her.

Chapter Thirteen

The following week, Lauren wove her way through the maze of kids lining the foyer of the church. Were all of them there to audition for the teen talent competition? Several were practicing vocal scales. Others stared at sheet music or zoned into whatever was playing in their earbuds.

Lauren squeezed past a group of girls harmonizing. A hand reached out and clutched her arm. Val. Her friend pulled Lauren off to the side. "Sorry, I should have told you to come in through the staff door at the back." Val raised her voice above all the noise.

Lauren waved her arm towards the crowded space. "How many kids are here to audition?"

"Forty. We had to cut it off at that. Isn't it great?"

"That's amazing. I knew the kids were excited for it at the community centre. It's going to be a jampacked evening though."

Lauren followed Val into the chapel. She spied Aaron speaking with Tony at the back of the room and her steps slowed. His blond hair was messed in the right places, and his dark jeans and black T-shirt fit him nicely. And there was the tattoo peeking out from under his sleeve. He was every inch a rockstar. He and Tony laughed before Tony spotted her and Val. The two men strode up the aisle.

"Great. You're here." Tony smiled at Lauren, not seeming to notice Val.

"Yep, we're both here." Lauren gestured to Val.

"Oh, Val, can I ask a favour?" Tony checked his clipboard.

Lauren groaned. The guy was oblivious. As Tony and Val chatted, Lauren turned to Aaron.

Tonight, his eyes were the colour of sapphires. Lauren hadn't seen him since the karaoke duet, although he'd texted to set up a rehearsal time for their song. As their gazes locked, goosebumps popped on Lauren's arms.

"Hi." Aaron smiled—not his thousand-watt smile meant for fans but a real smile that made Lauren feel like she was in on a secret.

"Hi." She breathed out the word. To her side, she saw Tony glance between her and Aaron.

A petite blonde woman came up beside him, phone in hand. "Can I get a picture of all the judges?"

"Just a sec, Audra. I don't think Marisa is here." Aaron gestured to Lauren. "This is Lauren, one of the judges. And this is Audra. My agent sent her to take pictures for social media." Aaron's smile was tight.

The spell of seeing Aaron faded, and Lauren swallowed the retort on the tip of her tongue. She nodded to the young woman as Marisa jogged up to them.

"Hi, everyone. Sorry. My babysitter was late." Marisa dropped her large tote on a chair. "I'm so pumped about these auditions."

Lauren smiled at her co-judge's enthusiasm. It was contagious.

Tony checked something on his clipboard before tucking it under his arm. "It's almost showtime. If you have any questions, ask Marisa. She's done plenty of auditions. Audra, you can take photos from the side, but please be discreet." Tony waved his hands over his head to get the rest of the room's attention. "Okay, everyone, let's get this show on the road. I'd like to be home before midnight." He directed orders to people, and soon the room emptied of unnecessary people. Only the three judges sat in the front row. A table had been set up in front of their seats. Audra took a seat a couple of rows back.

"I see you brought 'your people' tonight," Lauren muttered out of the side of her mouth.

Aaron's jaw tightened. "I didn't have a choice. My agent sent her, and it was part of the deal."

"Yes, the deal." Lauren couldn't help the sarcasm.

Aaron ran his hand over his head. "I can't help it. It comes with the life I lead. I have to do things I don't necessarily want to."

Lauren's heart softened. "I know the feeling." She'd had to do a lot of things as a pastor's wife that she didn't want to do. "Sorry."

"It's okay. I wish it wasn't like this either. Let's just focus on the kids, okay?"

"Yes." Lauren shook out her hands. He needed to turn the wattage down on those blue eyes. She inhaled then slowly blew out her breath, hoping to calm her jumbled insides. Between her growing attraction to Aaron and what appeared to be jealousy on Tony's part, Lauren's anxiety spiked. She didn't need a man to complete her life. Yet here she was, daydreaming about a guy who would be bad news in the end. Meanwhile, another guy, who would have been perfect for her in another lifetime, was obviously interested.

Aaron whispered, "Remember, they're more nervous than you are. Be kind and honest. You'll be great."

"I'm afraid I'll make a mistake and pick the wrong people."

"That's why there are three of us. You'll know who to pick. You'll feel it here." He pointed to his heart.

"I hope you're right."

"I won't steer you wrong." The cocky smile was back, which brought Lauren back to reality. She leaned forward, shoving all worries out of her head, as the first teen arrived on stage. Now was the time to enjoy the performances and choose an up and coming star.

An hour, and fifteen auditions later, Aaron rested his chin in his hands. Thankfully, not everyone sang their whole song. If by a few lines in, they could tell the performer wasn't going to make the cut, Aaron stopped them. So far, there had only been a few of those.

Aaron gathered his thoughts as the teen who had just performed shuffled forward on the stage. He'd played several great riffs, but his voice squeaked. Give him a year to get out of puberty and he'd be a contender. How to tell him that without snuffing out his dreams? Aaron held up his hand. "Thanks..." he shuffled the papers in front of him. "Troy, you've got great skills on the guitar. I enjoyed hearing you play. The voice needs work. Lessons would help. After that, you'll be ready for anything."

The kid ducked his head. *Shoot.*

"Definitely got skills, Troy. Polish up your voice with lessons and practice. I'd pay to hear you play guitar any day, right now."

Good save, Marisa.

"Absolutely. Take voice lessons and maybe work on control. We have a choir at the centre. It's a great place to learn this if you can't take private lessons. Just a thought. Listen, you've got a lot to work with. Don't give up." Lauren smiled.

The kid stared at Lauren. A small lift of his lips. Good, he was seeing past tonight and into the future. That's what they wanted. "Thanks."

"Don't give up, Troy. For us..." Aaron glanced at the two women, who shook their heads. "It's a no. Thanks for coming out. It takes a lot of courage to stand on stage and put yourself out there. You should be proud of yourself."

The kid exited the stage.

"Good idea about the choir." Aaron nodded at Lauren.

Lauren covered her mic. "I've seen him around the centre. I know he can't afford lessons, but the choir is taught be a professional. So, he'd learn how to work his skill and get great tips. Plus, it's free."

"I hope he takes your suggestion." Marisa sighed. "I hate telling them no." She groaned.

"Goes with the territory. If you want a career in music, you've got to grow a thick skin. I remember being told by a radio DJ that I'd never amount to much. I was twelve and trying to get him to play my demo. Accepting rejection and learning from it is a big part of the music journey. It can motivate you to improve or, in my case, prove that DJ wrong." Aaron sipped from his water bottle.

Tony appeared onstage.

"Hey, we're going to take a ten-minute break. A reporter from the local neighbourhood paper, *Glebe Chronicles*, is here. Can you guys answer a few questions?"

Aaron's pulse kicked up a notch. "Why not let Marisa do the interview?"

Marisa nodded her head enthusiastically. "I don't mind."

"He wants to talk to you specifically." Tony tapped the table. "It'd be good press for your album."

Wasn't that why Audra was here?

"Right. Thanks." Aaron unclenched his fists under the table. Where was Audra? It wouldn't be good for her to hear anything and post it. That kind of publicity Aaron didn't need. He glanced at his phone, seeing a text from her. She'd left, saying she had enough for a couple of posts. Aaron breathed a sigh of relief.

The youth director motioned a young man in. If Jimmy Olsen was a real person, this guy was him—or how Aaron had always pictured the comic character.

"This is Dwayne. He does the entertainment beat." Tony glanced at his watch. "You've got ten minutes."

"Great." The young man's voice cracked, and the knots in Aaron's shoulders loosened. Dude was harmless. "Do you mind if I record your answers?" He held a finger over his phone.

"Go ahead." Aaron nodded. He wasn't going to answer anything if he could help it. Marisa and Lauren could do the talking.

Dwayne placed his phone on the table. "What are you looking for when it comes to moving the contestants to the next phase?"

Marisa jumped in, answering enthusiastically while Aaron stood, stretching his legs.

Dwayne turned his attention to Aaron. "Aaron, you're the celebrity on this judging panel. What advice do you have to offer music hopefuls?"

"Believe in yourself. Don't listen to the haters and practice, practice, and practice some more."

He asked Aaron to tell them about his solo album. Aaron slipped on his rockstar mask and answered all the questions just as Jeremy liked. Finally, eight minutes in, Jimmy, er Dwayne, scribbled on his notepad. "One last question if you don't mind." He stared at Aaron. "There are a lot of fans of The Light here in the city and I couldn't not ask you this. What's the real reason the band broke up? Curious minds want to know." The innocent expression dropped away. The kid, who maybe wasn't a kid after all, stared at Aaron.

Definitely not harmless. "We had separate goals and dreams. We had matured both musically and in age. We were going in different directions. So, it was natural to part ways." That was all true, and Aaron wasn't going to get into the rest of the story. At the time of Wade's death, the PR people had buried the story. Wade had been a roadie, not a band member. So, the interest quickly died. Aaron wasn't going to let this entertainment beat reporter poke a hole in the façade. "I'd be happy to tell you why the community centre was so impactful for me growing up here."

"That's been covered already numerous times on radio and TV." Dwayne waited.

Aaron locked eyes with him. If he hoped to make Aaron feel awkward, the reporter was going to have a long wait.

Dwayne returned to his questioning, "You disappeared from public life for a year until this album came out. I heard a rumour—"

"I needed a break. I was tired from touring so I've been selective in what I've chosen to participate in." Aaron tapped his watch. "I think our time is up. The kids are waiting for us to finish the auditions." Thankfully Tony appeared, confirming Aaron's words.

"Sure thing." Slowly Dwayne turned to Marisa and Lauren. "Thanks for your time. I might call with a few follow-up questions." His emphasized the last few words.

As Dwayne followed Tony out of the chapel, Aaron tipped his water bottle, gulping half. Crumpling the plastic, he threw it into the recycle bin by the door. Aaron returned to his seat.

The next hour was a blur. After the last audition of the night, the three judges sagged in their seats. "I have no idea how we're going to cut this to only ten moving forward." Marisa groaned.

Aaron tapped his finger on the scoring sheets. "Let's pick out who we would pay to see in concert—right now, not in the future."

Marisa straightened. "Sounds like a plan." They sorted through their notes. When they had twenty, they went through the pile a second time, narrowing it to ten, using the parameters of the judging sheets.

"We're agreed?" Aaron read the names aloud. Lauren nodded and Marisa gave a thumbs up. "Okay, let's give these to Tony, and he can have the joy of telling everyone."

Aaron stood, glancing around the empty sanctuary. No Dwayne in sight. The reporter could ask what he wanted. Aaron wasn't going to answer any follow-up questions.

Chapter Fourteen

THE FAST FOOD CHAIN drive-thru was busy for a weeknight, and Lauren debated abandoning the quest for a milkshake and cheeseburger. Deciding against the drive-thru, she pulled into a parking spot and got out of her car. After placing her order, she stood to the side, waiting. A breeze blew in as the door opened. Aaron entered the restaurant, and his eyes connected with hers, sending a jolt through her body. Now it wasn't just the cool air giving her shivers.

"Determining young people's futures made you hungry too?" His smile, the real one, lit up his face. It was like a magnet. Involuntarily she stepped closer.

"It did. I'll have to spend an extra hour on the elliptical tomorrow, but right now it's worth it."

His gaze travelled down to her toes and just as quickly found her eyes. "I don't think you have to worry." He cleared his throat as he directed his attention to the menu above, which Lauren was grateful for, as her face was probably redder than a lobster. When the server called their numbers, Aaron grabbed his tray as she picked up her take-out bag.

"Want to stay and eat with me?" He nodded at the near-empty eating area. "Or do you want to go home and enjoy the carbs and grease on your own?"

Go home. "Uh, sure. If we eat in the restaurant, the calories don't count, right?"

He leaned closer, his lips lifted in a half-grin. "Pretty sure that's how it works." Scruff now adorned his cheeks, which enhanced his good looks.

She should go home. Right. Now. Instead, her feet followed him to a booth in the back. It was a late night snack with a fellow judge. Nothing more.

He unwrapped his double cheeseburger and bowed his head. Lauren waited. She had stopped saying grace after Sol died, when her world flipped upside down and God vanished. His silence hurt more than she wanted to admit.

When Aaron was done praying, he lifted his burger. "Cheers."

She lifted her milkshake. "Cheers." His sleeve had slid up, revealing his tat. It was a musical note or rather, several. "I like your tattoo."

"Thanks. I got it when I turned eighteen."

"Do you have more?" Why would she ask that?

"Nope." He eyed her. "You?"

"No." Lauren dipped an onion ring in ketchup. "You grew up here in Ottawa, right? You mentioned that you used to hang out at the community centre."

Aaron unwrapped a second burger. "Yeah, our house wasn't too far from the centre. My parents weren't around much. Climbing the corporate ladder took most of their attention. I'd hang out with the kids and youth directors at the centre. They never made me feel like I was a nuisance or like I wasn't welcome. It was a safe place for me. I'm glad I can help out with this competition." Aaron picked at a crumb. His neck reddened

Lauren set down the half-eaten onion ring. "Wow. I didn't know. I thought you were just involved to promote yourself. I'm sorry."

"I know." He glanced away from her. "Jeremy, my agent, is in it for promotion. Honestly, at first, I wasn't crazy about the idea, but it's grown on me. That's not to say I mind the promotion. It all helps."

"How old were you when you won the spot in the band?"

"I had just turned seventeen. Eighteen by the time we made it big. I was the youngest of the group. Yet they thought I had what it took to be the lead singer."

"Wow. You were so young."

"We had six months of intense rehearsals, writing, and recording. I'd been writing and recording my own stuff since I was twelve. I had been rejected over and over. I spent more time begging radio stations to play my demo than I spent doing homework.

"Contrary to the entertainment rags, I wasn't an overnight wonder." He twirled his soda cup, the ice clinking. "It's a tough life. There were casualties." A line creased his forehead.

Lauren dabbed at the corner of her mouth with her napkin. "What do you mean?" Being a rockstar didn't appear like it was a tough a life: travelling the world, fame, money, doing what you loved.

"There were great moments. I've had experiences I'd never have gotten if not for the band's success. But it goes both ways. I loved performing, but I missed my friends and home. Even parents who work 24/7 are better than no parents at all. When I was on tour, I wouldn't see them for months at a time. Our relationship had never been great, and it got even more stunted because we never saw each other. It also didn't help that they seemed more interested in my success that in me at that point."

"That's awful. I'm sorry." Lauren thought of her own loving parents, who attended every piano recital and school concert.

"It is what it is. I've worked hard since I was a kid." He crumpled his burger wrapper. "Sometimes I think I'd like to settle and set down roots." He lifted a shoulder then dropped it. "You? Where did you grow up?"

"Toronto. I moved here not quite a year ago, after my husband died in a car accident." When he nodded, she said, "You knew that."

"I only recently recognized the name. I'm sorry for your loss."

"Thank you. Anyway, I grew up in the Big Smoke. My parents were great. I had an ideal childhood. Things kinda went south from there. Sol changed after we got married and he had success in the church. Our marriage was a casualty of ministry."

Aaron sipped his soda while remaining silent. He probably knew that too. The church world was small.

"I get why you'd have suspicions regarding pastors and ministry. We witnessed an unsavory side of ministry while we were on tour."

"I bet you did. Anyway, Sol and I..." She shook her head. "It doesn't matter. I'm trying to move forward. This is a new chapter in my life."

"That's great. And you don't have to explain anything. I understand grief. I lost my cousin a few years back. I miss him every day. When I say casualties in the business, he's one of them."

When he didn't add to the comment, Lauren moved on. It was obvious from his frown that Aaron didn't want to get into it. She wondered what he meant. She studied the man sitting across from her. He'd been surprisingly candid about his life and understanding about hers. Once again, she'd acted on an assumption. *You think I'd have learned my lesson by now.* First, Sol—assuming everything was okay in their marriage even though the red flags had been there. Now, Aaron.

Aaron leaned back against the booth. "Your wariness with church and pastors is understandable. I have questions for God, too. It's harder to walk out your faith than it is to talk about it. I hope someday you'll realize not all us pastors are like your husband...Are we good for the rehearsal next week?"

"Yes, I'll see you at the centre." Lauren stood. "It's well past my bedtime. I should go."

He scooped up his tray and they dumped their trash on the way out. "Thanks for keeping me company. I find it hard to wind down after an evening like this."

"How you did it every night —performing to sold out stadiums and churches—is a mystery to me." Lauren stifled a yawn.

"Not a healthy lifestyle for sure." A shadow crossed his face.

Before Lauren could question him, they arrived at her car. "This is me." They stood mere inches from each other, his body heat warming her. The temptation to step closer and soak in that warmth overwhelmed her. She missed being held, touched, cherished, but leaning into Aaron was sticking her toe into dangerous waters. "See you tomorrow." She practically dove into the driver's seat.

Saluting, he jogged to his truck. Lauren exhaled slowly. Tired from the long evening, she wanted to get home and go to bed. After talking with Aaron, she felt lighter. Maybe it was a step forward into her new beginning. Despite the little fangirl crush, she didn't need a man or God, but maybe she could use a new friend.

Chapter Fifteen

THE NEXT EVENING, LAUREN flicked the remote as she scanned her choices. *You'd think with two streaming services there would be something decent to watch.* Nothing appealed.

Val came out of her bedroom.

Lauren's mouth dropped open. "Va-va-va-voom! You look amazing." Val's red hair had been blown out, and she wore a black cocktail dress and four-inch high heels.

Val did an awkward curtsey. "Thank you, ma'am. I aim to please."

Lauren sat up on her knees, resting her arms on the top of the couch. "Who's the hot date?"

"Why do I need a date to dress up?" She raised a perfectly plucked eyebrow.

Good point.

Val pointed a red polished nail at Lauren. "Get dressed. You're coming with."

"What? No." Lauren gripped the top edge of the couch. "I'm tired. The auditions were exhausting."

"I'm not taking no for an answer. It's girls' night out. Come with Marisa and me."

"I don't have anything to wear." That wasn't a lie. Lauren's new wardrobe was sparse and practical. Val's cocktail dress showed off her curves. Lauren would be severely underdressed.

Val came around to Lauren and grabbing her hand, yanked her out of her seat. "Stop thinking. I have a closet full of clothes. They might be a little big, but safety pins and double-sided tape are miracle workers. Call me the MacGyver of Fashion." She chuckled as she dragged Lauren into her room. She flicked on the bedroom light and flung open her closet door. "Sit." She pushed Lauren onto her bed. Riffling through her packed closet, Val pulled out a black satin jacket, held it up, and threw it on the bed beside Lauren. Next, she yanked out an empire-waisted dress, looking between it and Lauren. After a moment, she shoved it back in, all the while muttering to herself.

"Aha." Val held a royal blue, sleeveless wrap dress. Val picked up the jacket and dress and pressed them into Lauren's hands. "Do you have shoes?" At Lauren's frown, Val dropped to her knees, rummaging through the shoes on the closet floor. "Here." She flung a pair of high heels into Lauren's already full arms. "When you're dressed, I'll do your hair and make-up."

Lauren stared at the clothes and shoes in her arms before heading to the bathroom to change. Her fingers rubbed the light fabric of the dress before slipping it on. Not bothering to check herself out in the mirror, she walked back to Val's bedroom.

Val circled Lauren. "Gorgeous. That colour is perfect on you." She pulled Lauren's hair into a ponytail, twisting it up.

"You're a miracle worker," Lauren joked.

"I'm only enhancing the beauty that's there."

Val stared at her a minute longer before grabbing a few bobby pins. After finishing the up-do, Val applied eye make-up, blush, and powder.

"Open your eyes." Val handed Lauren a hand mirror "What do you think?"

Lauren stared at her reflection, her jaw dropping. Her blue eyes popped, and her hair framed her face in a way that softened the angles. "Wow. I don't recognize myself."

"We don't see this Lauren often enough. You'll be turning heads all night." Val held up a hand. "I know, I know. You don't need a guy. That doesn't mean you can't flirt a little. Have fun."

Maybe Val had a point. This was a side of herself she'd like to know better. Over the years, Lauren had lost parts of herself. Sol had been very opinionated about what he found acceptable in her dress and how she wore her hair. Lauren had blindly accepted what he said as gospel. "Where are we going?"

"The Purple Plum. They have a brie dip that you'll be addicted to after the first taste." Val ran a lipstick over her lips and smacked them together. "You'll have fun. I promise."

"You invited Marisa. Who else?"

"Tony said he was stopping in with friends. Maybe a few others from church." Val busied herself with putting lipstick and tissues into her bag.

"Care to confess anything?" Lauren walked around to stand in front of Val. "You like Tony."

"No, I don't. We're good friends…Maybe."

"I knew it." Lauren smiled triumphantly.

"Okay, I like him, but it's nothing. The feeling will pass."

"If you say so." Her smile faded as she remembered the few awkward moments with Tony that gave her the impression that he liked *her*. Should she say something to Val?

"It's hopeless. He doesn't see me. I'm just faithful Val. Good to volunteer and nothing else."

"Maybe you need to put yourself out there. Make him see you." Lauren slipped on her high heels. Maybe if Tony noticed Val, his interest would shift to her friend. Lauren couldn't figure out why the guys weren't beating down Val's door.

"I've tried. Got any suggestions?" Val dropped the make-up into her cosmetic bag.

"Let me think on it." And while she did, Lauren would hope that she'd mistaken the vibe she'd gotten from Tony and that he'd fall in love with her best friend.

The Purple Plum was standing room only. Men and women, who mostly appeared under the age of forty, stood in groups, waiting for tables while harried staff ran around taking drink orders and delivering succulent looking charcuterie boards.

Lauren scanned the room, not seeing Tony or anyone else she knew. Marisa had joined them shortly after they arrived, and now, the three sat at a tall table in the middle of the restaurant. A DJ spun jazz music in one corner.

"This is what I needed—an evening off." Marisa plucked a piece of cheese off the wooden plank. As she chewed, her eyes rounded. "Ooh. There's Aaron."

Lauren half-turned in her seat. Aaron stood by the hostess desk with Will and Janey. Aaron was either oblivious or was ignoring the stares of numerous women as his group followed the server to a table. The man commanded the attention of the room. His good looks definitely made one take the first glance, but he had an It factor that had people taking a second look. It had shone when he sang to packed out stadiums, and it filled this small room tonight.

"He's certainly not what I imagined. He's pretty down to earth for being famous." Marisa inclined her head toward Aaron's party. Lauren didn't like the look on Marisa's face. Did she like Aaron? Stop being ridiculous. What did it matter if Marisa liked him or not? Lauren was single and she planned to stay that way. Still, Marisa had nailed Aaron's character. He had never been arrogant or used his fame to get what he wanted. Even in the interviews for the competition, it was always the hosts who brought up his album, not Aaron. Not like Sol at all, who always liked to boast about who he was and that his church was the largest in the province. Lauren turned away. She didn't want thoughts of Sol or her past life to ruin her night.

Val grabbed Lauren's elbow, directing her attention back to the entrance. Tony was standing at the hostess desk, searching the crowd. Spotting their table, he waved and weaved his way through the crowded room.

Marisa leaned on the table, chin in hand. "Someone's excited Tony's here."

Val smiled as Tony approached.

"Ladies." His slow smile had a sexy quality to it. She could understand Val's attraction, although it did nothing for Lauren.

"Hi, Tony." Val's dimples deepened as her cheeks turned a dark red. Tony seemed oblivious to Val's obvious interest. Instead, his focus landed on Lauren. She forced her lips into a smile.

"Enjoying our neighbourhood hot spot?" he asked her.

Lauren sipped her drink. "Val suggested we come here," she said.

"We can always count on Val's good taste." He chuckled.

Val's smile drooped a little. Lauren wanted to roll her eyes. Wow. The guy was really clueless. He'd effectively assigned Val to the friend zone. Lauren clenched her hands in her lap. She wanted to slap Tony upside the head. Even Marisa's eyebrows were raised.

"I see my friends over there. I should go. Have fun." Tony waved at a group of guys and girls several tables over. "Save a dance for me later." He glanced at Lauren as he said it.

Val's gaze didn't leave him as he walked away. Oh brother. This was worse than Lauren feared.

Lauren nudged her friend in the arm. "You should ask him to dance or go over to his table. Make yourself seen."

Marisa eyed them. "Tony, eh? He's a catch."

Val threw up her hands. "It's a lost cause. Apparently, I'm only good for helping and volunteering."

Marisa dipped a chip in the garlicky hummus. "He's too wrapped up in the kids and the community centre. Lauren's right. Go over there and make him notice you."

Val stuffed a cracker in her mouth. "Maybe later," she mumbled.

"Chicken," Lauren muttered under her breath.

"Hi, girls." Janey smiled as she came up to them. "Marisa, it's been ages. How have you been?"

"Busy, but my mom's in town. So, I've got a built-in babysitter. I'm taking a night off to play." Marisa laughed.

"Is this a night off for you too, Janey?" Val asked.

"Yeah, I needed a break, and Will was more than willing to accommodate me with a date night. How are you, Lauren? It's good to see you."

"Val dragged me here, but now I'm glad I came." The truth of the words surprised Lauren.

Val waved her hand toward where Will and Aaron were sitting. "I didn't know Will was Aaron's friend."

"Oh yeah. They grew up together. I always forget Aaron is famous. Or was." She smirked. "He's single, too."

"Not my type," Marisa laughed. "However, he is nice on the eyes."

Val nudged Lauren. "What do you say, Lauren?"

She glared at her friend while Janey raised a brow. "Ooh. You'd make a cute couple."

"Banish the thought."

Janey waved at Will. "I gotta go. Talk to you later." She hurried off.

The music turned upbeat, and a few people danced in the small space beside the DJ. "Let's dance." Val dragged Lauren off the stool and tugged her over to the dancers, Marisa following behind.

Lauren protested, "You're just trying to get out of talking to Tony."

Val smiled innocently. "Maybe. Let's go."

"I haven't danced in ages." At least not in public. Sol didn't approve of dancing.

Pastor's Wife Rule Number Five: Dancing isn't allowed.

Memories of the weddings she'd attended where Sol and she left early flooded her mind. Lauren headed to the dance floor. Rule number five could go jump in the lake.

Uncomfortable, Lauren swayed stiffly—at first. Two women came over and whisked Marisa away to the other side of the dance floor. The DJ put on another upbeat tune. As the rhythm washed over Lauren, she loosened up, remembering how much she loved to dance. Val hip-bumped her. Plus, her friend's laughter was contagious. Lauren smiled as they sashayed a few steps.

"We were the dancing queens in high school." Val shimmied her shoulders. Lauren rolled her eyes. Val was exaggerating. However, they did have a lot of fun as teens.

The music switched tempo and Val slowed her movements. Lauren turned to leave and ran into a hard chest. "Oof." Strong hands seized her shoulders to keep her from stumbling.

She rubbed her nose. "Sorry." Aaron's blue eyes bored into her. His crooked half-grin made her knees weak.

"I don't mind." Aaron chuckled, his breath caressing her cheek. His low laugh rumbled through his chest, reverberating over her like the crest of a wave. Goosebumps popped out on her arms.

She should move; yet her feet remained glued in place. His hands sent warmth throughout her arms and chest. And his eyes. She was pinned to the spot by his intense look. She shook her head, trying to break free from his spell. "I'm sorry. I'm a klutz, which is why I'm leaving the dance floor." She stepped out of his reach.

"That's too bad. I was going to ask you to dance." He held out his hand.

Lauren went to grab Val, only to discover her friend had vanished. Traitor. "Ah, I..." *Bad idea. Bad idea. Bad idea.*

"I won't step on your toes, I promise. Will you dance with me?" He continued to hold out his hand and his eyes searched hers.

How did she say no to that? "Sure."

Aaron's hand settled on her waist while his other hand clasped hers to his chest. The smell of soap and mint, as well as something else Lauren couldn't put her finger on, wafted around her, teasing her nostrils. The man smelled delicious. The room spun slightly and not from the dancing. *Bad idea.*

"It's nice to see Janey and Will here. Date night...for them, I mean." Why did she bring up the word date?

"Hired a sitter. They try to go out at least a couple of times a month. He's so busy with youth, but I admire him. He always makes time for her."

Lauren swallowed her jealousy. The past was in the past.

"You and Sol—" He snapped his mouth shut. "Never mind. It's none of my business."

"What were you going to say?"

"You and Sol didn't have children?"

Lauren breathed in. Exhaled. "No, Sol always had an excuse about why it wasn't a good time to start a family." It still hurt.

Did she imagine it or did he pull her closer? "I'm sorry." His breath tickled her ear, and tingles exploded along her neck and arms, leaving her breathless.

The music flowed into another song, but Aaron didn't stop dancing. If she admitted it, Lauren didn't want to stop either. Out of the corner of her eye, she saw Tony twirl Val. They looked like they were having fun. Lauren hoped they'd hit it off.

As the second song morphed into another slow song, she inhaled. She stared at the small buttons of his shirt, ignoring the lure of the open one at his throat. *He's not Sol.* But he was famous and he was a pastor. She stepped away, putting space between them.

"You okay?"

"Yeah, sorry. I'm..." she fanned her face. "It's hot out here... Sorry, but I need air." She whirled and headed to her table.

AARON STOOD ALONE ON the dance floor. What just happened? *She ran away from you.* Usually, women chased him and he was the one running the other way. Now he knew how it felt. Lauren sat at her table and gulped water, her profile to him.

She never glanced at the dance floor. He headed to his own table, his face heating.

"What happened?" Janey's eyes widened.

"Was it that obvious?" He winced.

"That she ran away?" Will snorted. Janey elbowed him in the ribs. "Ouch." He rubbed his side.

"No, not bad." Janey unsuccessfully tried to cover Will's bluntness. It *was* that bad.

"She said she was hot, needed air."

Janey pursed her lips. "Considering her history, she's maybe a bit shy."

Will whistled. "You know how to pick 'em."

"It's not like that. I didn't *pick* her. We're working together and she's new in town. I was only being friendly, that's it."

Will held his palms up. "Easy."

"I don't think she even likes me that much." He popped an olive in his mouth, hoping to stop the conversation.

"She wasn't looking at you like she dislikes you." Janey forked an olive. "And she's really nice and I love her style. As I told her that you'd make a cute couple."

"You what?"

Janey feigned innocence.

The woman had a point. Lauren was beautiful, and Aaron was partial to the pink tips. "I'm sure her life is complicated." *You don't need complicated.* Rebuilding his career and writing new music was where he should focus his attention. *What about settling down?* He shut down his thoughts. "She told me she doesn't want anything to do with church or God. From what I saw of Solomon Grace, he was a jerk. Can't say I blame her."

He spotted Lauren and Val leaving their table. Were they heading out? He rubbed his fingers on a napkin, hoping to erase the imprint of her soft hand in his. Her reluctance to talk about her marriage niggled at him. Sol Grace did sound like a jerk, even from the little she'd said about him. Aaron balled up his napkin, tossed it to the side of his plate, no longer hungry. Not every man in ministry was like Sol. Maybe he needed to show Lauren that there were decent men. In the name of men in ministry, he could do that, right? Was that a challenge he wanted to take on? He exhaled. After the way she'd bolted from him, he'd best get his brain examined. It was useless. Nothing was going to happen between them because she was running scared. And so was he.

"YOU LEFT HIM ALONE on the dance floor?"

Lauren closed her eyes and pressed her forehead against the cool metal of the bathroom stall door, hoping to shut out the incredulity in Val's voice on the other side.

"Lauren, stop hiding." She banged the metal.

Lauren opened the door and peered out at her roommate. "I want to go home. I'm calling an Uber."

"No, you're not. I'll take you."

"Val, I'm a big girl. I can find my way home by myself."

Val turned on the cold water faucet and snatched a paper towel. After wetting it, she wrung it out, handing it to Lauren. "Press this on the back of your neck. It'll make you feel better."

"I think I'm catching the flu."

Val rolled her eyes. "You're catching something all right, and it's not the flu." She smirked.

Lauren pressed the paper to her neck, letting it soothe her heated skin. Once she felt refreshed, she held up a hand. "Stop right there. I'm not catching what you're implying. I'm just out of shape."

Val wet another paper towel and held it out to Lauren, drips of water falling to the floor. "That's why you ran away. You didn't want to show Aaron how out of shape you are."

Well, when she put it that way. Lauren stared at the mini-puddles. Leaving Aaron alone on the dance floor had not been one of her finer moments. Being held by a man other than Sol and liking it had freaked her out. She patted her face, careful not to smear her make-up, hoping Val would drop the subject.

As the silence lengthened, Lauren waved a hand. "I'm not running away. Besides, I'm sure his ego can handle it." Not that she believed Aaron had a big ego. He had only been humble, kind, and respectful during the competition so far.

"C'mon, Lauren. Give the guy a break. Aaron's a nice guy."

Lauren blew out a breath. "I know. That's the problem. He's a great guy who's not only a rockstar but also one who works at Cartwright."

"So?"

Lauren tossed the wad of wet paper into the garbage. "I refuse to get involved with another pastor. I want freedom from all that."

"He's not Solomon," Val whispered.

Lauren rubbed her knuckles over her breastbone. How could Val be so sure? Dare Lauren risk her heart again?

Val laid her hands on Lauren's shoulders and turned her around to face her. "Remember your dad? He was a wonderful man and he was a pastor."

"God threw the mold out when he created my dad." He'd been the last good man of God. Lauren was sure of it. She skirted around her friend and left the bathroom. Scrolling through her contacts, she found the Uber app and started tapping. She didn't want to debate with her friend about the merits of pastors, God, or church. Lauren was done for the night. Maybe for good.

Chapter Sixteen

The next morning, shouts from the hallway of the youth centre made Lauren look up from her computer. She stifled a yawn. She had tossed and turned all night after getting home from the Purple Plum. Tony appeared in Lauren's doorway. "Hey, Lauren, got a minute?"

"Sure, come in." More kids ran by bouncing a ball.

Tony stuck his head out into the hall and shouted, "No balls in the hall, guys."

"Yes, sir." The thunk, thunk stopped. Tony rolled his eyes as he sat in the chair near her desk. "I'll have to repeat that a hundred times more before six-thirty."

"Yes, you will." Lauren chuckled. Tony uttered those words at least once a day.

"Would you mind helping me with several bags of donated clothes? The back to school sale is running this weekend. I have a bunch of donated stuff in my truck, and Will has a trunk-load as well."

"Sure." Lauren followed Tony to his vehicle. Will stood beside it, several large bags at his feet.

"I recruited help." Tony grabbed a couple of the bigger bags.

"Awesome. Hey, Lauren." Will handed her two large paper shopping bags.

"Are these all donations?" Lauren gestured to the dozen bags in the back of the trucks.

"Yeah, my wife, along with the other pastors' wives, run a clothing drive around the community. People donate the clothes, and we bring them to your thrift store here at the centre. Our volunteers have gone through them and tossed the worn and damaged items already."

Lauren was impressed. Cartwright certainly pulled their weight in the Glebe community. And she wasn't surprised that Janey and Isobel were involved.

"We'll have to do a couple of trips." Tony shut the hatch door.

Lauren hurried into the building with her load, following Will, while Tony brought up the rear. Volunteers were adding things to the racks in the room used for the thrift store.

Will set his stuff down. "Most of it will go. We do this every year."

Lauren's throat burned. "I didn't realize there was such a need." The neighbourhood was fairly affluent, wasn't it?

"A lot of people have lost jobs and the cost of living has steadily risen. For some, it's a choice between eating and buying clothes. And kids grow like weeds." He raised his eyebrows. "Like a kid will be here on Friday and on Monday he's three inches taller."

Lauren chuckled as she set the things in the corner of the room.

"Aaron's idea of asking for canned goods at the competition was great. It will help our dwindling pantry at the church." Will headed back outside.

Wait. That was Aaron's idea? She'd figured it was Will's or Tony's idea.

After the last bag was brought in, Lauren waved goodbye to Will and headed back to her office. Tony followed.

Lauren fingered her necklace. Why was Tony still here? "How did the kids who didn't make it take the news?"

"Disappointed of course. I encouraged them to cheer on their friends. Their turn will come one day in the future. It's not today though. The ones who want to be involved behind the scenes... I'm finding spots for them in different areas. Val is going to have a couple help with hair and makeup."

Lauren jumped on the opening. "Val's awesome. She could have a million-dollar salon, but she keeps her prices affordable and gives away haircuts to families in need." If she winked, would he get the hint?

"I'm not sure what we'd do without her." Tony leaned against the doorframe. "You're doing great by the way. It's not an easy job, being a judge. You know how to handle yourself with both the praise and the criticism." Tony smiled. "Did you have fun last night? The Purple Plum is a great little hangout."

"Oh, it was nice. *Val* loves it there."

"Seems to be popular with everyone from the teen talent competition." He scratched the back of his neck. "Not that it's my business, but is there anything between you and Aaron? Between karaoke and last night, it appeared like there might be."

Lauren shifted her weight.

Tony's lips flattened into a thin line before his easy grin was back. "Ah, you know what? Forget I asked. It's none of my business." He backed up a step.

"No, there's nothing going on." Nada. Zero. Especially not after she abandoned him on the dance floor. She turned away, hoping he hadn't noticed the redness crawling up her neck.

"I wondered if—"

"Hey Tony, we're ready to start the game. Are you reffing?" A tall boy poked his head around the door.

"Be right there." He opened his mouth then shut it. A moment ticked by. "Thanks for your help. Duty calls. See you tomorrow night." His tone seemed to hold a hint of regret.

"See you." Lauren collapsed into her chair. That was close. Grateful for the reprieve, Lauren was sure she didn't want to know what Tony had intended to say. He had seemed jealous of Aaron, but that couldn't be right. The look of relief that appeared on his face when she'd said nothing was going on was obvious. Shoot. She didn't need a man—not Tony or Aaron—in her life. This was her chance to have a new life, one she wanted, and she didn't plan on ruining it with a romantic relationship.

She wandered out into the foyer, the noise from the basketball game much louder out there. Tony made the travelling sign, and one of the kids threw his hands up. Tony just laughed. Her mother would have labeled him a "good guy." No celebrity status, and as far as Lauren could see, the guy didn't appear to be religious. He checked all her boxes. Too bad Lauren wasn't the slightest bit interested. Hopefully she'd imagined his jealousy.

Val sauntered onto the court and yelled at Tony. The kids cracked up. Tony gave it right back, his big grin taking out the sting. Val's dimples were on full display. Yeah, Lauren needed to shut Tony down when it came to any ideas about dating her.

She straightened her shoulders as she walked back to her office. *Focus on your job.* Lauren needed to forget romance—and men.

A sharp rap on the door jolted her out of her thoughts.

"Hey. Uh sorry. Didn't mean to scare you." Aaron stood in the doorway.

"No, it's okay. I'm a little jumpy. What can I do for you?"

"I've got time right now and wondered if you wanted to rehearse our duet?"

"Uh, sure. Just give me a moment." She shuffled papers around, sending a few flying to the floor. "Shoot." She bent over in her chair and swiped up the runaway documents just as Aaron knelt down. His face was inches from hers. His full lips were tempting. Her eyes locked with his. His breath tickled her cheek. The feeling of being in his arms last night while they danced wrapped around her. What would it be like to kiss Aaron Miles Scott? The thought shook her to her core. *Danger.* She turned her attention to the jumble of papers on the floor. "I'm such a klutz." She hurriedly stood, clutching the papers to her chest.

"You're definitely not a klutz." Aaron straightened.

Warning! Do not look into those gorgeous eyes. Promises she'd made to herself would lay discarded at her feet if she even peeked.

"I wanted to make sure you were okay. After last night. If I overstepped in any way…" His voice trailed off.

Prickly heat crawled up her neck, probably turning it a mottled red. Lauren smiled. "No. I'm fine. I overheated. Sorry I ran off." *Leaving you standing there alone.* Those unspoken words seemed to echo between them. "It wasn't you. I'll meet you in the practice room in five minutes."

He headed down the hallway.

Contrary to the promises she'd made to herself, she'd definitely see him around.

Chapter Seventeen

Aaron wrote down the notes he'd just played, humming them to himself. He read them over again before stroking them out. He tried again. It all sounded like what he'd written before. He rested his forehead on the edge of the guitar. *God, please help me.*

He shoved the guitar away, as no answer or creative spark hit him.

Lauren entered the practice room. "Sorry, the phone rang just as I was going to leave." Her flowy skirt and loose blouse added to her beauty. He'd noticed it in the office, but watching the material float around her added to the look—to her. Her bohemian style and pink-tipped hair had caught his attention from day one. If only he could get past her prickles. She was like a porcupine. Some days she had a spikey exterior, and other days she was fine. Still, it seemed to be spikey less and less. Maybe he was growing on her. He stared at his guitar to hide his smile.

"That sounded great. What song is it?" She set a few pages on the piano. She seemed to again be avoiding looking directly at him.

"I'm just fooling around." Maybe if he was honest about his own struggles, she'd be more open to him. "I've got a serious case of writer's block."

She raised her gaze, meeting his. Bingo. "Oh no. How do you cure it?" she asked.

"I wish I knew. It's more than just an off day or week. I haven't written anything new in years."

"I'm sorry. That sounds very frustrating."

"It is." Aaron's phone rang. He glanced at it and made a face. "I'm sorry. I have to get this. It's my agent."

Lauren nodded and Aaron walked to the far end of the room. "What's up, Jeremy?"

"Hey, how's my favourite client?" Jeremy didn't let Aaron answer. "I got you into the fair circuit."

"Uh, that's great." Aaron pumped a fist in the air. Things were looking up. Finally. "When does it start?"

"That's the thing, there are a few early gigs scheduled. So, we need you to leave next week."

Aaron stopped his pacing. Lowering his voice, he said, "I have the competition for the next three weeks."

"Just tell them you can't do it. This is too important. Talk to Tony. He'll understand."

He snuck a glance at Lauren. "No, I can't leave. I've already done the preliminary judging of the auditions. And it's been posted on socials that I'm involved with the competition."

Jeremy sighed. "We can spin the socials to our advantage. As soon as we announce the tour, people will forget the teen talent competition." Silence hung on the line. Finally, Jeremy spoke. "Do you want a professional career or not? Because as it stands, you are on the precipice of being forgotten."

Aaron didn't know the answer to that question any more. Two months ago, he would have jumped at this chance. Now? "Let me think on it."

"You have until tomorrow. Do not waste this opportunity, Aaron." Jeremy's tone was steely.

The call disconnected. Great. Now he'd ticked off his agent.

Lauren laid out sheet music. "Everything okay?"

"Yeah, fine." He ran his hands over the ivories. "Let's begin, okay?" Although he wondered if this was a waste of his time since he might not be around to actually sing with her.

Chapter Eighteen

THE FOLLOWING WEDNESDAY, THE sanctuary was packed for the first night of the competition. Aaron smiled as the crowd cheered for the first performer of the evening. It had been difficult to narrow it down from the forty to twenty-five. It was going to continue to get more and more challenging as the competition continued. He was glad it was the audience voting tonight. They'd post the results at noon tomorrow.

Aaron observed the girl onstage, whose appearance was not the only thing she'd changed. He sighed quietly, hating what he was going to do. She finished the song and applause rang out through the sanctuary along with a few whistles.

As the crowd settled, he held up his hand to grab her attention. "Andrea. Good job. You nailed your vocals. The guitar, while good, lacked emotion for me. At the audition, you were more country, and tonight there's not a hint of that. It's too bad because that country girl comes off more real and original than tonight's performance. At least for me. Why change it up?"

Despite her smile dimming, the girl nodded. "I didn't think the country songs would go over as well."

Aaron sighed quietly. "What do you enjoy singing the most?"

"Country."

"Then sing country. When you are yourself and do what you love, that's what counts, and ultimately, it comes across as a more authentic performance. I wanted to hear the country singer tonight. However, you have a great voice, and you can pull off country or pop. So, while it was good, for me it could have been better."

Lauren signaled her attention. "Great job. You have an incredible range of vocals. The chorus was strong. Kudos for trying something new and different. It takes courage. Part of experimenting with your sound is to gauge reaction. In this, I'm in agreement with Aaron. While this was a good performance, the other night rang truer for me. I saw a part of your soul in that audition and I wanted more of that tonight. I didn't get it."

A few boos echoed through the gym. Aaron held up his hand. "Wait now. This is constructive criticism, and as musicians, it's important to sift through the comments so you can decide the path you're going to take."

Andrea nodded. "Thank you."

Marisa chimed in with similar feedback, and Andrea hurried off the stage, her shoulders sagging slightly.

Aaron covered his mic and whispered to Lauren, "You agree with me? What is happening right now?"

Lauren narrowed her eyes, but the corner of her lips twitched slightly. "Don't get cocky. It was a one off."

"Whatever you say."

"I'm glad we're off the hook tonight to see who moves forward. This is more difficult than auditions for musicals." Marisa chewed the end of her pen.

"There are a number of talented young people. Seriously, I'm glad it wasn't just me that felt that way regarding Andrea's song. Her audition piece was raw and showed a part of her heart. Tonight's song bordered on fake. It felt like an act."

Lauren stared at him a minute before facing forward, ending the conversation. Suddenly her prickly side was out again. What had he done? Before he could ask, Will introduced the next contestant.

The woman was maddening. Aaron couldn't seem to do anything right. If she was irritated now, it was only going to get worse. After the show, Aaron had to tell them he wasn't going to be around for the finale.

A sour taste filled his mouth as Lauren shifted in her seat, the sweet smell of her shampoo wafting in the air as her hair swung around her shoulders. She wasn't going to take the news well; he was certain of it. Suddenly, he cared too much what she thought.

L AUREN WRAPPED HER ARMS around her stomach. Aaron's comment that the girl's performance felt fake was a sucker punch. The last couple of years, she'd pretended and performed to people's expectations. She and Sol had been well rehearsed at creating great appearances. Lauren could give a masterclass in faking it. Maybe like Aaron had seen in Andrea, people had thought she was a fraud. She had tried to live up to Sol's expectations of "a godly wife."

Aaron nudged her elbow. "What gives?"

Lauren swallowed around the lump in her throat. She opened her mouth to say, "Nothing," but changed her mind. If she wanted to be real, she needed to start being honest. "It's what you said just now. About being fake. Made me think back to being a pastor's wife. I faked it a lot. I wonder if people saw me as disingenuous."

Aaron locked eyes with her. "I didn't know you then, but in the here and now, you're completely genuine. If that helps."

"It does. Thank you." Maybe being vulnerable once in a while wasn't a bad thing. Before she could ponder that more, the melody to one of The Light's hits filled the sanctuary. The teen belted out the lyrics. Lauren winced.

You take me as I am,
No matter how messed up I've been.

That was certainly true in her life. God saw her. As is. Maybe she needed to quit hiding from him, too. Could she do that? If Aaron responded to her openness, maybe God would too. She shook her head. *Focus.* This was going to take time to figure out. Now wasn't the time. If the teen finished the song and she hadn't listened, it wouldn't be good.

The song choice surprised her. Choosing one of Aaron's songs was not advice she'd have given. She snuck a glance at Aaron. His face was blank.

The last chord resonated and the crowd went wild. Aaron's eyes locked with her own. He'd caught her staring. Shivers spiraled down her spine. A grin spread across his face. He clapped and whistled with everyone else.

As the roar died down, Aaron held up his hand to draw the guy's attention. "Justin, great performance. You're an accomplished piano player for someone so young."

The teen grinned widely.

"Your vocals need work." Aaron consulted his notes. "Overall, a good job. It's a gutsy choice to take one of my songs and sing it. I enjoyed it."

The crowd chanted Justin's name. Lauren inhaled deeply, waiting for the noise to calm. At a lull, she dove in. "Your piano skills are out of this world. I wasn't thrilled with the song choice. I thought you could have picked one more suited to your vocal range."

A few fans booed.

While they waited for the next contestant, Marisa turned to her and Aaron. "Wow. I'm surprised he picked one of your songs."

Aaron chuckled. "There's always one. It doesn't bother me. It can backfire for them though."

Lauren wondered what had possessed him to write the words to the song. She realized she didn't really know much about him other than what was already in the news.

"I can't believe we got through all the performances tonight." Lauren sighed as Will ended the evening.

"It was a lot." Marisa stood and shook out her legs. "I don't know how the audience is going to choose only ten for the second night of performances. I want them all to move forward."

"Right?" Lauren nodded.

Aaron fidgeted with his papers, dreading telling them he was leaving the competition. He'd put it off since the weekend.

"What's up?" Marisa fisted her hands on her hips.

He scratched the back of his neck. "I've got news. My agent got me booked into the fair circuit. I'm so sorry, but I won't be here for the last two nights of the competition."

Heat burned through Lauren's chest. "What about the coaching? That's the next part of the performances. We're all supposed to coach the top ten."

Marisa frowned. "Does Tony know?"

"I'm going to tell him now. I don't have a choice." If he didn't do the tour, he was going to lose a lot of promotion. "You guys will have to split the ten. I'm sorry to give you more work, but you're both more than capable."

"Don't try and schmooze us." Lauren crossed her arms over her chest. "Did you care at all about the kids? Our duet?" Lauren made a face. "You don't have choice? There's always a choice. You've chosen to leave."

Marisa glanced between Aaron and Lauren.

"You don't understand." The pressure to meet expectations from his fans and Jeremy. His own desires and dreams. To make it up to Wade. "I'll be back on Sundays for church except for the last couple of weeks."

"Well, that's great for you. Not so great for us." Marisa sighed. "I wish you well. It was great working with you, and I'm sad you won't be here for the rest of the competition." She smiled, although she didn't look happy as she walked away.

Lauren grabbed her purse, not feeling as generous as Marisa. "In the end, you did exactly what I'd expected you to do. It was always all about you and your career. Thanks for not disappointing."

"You have no idea what I've sacrificed. I don't have a choice if I want to sell albums and have a professional career."

Lauren's hard stare cut him. "Right. Good to know." She stalked away.

Aaron shoved his hand through his hair. Jeremy had given him an ultimatum: either go on the tour or find another agent. He needed Jeremy and he needed to sell albums, even an album he didn't like. If he ever wanted to write and produce new music, he couldn't let Jeremy go. Tony approached and Aaron's shoulders curled forward as he shoved his hands into his pants pockets. He hadn't wanted to disappoint anyone, and now he'd gone and done it to everyone, including himself.

At 4:40 in the morning, Aaron accepted the fact he wasn't going back to sleep and sat up in bed. Lauren's accusations and Tony's disappointed expression had haunted his thoughts and chased away sleep. Not to mention he should have told them sooner so they could find another judge. He pulled on his running

shorts and a T-shirt. Heading out into the empty streets, he hoped he could outrun his thoughts.

Five miles later, Aaron's legs were burning, but his mind had calmed. He walked the half block to his favourite café. He ordered a protein shake and waited while the barista made it.

"Excuse me. Are you Aaron Miles Scott?" An older woman, probably in her sixties, smiled at him.

Inwardly sighing, Aaron forced a smile. "I am." He didn't want to deal with a fan.

"I don't want to intrude. I'll only take a minute of your time. I want to thank you for all your work on the Glebe Centre's teen talent competition. My grandson auditioned and made it through to last night. I can't tell you how much this has meant to him. He's shy, but he wanted to try out. When he made it to through the auditions, it gave him more confidence. He's going to try out for his school musical this year. I know he especially appreciated your advice and remarks."

Aaron blinked. He'd expected an autograph or selfie request, not this.

The woman laid a hand on his forearm. "You're making a difference in these kids' lives. Thank you." She squeezed his arm gently. Aaron blinked back the burning in his eyes. Over the years, he'd listened to stories about how the band's music helped people or inspired them to change. It was always great to hear. This woman's story was different. It wasn't his fame or songs that had changed a person. It was speaking truth into a life, giving the boy a chance to do something. Building into people.

Warmth spread through his chest and he grinned. Maybe the choice to do the fair circuit or judge the finale didn't have to be all or nothing. He wanted to finish this competition because he was enjoying coaching the kids. Maybe a certain judge made him want to stay, too. Her late husband had already let her down. Aaron didn't want to be another Christian who put her second or disappointed her. He pulled his phone out of his zippered pocket and found Jeremy's number. For once, he was going to choose to do the right thing.

Chapter Nineteen

"What are you doing here? I thought you'd left." Lauren blinked in case she was seeing things. Maybe she was more caffeine- and sleep-deprived than she'd thought. The radio station's clock said it was almost 7:00 in the morning. She was there to do another interview, a follow-up, with Charlie Most. The first night of performances the day before had been so popular that Charlie had invited them back.

Aaron shoved his hands in his jacket pockets. "I spoke to Jeremy and convinced him that it's important to fulfill my commitment. I told him that I'd only miss two weeks of the tour and if the organizers cancelled because of it, then so be it."

Lauren assessed the man standing in front of her. The more she got to know him, the more he failed at the rockstar persona. "How did he take it?"

"He finally saw my point of view. It doesn't look good for me to quit after the first week. He convinced the sponsors to let me join two weeks late. They have a couple of local bands from the areas that are going to take my place for those weeks." Aaron pointed to the seat. "May I?"

Lauren moved her papers and bag off the cushion.

"I thought I'd join you for this interview if that's okay." He tapped the face of his watch. "And I'm five minutes early."

Lauren smiled. "I'd like that."

Aaron settled in close to her, his bicep brushing against her shoulder. And...she didn't mind. Her traitorous body had practically done a cheerleading routine when he walked into the room a few minutes earlier. "Since I'm going to be around, we need to rehearse our duet. Do you have time in the next couple of days?"

"I can make time." She folded her hands in her lap. "Thank you. I'm glad you came back."

Aaron leaned closer. "I should thank you. You gave me a kick when I needed it. I do care for these kids. More than any album. Promoting the album was about meeting obligations, but you and a grandmother made me realize what's really important, making a difference in a person's life."

"A grandmother?"

The producer came over to them. "Oh great, I'm glad you made it, Mr. Scott. You can both follow me."

Aaron whispered, "I'll fill you in later."

Lauren locked eyes with him, a buzz zinging through her. "I look forward to hearing it. Now let's promote this thing and raise a lot of money for the kids."

After the interview, Aaron offered to drop off Lauren at work since she'd taken the bus. As they walked out of the building, two gorgeous women approached holding out CDs. "It's really you! We heard you were here for an interview. So, we thought we'd come see if we could catch you," The brunette said.

"We're huge fans of The Light, and we've already bought your solo album. Would you sign our CDs?" The blonde, whose hair reminded Lauren of an old actress who used to do shampoo commercials, held out the disc case and marker. "Are you every going on a reunion tour?"

Aaron took the marker and case. "I doubt it. Who do you want me to make this out to?" He smiled. The women giggled.

While Aaron turned on the charm, Lauren stepped back, feeling like the odd person out. Aaron was so normal that she'd almost forgotten he was a celebrity. *You let your guard down. You forgot your mantra.* She didn't need a man for a fresh start.

The women walked away giggling. Oh brother. It would take a special woman to deal with that on a regular basis. And it wasn't her. Not that it was likely going to be a problem. Aaron didn't like her like that. No men, especially rockstars and pastors. The man standing in front of her represented both. *Danger.*

Aaron glanced at her. "You look annoyed."

"You wouldn't understand."

"Try me."

Lauren huffed. "It's so annoying how these women fall all over themselves trying to get your attention."

"Jealous?" Aaron smirked.

"Absolutely not. I feel sorry for them."

"They're fans. Without them, what would be the point of my career?" He tugged his keys from his jeans pocket. "Why does it bother you so much?"

Lauren swallowed. "Sol cheated. I guess I wonder if that's how Sol succumbed to having an affair. Women were always vying for his attention."

They arrived at the truck. Aaron stood in front of the passenger door, blocking Lauren from entering the vehicle. This conversation wasn't ending anytime soon.

"I'm sorry you had to go through that. Now I understand why that would bother you. I'm not going to lie and say it doesn't affect me. Because it's always a temptation. I think acknowledging that helps me be more real and proactive."

Lauren stared at the door. "Can I get in the truck now?"

"One more thing. I've never told anyone this. I stay accountable to Will. We meet weekly, chat, and make sure we're keeping our eyes up."

Oh.

"I'm not Sol." He waited a minute before opening the door for her.

Still. *Danger.* Lauren slid into her seat. Before shutting the door, she said, "Thanks for sharing that."

After Aaron settled himself in the driver's seat, they pulled away from the curb. His words wound on repeat in Lauren's thoughts. It was good he kept accounts with his friend. It didn't mean he couldn't fall to the temptation, which was why it was good for her to stick to her boundaries. She stared at his profile.

"You don't talk about the band much."

He scrunched up his face. "Sure, I do."

"No, you clam up. When they asked about a reunion, you just gave the accepted line. You did it with Dwayne, that reporter, too."

"I don't know if there will ever be a reunion. I'm not going to get their hopes up."

"That's not what I meant. You don't tell stories about the guys or what it was like to tour. It's like you're trying to forget your past."

Aaron's jaw tightened. Maybe she'd pushed too much, but it suddenly bothered her.

"You want to hear about the band? Okay, let me tell you. If we were caught alone with a girl, the church world said we were being immoral even if it was totally innocent. If we wore jeans that were too low, we were leading the youth astray. If we went to a party and alcohol was served, we were addicts. We lived under the judgment and scrutiny of both the church and the secular worlds. Most of those people were supposed to be on our side. It was not as glamourous as everyone thinks it was."

He ran a hand through his hair. "Most days I'm just trying to forget it and hope others do, too. Please don't judge me by what I did at seventeen, nineteen, whatever. I was a kid."

His voice was low and he sounded defeated. They stopped at a red light.

"I'm sorry. We all did stupid things as kids. I'm sorry people haven't let go of your past." She laid her hand on his arm. "I get it a little. I've lived it, too, as Sol's wife. People made assumptions based on their own expectations and the stereotypes I didn't fit into. My shyness and fear of making a wrong move came across as unfriendly. They said I was inhospitable and a snob." She finger-quoted. "He cheated because I wasn't a good enough wife." Her voice trembled on that last word. "And who knows what else."

Only a few feet separated them. What started as a face off, now felt like a team huddle.

He glanced over at her. "I'm sorry that happened to you. You didn't deserve that."

"It's over now."

"That's how I feel about my band days. Why keep reliving it? It's in the past." The light turned green. The truck moved forward.

"Weren't there any good times?" Lauren was curious.

"It's complicated. I want to move past that. Maybe start a new thing."

The truck pulled up in front of the community centre.

"Thanks for the ride." Lauren hurriedly jumped out of the truck. Suddenly, she related to Aaron and that was scary. She couldn't put enough distance between herself and Aaron. *Danger.*

Chapter Twenty

ONE, TWO, THREE, FOUR, *five*...

Would ten counts be enough to get his annoyance under control? Aaron leaned his hip against the side of the piano in the practice room at the community centre. Justin, the incredible pianist who had chosen The Light's song, had won the audience over, and they voted him into the top ten. For this round, Aaron's job was to coach him through his song choice for the next night of competition the following week. After listening to Justin's choice of song, Aaron wished he was spending his Saturday somewhere else.

Not for the first time, Aaron couldn't believe he'd drawn the rocker girl's name and not Justin's. The piano was Aaron's least favourite instrument to play. Lauren would have been a more suitable coach since she taught piano lessons.

"You play so well that I can't help you improve with that." Aaron leaned his hip against the side of the upright piano in the practice room at the community centre. "Instead, I want to focus on your choice of songs. What made you decide to do this song?"

"It's a favourite and it's piano-based."

Aaron nodded. "Here's the thing. It's good, not exceptional. For me, it's a cover of the original. It's not a great fit for your voice. Why not choose a different song and make it your own? Or at least jazz this one up and arrange it in your vocal range if you're dead set on it."

Justin squinted at his sheet music. "I'm not any good at being original. I'd lose the contest."

"What do you want more? To win or to grow musically? Because this is an opportunity to move out of your comfort zone and mature as a musician. I can help you. That's what I'm here for, to coach you."

The kid made a face.

Aaron searched for the words to motivate him. "You have a lot of potential. I think you're capable of doing a piece more original than you think. I'd suggest 'Walking in Memphis' by Marc Cohn."

"It's country." The young man snorted.

"Hardly. It will be easier to sing, and you'll hit the notes. If you think it sounds too country, make it jazzier. You could definitely do that with that song."

"I don't like jazz or country. I don't want to do it. My friends will think I'm some middle-aged guy, like you." Justin frowned.

Aaron shoved down his frustration, ignoring the dig. He needed to convince the kid that his suggestion was sound. Before he could argue further, Justin stood. "I'm good with my choice. It's the people voting, right? They're going to vote for a contemporary song, not an old one."

Aaron didn't miss the sarcastic tone. "It's up to you. If you need any help, I'm here."

The kid saluted and sauntered out of the room. Aaron ground his teeth. He had to let it go. It was the kid's choice.

"You look like that didn't go so well." Tony stepped into the room.

"Nope. He didn't want to hear what I suggested." Aaron closed the lid over the piano keys. "I'm not sure what I did wrong or if I could have said it differently."

"Justin, right?" Tony rubbed his jaw. "He's a tough one. His dad is a widower with a high stress job. He's a little intense. I'm not surprised Justin didn't listen to you. He only cares about what his dad has to say."

Oh.

"Don't be too hard on yourself. You do what you can and hope for the best with these kids." Tony left, leaving Aaron to his thoughts.

Hoping for the best was good. Yet it left things up to chance, didn't it? Aaron wasn't just going to hope. He'd pray for Justin and his situation. He'd rather leave it in God's hands. Justin may or may not come around, but Aaron understood what it was like to have parental pressure. Once he'd made it big, his parents had turned their attention to him and expected him to succeed. Big. Maybe he could connect with the kid on that level.

His thoughts turned to Ryan. Maybe he needed to rethink his approach with him, too. The kid was in a tough situation with his mom being sick. Maybe Aaron needed to be creative in his approach to him, too.

He pulled his phone from his pocket, scrolling to find Ryan's number. Maybe a little understanding would turn the situation around.

"I THINK THAT'S A wrap, Crystal. It sounds great. You've got a few days to practice." Lauren placed the sheet music into a folder. "Excited?"

Crystal packed up her guitar. Her blue hair, piercings, and "don't mess with me" expression hid a talented and surprisingly emotional musician. "I can't believe I made it this far. For a girl to play heavier music is unusual. I don't always get the respect. To make it to the top ten shows everyone that girls can rock, too."

Lauren high-fived her. "You bet we can. If you need anything before Friday text me."

"I will. Thanks for your help. I'm hopeful I can make it to the final night." Crystal settled her guitar over her shoulder and hurried out, her hair flying behind her. She passed Aaron on her way out the door of the community centre's gym. He sauntered over to the piano.

Lauren turned on the bench. "Spying? How long have you been out there?"

Aaron chuckled. "No, I'm not spying. It's not a competition between judges. We're not The Voice."

"I guess." She groaned, "I'm out of my depth."

Aaron jutted his thumb behind him. "From what I overheard, you're in exactly the right spot. She sounded like a pro today. She didn't the other night. My guess is that's because of your coaching and encouragement."

Lauren fingered the file folder in her hand. "I... Thanks. She's got real pipes there, and her guitar work is good. Did you know she's only been playing a couple of years?" Lauren mimed an explosion coming from her ears. "Other than spying, what can I help you with?"

"Nothing. I just finished with Justin." He, too, made an exploding gesture.

"Uh oh. What happened?"

Aaron filled her in on his session with the boy. "I thought it was a good suggestion." He sat down beside her on the piano bench. "Not off to a great start with the coaching sessions."

"Let me give it a try. I think you're onto something." Lauren set the folders down and ran her fingers over the keys. After a couple of attempts, she found the right notes and tempo. Her fingers flew across the keys. Warmth spread throughout her chest right to her fingertips. A smile crossed her lips, one she couldn't stop if she tried. She finished with a crescendo, the final notes ringing out.

Aaron sat slack-jawed. "How did you do that? That's exactly what I wanted him to do."

Lauren wiped a piece of dust off the keys. "I don't know. It's hard to explain. Justin wouldn't find it hard since he's such a talented a pianist. It was a good suggestion. Hopefully he'll come around."

She played the chorus again and Aaron sang softly beside her. Goosebumps popped on her arms as his smooth, velvety voice wrapped around her. She'd undervalued jamming. Resting her hands over the keys, she said, "It sounds amazing. I hope he changes his mind, although he'd never compete with you vocally." Ugh. Had she said that out loud? The grin on Aaron's face as he leaned toward her said he'd heard her loud and clear. He was so close; she could see a few freckles on his nose. Tingles travelled over Lauren's body as his warm breath caressed her cheek. Lauren's belly flipped and she wanted him to kiss her. Anticipated it.

"Lauren." Tony's voice interrupted the moment. The doors flew open as Lauren jerked away from Aaron.

"Oh, there you are, Lauren." Tony stood in the doorway. His brow creased. "Uh, Tyler, your next coaching session, is here."

Aaron checked his watch. "I was just leaving. Thanks for your help." He stood.

"No problem. I'm looking forward to hearing Justin and your other contestants." Lauren lifted her hand in a small wave.

Tony walked into the room. He didn't look too happy. "You know he's not going to stick around after the competition. His agent is trying to get him booked on tours. In fact, he was going to miss the end of the competition, but Jeremy arranged it so he'd stay. Otherwise, he'd be gone already."

Lauren crossed her arms over her chest. "I know. There's nothing going on. Aaron told Marisa and I he was leaving but changed his mind."

Tony shook his head. "It was his agent, not Aaron."

Lauren gathered her bag and music. "Nothing's going on," she repeated. "I need to get some other music. Excuse me." She hurried past Tony, not liking the way this conversation was going. Aaron had told her he'd asked Jeremy to make it happen, but Tony was saying it wasn't that way. This is why she shouldn't be almost kissing rockstars or even thinking about it.

"I'm busy. So, get to the point." Ryan's tone was cold.

Aaron pulled his phone away from his ear and inhaled. Exhaled. The guy wasn't going to make this easy. Aaron wanted to take the high road with him, but that didn't mean Ryan would reciprocate.

Aaron lifted the phone back to his ear. "I thought we could get together and try to work things out. I haven't communicated well and that's on me. I'm sorry." Aaron stood by his vehicle outside the community centre. It had been a long day of coaching, but other than Justin, the kids had been open and eager. It had inspired Aaron to call Ryan.

"I'm not interested in anything you have to say. You got the job because of your fame and nothing else. You don't deserve it. You have no idea what leadership is about."

Perhaps the kid had a point. Aaron pressed on. "You have all kinds of potential, and part of becoming a leader is letting yourself be mentored."

"By you?" Ryan mocked.

"Not necessarily. Perhaps Luke could do it." Luke was another worship leader. He and Ryan appeared to be friends.

"I'm a way better musician and singer than Luke and you know it. You're just keeping me down to feed your ego. The truth *will* come out. I'll make sure of it. You're no worship leader and everyone will know." The call ended.

Stunned, Aaron pulled the phone away from his ear. "Hello?" Nothing. He tossed the phone onto the driver's seat through the open window even though he felt like whipping it across the parking lot. What did Ryan mean by the truth coming out? He couldn't mean Wade. No, the kid was referring to Aaron's lack of experience. That must be it.

Aaron groaned. He was two for two today. Maybe Ryan was right. Maybe Aaron had no idea how to lead the worship team or even coach a teenager. Neither Justin nor Ryan had listened. *What am I doing?*

Chapter Twenty-One

FRIDAY NIGHT THE EXCITEMENT of the full house filled the air in the sanctuary. It reminded Aaron of his concert days just before the band walked onstage. He settled into his seat, anticipation filling him. *I'm glad I'm here for this.* Staying to finish out the competition had been the right choice.

"We sold out again tonight. The kids are probably dying of nerves. I'm only a judge and I'm nervous." Marisa lifted her shaking hand.

"They're performers at heart and this is what they love to do. They'll be fine," Aaron said. "I find it hard to believe you're nervous. You're doing a terrific job coaching the kids. And I can't wait to hear your contestants. Did Henry come tonight?"

"Yes, he's here somewhere with his grandparents. As for my contestants, I'm excited for them. All of them." Marisa studied him in the semi-dark. "What was the largest audience you played to?"

Aaron cracked his neck. "I don't know."

"You're lying. C'mon," she coaxed.

He popped the other side of his neck and noticed Marisa wince at the sound. "We played for the Dove Awards, which was broadcast around the US."

"Oh my gosh." Marisa's jaw dropped.

"It was a little terrifying." Aaron glanced at the stage. "Once I'm on the stage with my guitar, everything fades and there's no place I'd rather be." Or that's how he used to feel.

Marisa smiled. "I prefer backstage myself. This," she made a waving gesture, "is as in the spotlight as I want to be."

Aaron patted the empty seat beside him. "Where's Lauren?"

Marisa pursed her lips. "Come to think of it, I haven't seen her yet." She checked her watch. "Hopefully, she arrives soon. We've got five minutes until the lights go up."

As Marisa spoke, Lauren appeared. She took her time hanging her purse on the back of her chair and removing her light jacket.

Aaron's eyes narrowed. "What's up?" He leaned close, getting a whiff of her light perfume. He didn't know what it was, but he liked it. A lot.

"Nothing."

She was avoiding him. "How come you won't look at me?" he pushed.

Lauren faced him. "Was it your decision to stay or Jeremy's?"

"Mine. Why?'

Lauren released her grip on the edge of the table. "Never mind."

Before Aaron could pursue the conversation, Will welcomed everyone to the Top Ten Night. The first two contestants were Marisa's and Lauren's respectively. Both performed well. The audience were going to have a tough decision narrowing it down to the final three.

The judges had each coached three performers, and Aaron had taken the extra teen in hopes he'd get bonus points from Lauren. By her feisty entrance tonight that wasn't happening.

Aaron sat up as Justin entered from stage right. The young man sat down on the piano bench.

Will leaned his hand on the top of the piano lid. "Justin, what song are you performing and why did you choose it?"

"I'm singing and playing Coldplay's 'Fix You.'"

Will motioned for Justin to take it away. Aaron listened, trying to keep his mind open. Justin was only a kid, a kid with parental pressure on him. Perhaps Aaron was wrong in suggesting Marc Cohn. And he hoped Justin did prove him wrong.

As Justin finished the piece, the crowd cheered. Aaron didn't love it, but the crowd did, which was all that mattered. They were the ones voting tonight. Once everyone had settled in their seats, Marisa spoke. "Great job, Justin. You are an insane pianist. I'd love to see you take more risks. It was good but a bit boring. A decent cover."

Lauren's comments were similar, which was what Aaron had suspected. A chorus of boos filled the church.

"Justin, a good cover. Your technique on the piano is exceptional. Vocally, it was okay. For me, the song was good. That's all," he said.

More loud boos. Aaron winced as the kid frowned before trudging off the stage. Maybe Aaron should have gone to the fair circuit early instead of disappointing teenagers at the competition.

Lauren reached under the table and squeezed his hand. "Hey, you weren't wrong. There are times we need to hear the hard stuff so we can move forward."

"I feel like a schmuck." Still, he'd been told harsher things in his career.

"You're not." She smiled and let go of his hand, turning her attention to the stage once again. He stared at her profile a minute longer. She was beautiful, inside and out. And at the moment, he didn't try to squash the thought. He liked Lauren Grace.

CRYSTAL BOWED AND LAUREN whistled through her fingers. Her young protégé was the last of the ten contestants tonight. The girl had rocked her song and wowed the crowd. Marisa spoke into her mic. "Wow, girl. You are going places. That was unbelievable. I'd pay to see you sing and play."

Aaron nodded. "Well done, Crystal. An outstanding performance. Great vocals. Your grittiness fit the song well. I loved it. Good guitar, too. You're the real deal."

Lauren blew a kiss. "You rocked that. You proved that girls can sing and play hard rock and do it well. Bravo!"

Crystal waved to the audience, who roared their approval as she ran off the stage.

The spotlight hit Will. "And that wraps up our evening. Ten performances, and now, guys and gals, we are voting for the top three. You have twenty-four hours to do so and the winners will be announced tomorrow night on our podcast, 'Youth Alive.' How you can tune in is up on the screen. Thanks for coming and goodnight." Will saluted and the lights went out. A minute later, the houselights came up, blinding Lauren. She blinked several times.

"Ow. Is there not a better way to do that?" Aaron complained, rubbing his eyes.

"Seriously, they're going to blind us. Or give us a migraine." Marisa shaded her eyes.

Tony appeared out of Lauren's blind spot, and her heartbeat ticked up. Not now. She hurriedly stuffed her papers in her tote. Why was she acting like she was in middle school?

"Hey, guys, great show. You did amazing work with the kids." Tony gave them the thumbs up. Lauren slipped the bag over her shoulder. "Lauren, you got a minute?"

"Sorry, Tony. I gotta run." Was that disappointment on his face? She pretended not to see it or the too-observant glance from Aaron. She waved to the group and hurried off. Val was cleaning up the makeup and hair area and didn't notice Lauren. She hurried by, hoping to slip out unseen.

The fresh outdoor air hit her in the face as she strode out the front doors of the community centre. Using the key fob to unlock her car, she jogged over to her SUV. She fumbled with the door handle, opening it on the second try only to see an arm stretch out and shut it. She whirled around. *Please don't be Tony.*

Aaron stood there. Oh.

"Where's the fire? I practically had to run to catch you."

"No fire. I just need to go home." She peeked over his shoulder. No Tony. She let out a tiny breath.

He crossed his arms. "Why are you hiding from Tony?" He glanced over his shoulder. "It is Tony, am I right?"

Lauren tugged on her door, wanting to escape. Aaron held it shut. "I'm not. What makes you say that?" She blew a piece of hair that had come undone.

Aaron shifted his weight, resting his back against the door, the door she wanted to open so she could leave. She wasn't going anywhere. "You're a bad liar." His eyes roamed her face. "Did he—"

"No. He's a great guy and nothing but a gentleman." She pushed the annoying strand away. Ugh. "I think he'd like to get to know me better, in a romantic way, and I don't share those sentiments."

"I see." Aaron stared at her lips. "Is there someone else?" He leaned in slightly, his warm breath teasing her. She wanted him to kiss her.

You don't need a man. The thought was like a splash of cold water in the face. She blinked, breaking their connection.

Aaron cleared his throat. "Why don't you tell him? You're a grown-up. Have the decency to be honest with him—and yourself." Aaron backed up a step, releasing his hold on the door.

"You're right. I need to act like a grown-up." She sighed and opened her car door. People walked to their cars or milled around in groups, chatting. She tossed her bag onto the passenger seat, wanting to end the now-awkward conversation. "Val is interested in him."

A soft breeze ruffled Aaron's hair as he stared across the parking lot. "Why don't you let it play out and see what happens? Maybe he's being friendly. He's that type of guy."

"Could be. I don't want either of them to be upset with me. I'm short on friends."

Lauren settled into her seat.

"I'll be your friend if you let me. Since you're short on friends." His tone was low and intimate, sending shivers down her spine. Lauren diverted her gaze to the door handle. Much safer.

"I guess I'm not in a position to be choosey." She grinned, glad to be back on solid footing.

He chuckled softly. "Not much of an endorsement, but I'll take it." He stayed a minute longer before he stepped away from the car. "I left my stuff in the gym. I need to go and retrieve it before it gets chucked into the Lost and Found." He spread his hands out. "Put the poor guy out of his agony."

Lauren wondered if Aaron was talking about someone other than Tony.

Chapter Twenty-Two

THE NEXT DAY THE corner farmer's market aisles were jammed with people carrying canvas bags in varying degrees of fullness. Lauren squeezed by young families with babies strapped to their fathers' back and mothers holding tightly to their toddlers' hands. Lauren picked out a half dozen oranges and dropped them into her mesh bag. After a second elbow to her ribcage, she decided to pay and leave. Saturday and shopping didn't mix. She needed caffeine.

"Busy place, eh?"

Lauren's heart thudded at the familiar voice. "Hey, Tony. Way too busy for me."

"Not a fan of crowds?"

"Not my favourite." She tamped the urge to elbow her way out of the store. That would be rude especially since she worked for him. Maybe she was imagining his interest in her.

"I find it ebbs and flows. Wait five minutes and it won't be as bad."

"I'm good with my oranges." She lifted her mesh bag full of the fruit. A couple with an infant in a baby backpack squeezed past them, forcing Lauren to step closer to Tony.

He squeezed her elbow. "C'mon. You've come all this way for healthy food. Don't chicken out now."

Lauren bit her bottom lip as she considered the two bowls of ice cream she'd consumed the night before. Yes, she'd come for healthy food to counter the sugar she'd consumed. "You're right despite the fact I'd rather have coffee." She eased away from him.

Tony chuckled. "Left the house without caffeinating?"

"A very bad decision." She picked out bananas and a basket of blueberries, imagining a cold smoothie. Healthy ice cream. That thought made her smile as she lined up behind Tony at the cash.

He nudged her gently with his elbow. "Not so bad, right?"

"Livable." She eyed his items as he placed them on the cashier's counter: brown eggs, milk, spinach, apples, and oranges.

"Do you always eat your fruits and veggies?"

He ducked his chin. "I'm a health nut. It's hard with the youth, and I do indulge in a slice of veggie pizza or a burger. As a kid, I was heavy. So, now I try to stay fit."

The guy could be on the cover of *Men's Health*, and his kindness only added to his appeal. In another lifetime, maybe Tony would be perfect for her. Too bad there were no butterflies or tingles in her gut.

He waited while she paid for her groceries. Lauren had half hoped he'd leave. No such luck. They wandered out together into the cool morning.

Tony held up his canvas bag. "I make a mean omelet. Want to join me?"

Heat crawled up her neck as she searched her mind for an excuse. Her mind was empty. "Oh, uh, I should probably go. Val will wonder where I'm at."

The hopeful expression on his face flatlined. Finally, he smiled, but it appeared forced, and it never reached his eyes. "Sure. Maybe another time?"

She wound the handle of the mesh bag around her fingers. No time like the present to set him straight. "I'm sorry, Tony. I don't think so. I'm not ready..." She stopped, then started over. "I think you're a great guy, and you're going to make some girl very happy, but I'm not that girl. I'm sorry." *Val might be.* The temptation to say something was real, but it wasn't her place. Val would not approve.

His chin dipped. "I understand."

She laid her hand on his forearm. "I hope we can be friends." Was that a wince?

His dark amber eyes met hers. "Sure. I hope this won't make it awkward at work?"

"Not at all."

He stopped at a side street. "I turn here. Have a great weekend." He strode away.

Lauren sighed. Being a grown up wasn't what it was cracked up to be.

Aaron checked the order of service as Sunday morning service wound down. The high from Friday night's competition hadn't dimmed, and he hoped Ryan didn't pop a hole in his bubble. One more song to go. The kid had kept to the order of service. No outrageous music. The opening chords of the song suddenly turned staccato, and Ryan and the singers were hopping around.

No. No. No. The beat of the rap song that Aaron had vetoed echoed throughout the auditorium. Aaron's fingers crumpled the paper in his hands. Will sucked in a breath next to him. Aaron could feel eyes boring into the back of his head. He glanced at Ed, whose face was a blank slate.

Ryan sang out the last of the chorus while locking eyes with Aaron. After finishing, Ryan leaned into the mic. "We hope you enjoyed that number. We believe God likes all kinds of music."

Aaron clenched his teeth at the kid's cocky grin. What Pandora's Box had he just opened? The worship team came off the stage as Ed strode to the podium. Ryan smiled smugly as he sat next to the other team members. Several people around him were frowning or had crossed their arms over their chest. Aaron recognized the body language. Great. A few people glared at Aaron. Even better.

Aaron braced himself mentally for the earful he was sure to hear after the service. He didn't hear a word of Ed's sermon. Instead, Aaron ruminated on what words he'd be having with Ryan when he saw him. After Will issued the benediction, Aaron beelined it for Ryan.

Before he could reach the kid, Ed stepped into Aaron's path, holding up a hand. "Hold on now, son. Let's cool off first so we don't go spouting words we might regret."

Aaron's nostrils flared while he kept his lips firmly clamped. Ed was right; he needed to cool down. Aaron followed his boss as Ed led him to the far side of the auditorium. "I'm not happy with the choice either. However, storming over there isn't going to help the situation. Take a breath and we'll deal with Ryan when cooler heads prevail."

Aaron noticed Ed's wife eyeing them. Ed waved at her. "Agree?"

"Sure. I'll talk to him tomorrow."

Ed nodded and hurried over to the woman. Aaron pivoted away from the worship team and headed out to the foyer, where Will waited by the glass front doors, his toddler, Matty asleep in his arms. Janey, herding Ella, approached her husband just as Aaron came up to them.

"I'd say by the expression on your face that wasn't what you'd planned." Will planted a kiss on Matty's head before releasing him to Janey. He turned to Aaron. "That was something."

"It was something alright." Janey nodded, her eyebrows hiking up.

Aaron scrubbed his face. "Can we not...?"

Matty leaned his head into the crook of Janey's neck. She spoke over his head. "Sure. We'll give you a reprieve, but it's not over. It's just getting started."

Aaron's shoulders sagged. "I know. Hot Topic Number One: why the new music director allowed rap in a church service."

An older woman dressed in a white pantsuit marched toward Aaron. He groaned. It was already starting. Mrs. Beattie, chair of the elders' board.

"Mr. Scott, may I have a word?" Her red lipstick made her lips a prominent thin line across her pale powdered face. Did he have a choice?

"Sure, Mrs. Beattie. Why don't—"

"That music was disrespectful, unchristian, and way too loud. Especially on communion Sunday. What are you going to do, or is this what we can expect from a rockstar director of worship?" She glared at Aaron. "I told Ed he was ridiculous for hiring the likes of you." Several heads swung in their direction. So much for having a private conversation. Aaron sighed.

"Maybe you can lower your voice, Mrs. Beattie. Not everyone needs to hear this conversation."

Her lip curled up. "Don't be smart with me, young man. I asked a question and I want an answer. And if you don't have one, I'm lodging a complaint with Ed."

Blood whooshed through Aaron's temple, and he thought his head might explode. "I hear what you're saying Mrs. Beattie, and your complaint is noted. Pastor Ed and I will be addressing your grievances." He checked his watch. "The service has only been over fifteen minutes. You need to give us time to talk it over."

Mrs. Beattie harrumphed and crossed her arms. "I expect a phone call. Tomorrow. Even though you didn't play the music, you're in charge, Mr. Scott. The buck stops with you. If you think you can charm everyone and get what you want because you have a Dove award, I assure you, you are sorely mistaken."

She whirled away, leaving a trail of strong perfume in her wake. Shoulders sagging, Aaron slowly faced his friends.

Janey wound her arm around Aaron's and gave a comforting squeeze. "It will be okay."

"It's only the beginning," he said as his phone buzzed in his pocket. Aaron turned off the device. The tsunami of complaints, accusations, and condemnations would only build speed until they crashed, and he didn't want to be around when it happened. He wanted to kill Ryan.

Will clapped his shoulder. "It will blow over. That's the thing about church. There's always a new thing for them to complain about right around the corner," he joked.

Nausea rolled through Aaron. *I told Ed he was ridiculous for hiring the likes of you.* Mrs. Beattie's words reverberated through his mind. He should never have taken the job. His fame had taken the focus off God, and Ryan obviously wanted to ruin his fledgling career at Cartwright. He sighed. At least being involved in the fair circuit would give him a distraction from all this drama.

Chapter Twenty-Three

Lauren balled a pair of socks from the piles that surrounded her. She usually found the smell of clean laundry soothing. Not tonight. Lauren folded a pair of jeans while surreptitiously watching Val flick through the TV channels. Sunday night wasn't the best for TV shows. "What about that new sitcom with the freshman at college?"

Val shook her head and switched the channel. Lauren refolded a shirt. Val clicked the remote and the TV went black. "I don't want to watch anything."

"Do you mind if I watch a show?"

Val chucked the remote to Lauren, who caught it with one hand. Instead of clicking the On button, she stared at the black oblong shape in her hand. Her roommate wasn't herself and Lauren needed to find out why.

"What's wrong? You seem off today." Lauren dropped the remote and picked up a tank top, folding it in half. Val had been mopey since she'd returned from church.

Val scooped out a handful of popcorn from the bowl that sat on the coffee table. She popped a piece in her mouth and chewed. "I think Tony might like someone."

Lauren's fingers tightened around the shirt. "What makes you think that?" *Tell her.*

"He asked *you* out," Val whispered.

Lauren exhaled loudly. "I said no. I'm not interested in him that way." She tossed the shirt into the laundry basket.

"That makes it worse. He asks you out and you don't even like him. Meanwhile, I've been pining for him for two years. He barely registers my existence. The worst part is that you didn't tell me he asked you out."

"I'm sorry. I should have told you. I was afraid to." Lauren set her elbows on her thighs and laid her head in her hands. Val had worked most of yesterday, and Lauren hadn't seen her except in the morning. It was a convenient excuse to stay silent and hope it all went away. But it was a coward's way out. She didn't want to be that person anymore. "I should have told you. I knew you'd be disappointed and I was worried you'd be mad at me."

"I'm upset because you *didn't* tell me. Of course I'm disappointed. It sucks that he's into you. I know you didn't encourage it. I would have preferred for you to tell me instead of Marisa. Tony seemed depressed when she talked to him yesterday. So, she asked what was wrong."

Lauren sat mute. What could she say that would possibly make this better?

"I'll get over it." Val stood. "I'm going to read in my room."

"Wait. It hurts today. However, someday, a guy will come around who sees you and will sweep you off your feet. I know it."

Val slumped onto the couch. "When? I'd like a timeframe please." She chuckled, but it held no warmth or humour. "It's lonely at times. I've liked Tony for a long time. I'm like his kid sister or the cliché girl next door who he's totally blind to. I feel like I'm in a bad rom-com."

Lauren shook her head, taking in her vivacious and gorgeous friend. With her red hair and big blue eyes, Val was a knockout. And Tony was an idiot. "You're anything but the girl next door. And Tony is blinder than a bat." Lauren shuffled the laundry piles around. "I used to get lonely even though I was married. Sol and I didn't connect the last couple of years. Obviously. I'm right there with you in the lonely department. Maybe we can help each other through these feelings?"

"Thanks. Let's start by going to get ice cream. We can drown our sorrows in rocky road and peanut butter. Then you can tell me what's really going on with Aaron Miles Scott."

Lauren stood, reached out, and grabbed her friend's hand, pulling her off the couch. "There's nothing going on."

"There should be."

Lauren wasn't so sure. Aaron Miles Scott had *danger* written all over him, and Lauren was afraid to get too close.

"For now, Ryan, you're off the schedule." Aaron kept his voice low and calm. After speaking with Ed Monday morning, Aaron had determined this was the best way to handle Ryan's behaviour.

Ryan's eyes bored into Aaron. "You're overreacting. People enjoyed it. It takes time to adjust to new things. You said it yourself."

Aaron picked fictional lint off his jeans. "I disagree. Did you receive complaints? Because both Ed and I fielded calls, texts, and emails most of yesterday. I agree that it takes time to adapt to new ideas. In time rap might find a place in a Sunday morning service. What concerns me is your attitude. Were you not listening when we spoke on servanthood at the leadership meeting? Being a worship leader isn't so you can perform your own playlist. It's about guiding people to the throne of God. You're submitting to God and people, and your resistance to any sort of instruction or teaching is concerning." Aaron stared at the kid in front of him. "You need to adjust your attitude and the ego has to go. Did you at any point ask God what he wanted you to play? Worship is praising God. Leadership is servanthood first. What I saw yesterday wasn't either of those. It was The Ryan Walters Show. Am I wrong?"

Ryan studied his fingers, one shoulder lifting slightly.

"Ryan, this is an opportunity to grow as a leader, hone your skills, and see where God is leading. Maybe rap is part of his plan. I don't know because I'm not God. You've got talent in spades, Ryan. What I'm seeing is that you're not ready for the responsibility of leadership."

Ryan rolled his eyes and Aaron prayed for calm and a guard at his mouth.

"I don't need to hone my skills or grow. I'm one of the best musicians you've got, and I doubt there's much you can teach me. You're a washed-up boy band member." Ryan spit out the last words.

"If that's how you feel, perhaps you need to take a break because I'm not going anywhere."

Ryan's glare reminded Aaron of a dangerous animal. "We'll see about that." He stalked out of the office.

Panic climbed up Aaron's throat. Ryan's comment planted itself and festered in his brain. What had he meant? Wade. No one knew what had happened to his cousin. Aaron was being paranoid. He needed to focus on the positive, which was that Ryan was out of his hair for a while. Even that thought didn't ease the tension in his shoulders. He'd run into Ryans before and it was always hard. Usually, they caused trouble.

The buzzing of his phone in his pocket roused him from his thoughts. After he fished the device from his pocket, he saw Lauren's name.

> **Lauren: Marisa has "easy" dance moves to teach us for our song. <Yikes! Emoji> Can you meet?**

> **Aaron: Sure. Send me the details.**

> **Lauren: Glebe Playhouse, 6pm**

> **Aaron: Gr8t C U**

A chance to dance with Lauren? Aaron was all in.

Chapter Twenty-Four

Her brain said one thing while Lauren's feet did the opposite. "Could you show me that again, Marisa?"

Marisa walked across the hardwood floors of the rehearsal room in the Glebe Playhouse, to Lauren. Heat crawled up her neck, setting her face aflame. Marisa made it look so easy. Lauren tried to mimic her, flubbing the moves again. She caught a glimpse of her awkward movement in the mirrors that lined the walls. She wanted to die because Aaron stood off to the side, witness to her complete humiliation. At least Audra wasn't around to preserve her disgrace on socials.

"Can I suggest something?" Aaron walked over. Mr. Boy-Band had no problem with the dancing. He'd performed much harder routines with The Light. Lauren knew from watching all the videos on YouTube.

Marisa gestured for him to take the lead.

"Can we drop the formal steps and just move to the music. Maybe Lauren stands here, and I move from one side to her other. I could twirl her out to the other side. That's moving her in a natural flow without a lot of choreography."

He sang his line and circled Lauren before grabbing her hand. He pulled her in close, giving her a tantalizing whiff of his cologne before whirling her away from him and then back again.

Marisa clapped. "That's better. I want you both to be comfortable. So, if this works, let's do it."

Lauren silently breathed a sigh of relief. This, she could do, and she might even have fun. Sol hadn't danced, and so, Lauren hadn't either. She didn't know if she was just rusty or she'd forgotten how to dance. And she was already freaking out about singing. Doing both had seemed impossible until Aaron saved the day. As they took their places again, Lauren whispered, "Thank you."

He squeezed her hand. "I've got you."

Warmth seeped through her chest. Miraculously, she believed him. He wouldn't let her down. In fact, he hadn't let her down yet.

They walked to their opening positions: Aaron at centrestage and Lauren off in the wings. She'd enter when it was her turn to sing. Before she headed off to the side, Aaron whispered, "You inspire me, you know."

"What?" She moved closer to him.

"I think you're brave."

She waved her hand. "I am not."

"You're out there taking risks, doing what's uncomfortable. It's admirable and inspiring. You should be proud of yourself."

Heat flamed over her face. "Thanks." Surprised by Aaron's words, Lauren hurried to her spot in a daze. Brave was not a word she'd use to describe herself. She'd let Sol manipulate her for years.

The events of the last month scrolled through her mind. Lauren had stepped out of her comfort zone by being a judge and doing the interviews for the local news. Maybe things were changing. It wasn't that she wasn't scared; she definitely was. But as her dad used to tell her, "Do it scared, Sweetie." She glanced at Aaron as he sang his first line. Yeah, maybe she could be brave.

"Y OU DID GREAT IN there, Lauren. Don't be discouraged." Marisa gathered up her ballroom dance shoes. "I'm glad Aaron had to hurry off because I wanted to encourage you."

"Ha." Lauren laughed. "I didn't do very well, but thanks anyways."

"I'm being serious. Kudos for trying."

"Thanks for being flexible with the moves. It helps."

"If it works, then why not?" Marisa called to her son, who'd been playing in another room. Henry gave a small wave to Lauren. The kid was cute. "I'll take the tablet now." Marisa held out her hand.

"Aw, Mom," Henry whined, but he handed it over.

"Grab your bag and let's go." Marisa waited as Henry picked up his backpack from the floor. Then she locked the door behind them.

"Thanks for your patience, Henry." Lauren smiled. "I really needed your mom's help tonight."

The boy drew a circle with the toe of his shoe.

Marisa rolled her eyes at Lauren. "What do you say, Henry?"

"Thanks." Henry threw the word over his shoulder and got into their car.

"I try to teach him manners, but ten-year-old boys are an entity of their own." Marisa sighed.

"You're doing great." Lauren hit the unlock button on her fob. "Henry's a great kid. I see him around the community centre. He helps Tony pick up when the after-school program is finished."

"I don't know what I'd do if we didn't have the centre. I really hope we raise a lot of money. I realize it's for the teen programs, but Henry's just a few years off. The extra funds benefit everyone because it means the younger kids have something to look forward to. The centre means the world to us. Henry gets to see good male role models in Tony—and even Will—when he visits. A lot of us single moms couldn't work full-time if it wasn't for the after-school program."

Aaron's words flicked through her mind. The woman standing in front of her was brave. "You're a good mom. And I'm so happy that I get to be a part of both the community centre and the talent competition. It has really opened my eyes to the needs of the neighbourhood."

"I'm glad you're a judge, too. I was a bit intimidated by Aaron at first, but he's a good guy. I think you two would make a good couple."

"What? Oh, we're not—"

Henry banged on his window. Lauren could have kissed the kid.

"I gotta run. Poor kid is hungry." Marisa opened her door. "When you celebrate your first anniversary together, remember what I said." She laughed as she climbed into her vehicle.

Lauren shook her head, smiling. She had no idea what the future held, but it certainly appeared brighter than it had in a long time.

Chapter Twenty-Five

THE NEXT DAY, AARON strummed his guitar, picking out chords to a melody in his head. He pulled the pencil from between his teeth and scribbled down notes on the sheet balanced precariously on his knee. The melody seemed to have a life of its own, and he could barely write it fast enough before the next line forced its way into his consciousness. It felt good to be inspired. And terrifying. He was afraid that at any moment the melody would fade and he'd be left staring at a blank or partially blank page.

Will popped his head around the corner. "I brought—" He stopped short. "Are you writing?"

Aaron couldn't help but smile. "Trying to."

Will set a coffee on the table and backed up. "I won't disturb you."

"No, it's okay. These kids—and Lauren... They inspire me. It's still just a mess of notes, but it might turn into something." Aaron set his guitar down. "What are you up to?"

"I have to drop off a few groceries for a family who's struggling. Care to tag along?"

"Sure." It would be a relief to walk away for a few minutes. He needed a distraction. Briefly the thought of calling Audra to come along crossed his mind. Aaron shoved it away. Jeremy would love it, and it might make up for Aaron's stubbornness about staying for the competition, but it would make Aaron uncomfortable. This job was about more than Aaron or his ambitions.

Fifteen minutes later, Will parked by the curb in a low-income neighbourhood. Aaron grabbed several bags and followed Will up the walk. Although the house and lawn were neat and tidy, the house needed a fresh coat of paint and the railings along the porch were hanging loose. Will knocked, and a woman opened the door, her face as washed out as the paint on the exterior of her house.

"Hi, Mrs. Brockstone. I've got groceries for you." Will introduced Aaron.

"Thank you, Will. Please set them on the counter." The woman led them into the house, which was neat as well. Aaron noticed the worn patches on the sofa. A knitted blanket lay over the back. A teen lolled on a chair, engaged in his phone.

"Hey, Eli." Will waved to the kid, who nodded.

"Please let me make you coffee."

Before Aaron could refuse, Will accepted her offer. He glanced at Aaron and subtly dipped his chin.

The woman smiled and set to work filling a carafe with water.

"I'm so glad you've joined the staff at the church." Mrs. Brockstone scooped coffee into the filter. "We loved your singing in the band. My husband was a real fan."

"Thank you. I love my job. Your husband *was* a fan?"

"He died three years ago in a car accident."

"I'm so sorry."

"I am too." She pulled three mugs down from the cupboard and poured the coffee. "He was T-boned by a young kid who was fooling with his phone."

Aaron glanced at Will, who didn't look like this was his first time hearing this.

"Last week, I had to give a victim impact statement. He's up for early parole. After speaking with my sons, who are eighteen and twenty, we decided not to do it."

Aaron's eyes widened.

She handed him a mug. "He's the same age as my oldest child. He comes from a terrible family life. The boy needs a second chance more than time in jail. We forgave him long ago. I felt it was time to live out that forgiveness. It's amazing how light I feel."

Aaron stared at her. Forgiveness. "That kid is incredibly lucky."

"It's what Jesus asks of us. He's forgiven me. Shouldn't I forgive this kid?" She shrugged like it was that simple.

Aaron cleared his thickening throat. "You think he deserves it?"

"Do you? Do I? Jesus gives it if we're willing to accept it." She sipped her coffee.

Aaron stared at the table that had a few chips in the Formica while Will asked her about her sons.

Her words stung. After a few more minutes of chatting, Will rose. "We need to get going. Thank you for the coffee."

"I always love to see you, and I'm so happy to meet you, Aaron." Mrs. Brockstone clasped his hand.

"Thank you." Aaron followed Will to the car. He had no words.

Will turned the key in the ignition, letting the engine idle. "Amazing, eh?"

Aaron stared at the house he'd just left. "I'm not sure I could be so gracious in the same circumstances."

"You're right. You couldn't be. You haven't been."

Aaron faced his friend. "Okaaay. You have my attention."

"Wade. You've never forgiven yourself for what happened."

Aaron huffed out a breath. "C'mon. This is different. Is this why you brought me here today?"

"No. But it could be why God placed the idea to invite you in my head." Will tapped his fingers on his jeans. "You know why you can't write?"

Nope. He was tired of analyzing it.

"I think you're blocked because you're filled with guilt, anger, and other bad feelings. They've taken over your insides and stomped on your creativity and soul. You can't let anything good in because the guilt is taking up all the room."

Aaron's jaw dropped. "That's ridiculous."

"Is it? You can't let it go because you need to punish yourself. When are you going to stop?"

"I don't need to punish myself. I'm not. Wade didn't get a second chance. I have to own that."

"There's a difference between owning something and continually beating yourself up over it."

Aaron lowered the window, letting the cool breeze wash over his face. "Can we go?"

Will pulled out into the street. Aaron clamped his jaw shut. He didn't want to hear Will's opinion. Wade wasn't the reason Aaron had writer's block. Hadn't he had a breakthrough earlier? He just had to try harder—and he would.

Aaron hurried through the centre, hoping to catch Lauren before she left for the day.

"He's a washed-up wannabe rocker."

Aaron halted just outside the gym.

"Who listens to Christian music anyway? The Light—what a stupid name."

"Apparently, he was quite the partier. Ryan told me. What a hypocrite."

"A player, too. That's what I heard."

Heart thumping, Aaron backed up the way he'd come. He shouldn't be eavesdropping. They didn't know he was there. Turning, he strode down the hall to the front doors. The kids' words overshadowed the good Aaron had felt after visiting with Mrs. Brockstone. And the teens didn't even know about Wade.

Chapter Twenty-Six

THERE WERE NO EMPTY seats in the sanctuary on the final night of the competition. It had come down to the final three, Justin, Crystal, and Jamal. Coincidentally, the audience had voted a contestant from each judge. The sense of anticipation in the air made bumps rise on Lauren's arms. Each section held fans for one contestant—Justin's on the right, Crystal's in the centre, and Jamal's to the left. Signs with "We heart you Justin," "Rock on Crystal," and "We vote Team Jamal" were waving around the room.

"Don't overthink it." Aaron came up beside her.

Lauren side-eyed him. "Easy for you to say. It's not the judging that's making me nauseated. I haven't sung in front of a crowd this big in forever."

"You nailed it in rehearsal. I'm the one who should be worried because you are going to totally upstage me." He gently nudged her shoulder with his. "There's goes my career." He smirked. "You don't need to be nervous because I've got your back."

Afraid to open her mouth in case she vomited, Lauren nodded.

"Ready, you two?" Will came up to them.

Lauren froze.

"Yep." Aaron grasped her hand, his warmth flooding her. He locked eyes with her, and she felt herself calm. Well, at least she thought she wouldn't barf.

"Go out and knock their socks off. I'll welcome everyone after you're finished." Will saluted as he backed away.

"Come on. Let's go have a little bit of fun." Aaron tugged her forward, and the next thing Lauren knew, she was centrestage, the music filling the room and her hand in Aaron's. His smooth voice filled the sanctuary, and she focused on that. When it was her turn, he squeezed her hand. She opened her mouth and the words came out. Singing with Aaron was like dancing with a really good partner. She just followed his lead, and before she knew it, the song was over. They stepped off the stage. Aaron turned to her. "That was amazing."

Lauren laughed, and before she could stop herself, she kissed his cheek and hugged him. "Thank you."

Aaron squeezed her gently. "My pleasure entirely." He smiled as he let her go.

"I forgot how much I loved singing and performing. Tonight, once we began, I just had fun." It had been a gift.

"Me, too. For once it wasn't about me and putting on a show. I enjoyed it very much."

Will motioned for them to take their seats. They hurried to sit beside Marisa, who gave them a thumbs up.

Will introduce the three finalists.

"Good evening, ladies and gents. We're glad you're here with us." The crowd roared, and Will waved his arms, igniting a bigger cheer from them. "I see you're in excellent form tonight. Let me introduce to you my friend, Tony, the youth director over at Cartwright Community Centre."

A cheer rose from the crowd along with some catcalls. Tony had a great reputation in the community, not only because of his job but also because he cared about the kids he worked with. It showed in his interactions with the teens and their families.

Will pointed to Tony. "I see you know him. He has played an integral part behind the scenes of this competition. Thank you, Tony." The crowd got even louder. "And right now, he's going to fill you in on a couple of programs related to this competition that will be happening at the centre in the coming weeks." He passed the mic to Tony.

"Hey, friends, thanks for being here tonight and supporting our finalists. I have a couple of announcements. We have two new programs starting in September. First, our girl Stella is teaching hip hop lessons after school on Tuesdays and Thursdays. You can go to our website and sign up, or come visit us at the centre, and we'll sign you up there." Tony held up two fingers. "Second thing is a music jam session. Check the website for the details." He jogged off the stage, leaving Will standing front and centre.

"Finally, I want to thank you for all the canned food and donations you brought in. Cartwright's pantry is filled to the brim, and we have enough money to buy more food as needed. Thank you so much for meeting this growing need in our community.

"Now the reason we're here. The three finalists. Justin, Crystal, and Jamal, come on out." The three teens, dressed to rock 'n' roll, ran out on stage. Lauren whistled, her heart light for the first time in a long time as anticipation hummed through her.

Justin, dressed in dark jeans and a tuxedo-stamped T-shirt, bowed low. He'd just squeaked into the final three. Jamal—in his dark jeans and white T-shirt, which looked professional yet hip under a tuxedo jacket—waved to the crowd, sending girls into hysterics. Aaron chuckled.

Crystal won the prize as a rock princess. She wore her blue hair up in a spiked mohawk reminiscent of the 90s. Her leather boots came up to her knees. She had on a frilly tutu with leggings and a sleeveless tank.

Justin, Jamal, and Crystal high-fived each other. Lauren loved seeing the comradery between them. Despite the competition, they supported and cheered for one another.

"You guys can go and get ready while we give the audience a special surprise. Don't worry. We're taping it so Justin, Crystal, and Jamal, can watch later." Will pointed to Aaron, who groaned beside Lauren. As she turned to face him, he was gone, striding to the stage. Marisa's eyebrows shot up as she locked eyes with Lauren. "What's going on?"

"I have no idea."

Aaron picked up a guitar and sat on a stool that had been brought out by a stagehand.

"We've asked Aaron to play a song for us tonight. Aaron once played with a band that won a Dove award and was nominated for a Grammy. He has a new worship album out. What you probably don't know, unless you were a superfan, is that Aaron wrote most of the band's songs. He's going to sing some new music."

Aaron strummed and tuned the strings as he spoke into the mic. "It's good to be here—on this stage. These kids have inspired me. Their courage to try out, get on the stage, do what they love. Thank you. If you can do it, I can too. I pulled out my pen and paper recently and wrote this song."

Aaron's rich voice filled the auditorium. While Lauren knew he had instrumental skills, it was his voice that drew her. His tone was rich and smooth. Heat radiated from her chest, warming her whole body, as she sat transfixed. He might as well have been a pied piper. For a minute, the crowded auditorium faded, and it was only Aaron playing his guitar.

The last note resonated across the room in a ripple effect. As if a tidal wave broke, the crowd rose to their feet, whistling and cheering and stamping their feet. Lauren stood, her palms stinging from clapping. Aaron smiled shyly, quickly handed his guitar to Will, and gave a slight bow. As he neared the judges' seats, Lauren noticed his flushed face.

Marisa wrapped him in a bear hug. Despite the fact she was tiny, she packed a wallop in the hug department. Lauren knew from experience. Aaron laughed as she finally released him. He waved one last time before sitting. Lauren tapped him on the shoulder. He faced her, smiling hesitantly. His humility only added to his appeal. He wasn't the self-serving artist she'd accused him of being. In fact, he was just the opposite.

"I don't have words other than that was incredible. I loved it," she whispered.

Aaron wiped a trickle of sweat from his brow with a tissue. "Thank you. It means a lot. And it had nothing to do with promoting my album. These kids honestly inspired me and that song just came to me." He laughed. "I was nervous."

"To play in front of this little crowd?" Marisa asked.

"Yeah, I was," he admitted.

Lauren liked that he was honest enough to admit it.

Justin followed Will onto the stage. A hush fell over the crowd.

"Here we go," whispered Marisa. "Buckle up."

Lauren gripped her pen so tightly to stop her hand from trembling that her knuckles turned white. She loosened her grip a little and wrote *Justin* across the top of the paper. Buckle up indeed.

Chapter Twenty-Seven

Aaron sat with Lauren and Marisa in a room off the sanctuary used for guest speakers and musicians. The chorus of voices of the contestants as they performed an ensemble number drifted into the otherwise silent room. "Can we go watch them?" Lauren glanced longingly at the door leading to the platform.

Marisa had worked with them on the musical number the past couple of weeks. Aaron had seen the dress rehearsal earlier. It had blown him away. "No, we have to decide on a winner." Marisa pursed her lips and stared at her papers.

"Don't you want to see your kids?" Lauren tapped her pen against her full lips. He shifted in his chair when he realized he was staring. *Get a grip, man.*

"I want to choose a winner." Marisa drummed her fingers on the papers.

"Can't we say it's a three-way tie?" Lauren laid her forehead on the table. It would make their jobs easier for sure. It wasn't the answer. Will stuck his head in the doorway.

"By the looks of it, we don't have a winner yet."

"No," Aaron muttered.

Will checked his watch. "You've got five minutes."

Aaron chucked a wadded-up piece of paper at him, and he ducked out of the room. Aaron ran his hand through his hair. "Let's go over our judging sheets one more time." They had Justin and Crystal in a tie. They needed to break it.

"Can't we do a tie breaker?" Lauren lifted her head.

"How? It would add another hour onto the night." Aaron closed his eyes. "Why don't we go over their other performances? Who's grown the most?" He opened his eyes.

Marisa bit her thumbnail. "Justin pulled it off tonight. His song choice was good. Obviously, the kid had a change of heart about your suggestion, Aaron. I'd say he's grown. He's taken risks that Crystal hasn't."

"Crystal risks it each time she steps onto the stage. And Jamal is good, but doesn't compare to the other two," Lauren said. Justin had been good. He'd definitely had a change of heart and took Aaron's suggestion about doing a jazzy version of "Walking in Memphis"—and nailed it.

"Let's keep it to musical ability and performance. We keep it simple or else it's too complicated." Aaron crossed his arms on the table. "Justin is a better musician. He got top marks for his playing. While his voice isn't as strong, the pitchiness is gone."

"Crystal is both a strong singer and a strong guitarist. I would say she's the winner." Lauren tapped her nail on the paper in front of her.

"Agreed." Marisa nodded.

Aaron sighed. "Agreed. As far as this competition goes, Crystal is the stronger performer."

"But?" Lauren rested her elbow on the table and cradled her chin in her hand.

Aaron folded his papers in half. "Personally, I wanted Justin to win. It showed a lot of maturity to change his mind and do what he didn't want to."

"Or he just wanted to win." Marisa tapped her pen. "Runner-up isn't too shabby. He receives fifteen hundred dollars."

"Yeah, I know."

"So, we have a winner?"

"We have a winner," Aaron and Marisa said in unison.

Lauren smeared lip gloss on her dry lips as Will opened the door. "Ready? Who is it?"

Marisa shook her head and smirked as she brushed by him. "We're not telling. You'll have to wait."

Will threw his head back, groaning. "The crowd is growing restless. All the kids are on stage. The three finalists are off to the side." Will pulled open the door and the crowd went crazy as they entered. People waved signs for each competitor and chanted, "Crystal" or "Justin" or "Jamal." Warmth rushed through Aaron. Lauren's hand brushed his as they walked. Without thinking, he grabbed it. She glanced at him, keeping her hand in his. A sigh escaped her lips. Her prickly outside seemed smoother tonight. Maybe this was the beginning of a turn-around.

Lauren kept her eyes focused straight ahead and didn't make eye contact with anyone, afraid she'd give away the results. Or that she'd see them staring at her holding Aaron's hand. At the stairs, Aaron let go. The desire to grab his hand back warred with the need to quash any gossip that might arise about a romantic relationship. Even Lauren didn't know the answer to that.

She followed Marisa up the stairs with Aaron behind her.

"Here we go, the moment everyone's been waiting for, and these cruel judges wouldn't even give me a hint," Will joked. The crowd booed in a cheerful way as he handed the mic to Aaron, who was the spokesperson for the judges.

"Thank you. It takes courage to audition. Period. You should be proud of yourselves. We are so proud of each of you. No matter where you landed, if this is what you want to do, don't give up. Take a few lessons. Work on your craft. Keep going and don't stop believing in yourself."

Aaron motioned the three finalists forward. "I'll get right to it. The winner of the Cartwright Community Teen Talent Challenge is..."

A hush fell over the large auditorium.

"...Crystal Symthe."

The auditorium erupted with whistling, clapping, and cheering. Crystal stepped forward, and Aaron presented her with an envelope and a small trophy. Lauren hugged the girl. Crystal wiped away a tear. Lauren hadn't expected that from the teen.

Next, Aaron handed envelopes to both Justin and Jamal, shaking their hands. Lauren and Marisa followed Aaron as the other contestants swarmed the three finalists. Lauren backed up to the stage wings, awed by the excitement and joy. It was good to see a happy occasion in a church setting even though it wasn't a religious event. Calm wrapped around her. She felt at home here in this place of worship. She glanced at the smiles on the kids' faces. God cared for these kids more than she did. The truth of it resonated down to her core.

"That's a wrap." Aaron stood beside her. "Wasn't so bad, was it?"

"I actually enjoyed it. Thanks for volunteering me. You did me a favour." She nudged his shoulder.

"Aaron?" Justin approached. "Uh, I wanted to thank you. I know we didn't see eye to eye on the songs. I've learned a lot, mostly from you. It takes me a while before I warm up to an idea. My dad is kinda bossy, so I resist suggestions. Thank you for sticking it out."

"Anytime. Thanks, Justin." Aaron shook the young man's hand. "Good luck." The teenager walked away.

Aaron faced Lauren, eyebrows raised. "I admit, I wasn't expecting that."

"You made a difference. This experience is going to help these kids. Seeds have been planted. Now we watch them grow." Lauren glanced around the room.

"That's a good analogy. I wish I hadn't been so self-absorbed when I was younger." His lips thinned as he stared at Dwayne the reporter talking to Crystal.

"I should go. Walk you out?" Aaron motioned to the exit.

Lauren lengthened her strides to keep up with him. "Hey, it's not a race. Why are you avoiding the reporter?"

Aaron turned a corner into the office area. He unlocked a door near the end of the hallway. "Come in."

His office was neat and a couple of guitars sat in stands. A faint hint of his soap tickled her senses. If her office smelled this good, she'd never leave it.

"I don't like talking to reporters. They always want to dig through my past with The Light. As you once reminded me, this is about the kids." He grabbed his jacket off the back of his desk chair.

Lauren studied him. A sense that he was keeping something back poked her. *It's none of your business.* The guy was allowed his privacy.

"You did fabulous tonight." Aaron interrupted her thoughts. "You should sing more often."

"I couldn't have done it without you." Lauren toed the carpet.

"I don't believe that for a second. You would have figured it out. However, I was happy to help." He lifted her chin so she had to look at him. His eyes roamed over her face, and he ran his knuckles over her cheek, exploding every nerve ending he touched. "You are one of the most courageous, intelligent, and beautiful women I know." He leaned close and softly kissed where his knuckle had just caressed her skin.

Her body lit up and her knees actually weakened slightly. She let out the breath she'd been holding.

He smiled, the one that lit up his eyes. "I'll walk you to your car."

She nodded, words eluding her. They headed out the staff entrance and Aaron stopped at her car while she unlocked it. He opened the door for her and she got in.

"I leave for the fair tour tomorrow and I'll be gone for a couple of weeks."

Lauren finally managed to get her brain and mouth to cooperate. "Good luck. I hope it goes well."

"I'll see you in a few weeks." Aaron shut the door and stepped back. Lauren pulled out of the parking lot. She caught a glimpse of Aaron's reflection in her rearview mirror. He was waving.

She hoped the next few weeks passed quickly.

As he stood watching Lauren drive away, Aaron dared to let himself think about a dream he'd never had before. He wondered what it would be like to come home to her after the fair circuit. Her light floral scent lingered in the air.

"The guy is so full of himself." The voice drifted out over the emptying parking lot. Aaron turned but couldn't see anyone.

Another person laughed. "He's a washed-up boy band singer. What's he so cocky about?" Ryan's voice was loud in the dark. "And he's got a pretty checkered past."

"What do you mean?"

"I've got a friend who says his older brother knew the drummer of The Light. Despite their good boy Christian image, there were pretty scandalous things going on behind the scenes."

"Like what?"

"I don't have all the dirt yet, but I think it's big." The voices faded as they moved away.

Aaron squeezed his hands into fists. *No. No. No.* He walked toward a couple of vans and a pickup where he thought the voices were coming from. Just as he neared the pickup, it revved its engine and pulled away. Laughter echoed in the night. His good mood wiped away, he headed back to his vehicle. What did Ryan know? Sick, Aaron sagged behind the wheel and groaned. He had to find out what the kid knew before he destroyed Aaron's career.

Chapter Twenty-Eight

Two weeks had passed since the end of the competition, and the last time Lauren had seen Aaron. Although he'd been home Saturday and Sunday for church, he had to run back to the fair tour on Sunday night. While home, he'd spent the two days catching up on work. And it wasn't like they'd gone on a date. However, he'd been in her thoughts constantly. Who was she kidding? She missed him. Maybe she was falling for the guy.

"Lauren." Phil, the director of the community centre knocked on her office door, interrupting her thoughts She turned to the open door and stopped short. Her boss stood beside two officers. All the air whooshed from her lungs. She stood.

"What can I do for you?" Her voice wobbled.

"These are Canadian Revenue Agency Criminal Investigation Officers. They wanted to speak to you." Phil had a great poker face. So, she couldn't tell what he was thinking.

Canadian Revenue Agency officers not police. "You wanted to speak with *me*?"

A hulking bald guy stepped into the office. "I'm Officer Hogan. We need to speak to you regarding your late husband's affairs."

The words "late husband's affairs" caught Lauren's attention. Solomon.

"If you need anything, Lauren, I'll be in my office." Phil tapped the doorframe before heading down the hallway.

"Have a seat." Lauren motioned to the two chairs on the other side of her desk. The officers declined the invitation. Just as well. Lauren didn't think the chair would hold the big guy. His partner was a tall woman, whose severe hairstyle didn't suit her heart-shaped face and hazel eyes.

The woman spoke up. "I'm Officer Van Hassen. Do you mind if we record this?" She held up her phone.

"I guess not." Lauren wrapped her arms around her waist then dropped them to her sides. She didn't know how to act. The last thing she wanted was these officers thinking she was hiding money or information. She blew out a slow breath, waiting for them to continue.

"Ms. Grace, we're investigating the York Community Church's books. An anonymous person tipped off the CRA. The treasurer found irregularities in the bookkeeping. Evidence is pointing to your late husband."

"I don't understand." Lauren clutched the edge of her desk. What did this have to do with her?

Officer Van Hassen studied Lauren. "We believe your husband, Solomon Grace, stole hundreds of thousands of dollars from the church before he died." Officer Hogan dropped the bomb as if he was discussing the weather.

Lauren blinked, trying to wrap her mind around his words. "I'm sorry. Can you repeat that?"

"Evidence is pointing to your husband skimming up to five hundred thousand dollars from the church. We want to ask you a few questions."

Wait. What? "That's impossible. We never had that kind of money." Even as the words came out of her mouth, doubt assaulted her. Sol had been paid a very good salary, but Toronto was an expensive city to live in. Their house wasn't paid off. They leased their cars. Yet Sol travelled a lot—to conferences as well as speaking engagements. He liked nice things, especially clothes. He always told her he got his suits on sale. The dinners at fancy restaurants. Not that he took her out much, but she'd found receipts in his pants pockets. He'd told her it came out of his expense account. She hadn't given it much thought until now. York Community had money, but could the church have afforded trips to California and New York every year, not to mention conferences in BC and Alberta?

"Ms. Grace?"

Lauren stared at Hogan. "You think Sol stole money from the church?"

"Yes. Your husband had a credit line through the church, which was supposed to be used for discretionary benevolence funds. Over the last four years, your husband used it to pay himself rather than help those who needed it. Last spring, the treasurer contacted one of the supposed recipients who hadn't received any of the funds that were supposed to go to him and his family. Upon further investigation, we discovered Pastor Grace skimmed off the top of the money that was to go to the families. Plus, some of the families were fake."

Pain shot through Lauren's temples. With shaking fingers, she rubbed her head. "Where is this money? Solomon's estate has been settled. It paid for the mortgage, and the rest, which wasn't much, went to the church. Do I need a lawyer?" Her heart raced and blood rushed her head. Lauren sat.

Van Hassen handed Lauren the water bottle sitting on her desk. "Take a drink. We're not arresting you. At this time, we only want to ask you a few questions. As for the money, we think it's in an offshore account."

Lauren unscrewed the cap and gulped a mouthful. *I hate him. If he did this…* Carefully, she set the bottle down. They could ask whatever they wanted. She had nothing to hide.

Officer Van Hassen hit the record button. "What kinds of conversations did you have with Pastor Grace regarding money?"

"Other than the monthly household budget? Once I asked him how the church afforded his business-related trips." She'd wanted to go with him in the early days of ministry. He'd shut her down, saying the church couldn't afford to pay for her to go. A lie because he'd taken Brittany on at least one of those trips according to church gossip. She dug her nails into the palms of her hands.

"What did he say?"

"He told me it came out of an expense account for those purposes."

"How many trips did he take a year?"

Lauren explained the trips to the US and Canada. "If he was the guest speaker, it didn't cost him anything. He travelled several weeks a year."

"How long was he away?"

"The big trips were for a week. The rest, only two or three days. He had to be back to preach on Sunday."

Van Hassen wrote in her small black notebook. "What was your household budget?"

Lauren told her. The budget wasn't out of range, based on Sol's salary.

"We will need a copy. Did he ever give you expensive gifts?"

"No. Nothing out of the ordinary. Flowers. Jewellery over the years. Nothing wild or expensive." Lauren ducked her chin and studied her fingers. Just say it. "He had an affair. I found out after he died."

"I'm sorry." Van Hassen voice gentled.

Officer Hogan cleared his throat. "I'm sorry to ask this. But do you know the woman?"

"Brittany Clarkson."

Van Hassen wrote in her notebook. "We may need to talk to you in the future."

"I understand." Sol had broken her heart once again.

"If you have any hidden money, now is the time to tell us." Hogan's eyes were gun metal gray.

"If I had hidden money, do you think I'd be sleeping on my friend's couch and working at a temp job?" Lauren snapped her mouth shut so it wouldn't get her into trouble with the CRA.

"Is there anything else you can think of?" Van Hassen sat down on one of the chairs.

Lauren chewed the inside of her cheek. *Think. Think. Think.* The USB stick. "A USB stick. He always carried it with him. Told me it had his sermons on it. I put it in his bedside drawer once without telling him and he freaked out because he couldn't find it."

"Do you know where this USB stick might be?"

Lauren pressed her fingers to her temple. "He would have had it on him when he had the accident because he always carried it with him after I did that. The hospital gave me a bag with his personal items. It should have been in there." What had she done with his things? Her memories of the days after the car crash were foggy at best.

"Do you know where the bag is?"

"No. They gave it to me and I can't remember what I did with it." The last word trailed off. She remembered setting it on the bedside table on Sol's side. What had she done with it from there?

"Take your time. I'll check in in a couple of days. In the meantime, if you find it or think of where it is, please call my cell." He wrote on the back of his card. "This could be important."

"I will."

Thank you for your time. We'll be in touch if we have more questions." Van Hassen followed her partner out.

Lauren stood and the room spun. Grabbing the side of her desk, Lauren steadied herself as her brain sifted through this new information. Sol had stolen money and lived a double life with his mistresses. And now the CRA was questioning her. Heat spread up through her chest, and she snatched a pen, throwing it across the small office space. "Aargh."

Sitting on the edge of her desk, she cradled her head in her hands as sobs rolled through her body. He had ruined her life. Even from the grave, his selfishness was haunting her.

She'd been a fool. Why had her life turned out like it had? She'd tried to be a good wife and follow God. *Where are you, God?*

Silence.

Lauren leaned her head back and stared at nothing. Even the tears had dried up. All the steps she'd taken back to God disappeared. He never seemed to show up when she needed him. She was on her own.

Chapter Twenty-Nine

A KNOCK ON THE door jolted Lauren out of her daze on the couch, where she'd been for the past thirty minutes. Val was at work but had offered to come home when Lauren called to tell her what had happened with the CRA officers earlier that day. Lauren refused because Val was short-staffed.

Lauren peered through the peephole to see Janey and Isobel standing there, holding a large pizza and drinks. She quickly unlocked and opened the door. "Hi. What are you doing here?"

"We brought supper." Janey held up the pizza box. Lauren inhaled the aroma of cheese and freshly baked bread. "We hope you like vegetarian."

Lauren's stomach rumbled. "Love it." She remembered her manners. "Come in. Why did you bring dinner?"

Lauren stepped back and let the women in. Janey moved to the coffee table and set the drinks down and took the pizza from Isobel.

"Val called us. She told us what happened today." Isobel held out her hand. "Don't be mad at Val. She was worried when she couldn't get away and didn't want you to be alone."

"What happened? We won't repeat it. We're good at minding our own business and keeping yours to ourselves. We're a vault." Janey motioned to her and Isobel.

"No, I'm not mad. Just surprised." They had dropped everything to come over and bring dinner? Lauren stood staring, mute.

"Great. Do we need plates or can we just use napkins?" Janey held up a roll of paper towels that she'd tugged out of a plastic bag.

"Paper towels, definitely." Lauren chuckled, sitting down on a chair. Isobel pulled out cups and poured the soda pop.

"Thank you so much." A warmth thread its way through her body, warming her right down to her soul.

"When one of us suffers, we all do. That's being part of a community." Isobel handed her a cup. "You're part of our community, Lauren." She held up her cup.

"Whether you want to be or not." Janey piped up, her grin wide. "We hope you want to be."

"I think I do." Lauren held her cup up and toasted with the two women. Suddenly the weight of the world wasn't crushing her. She remembered her anger at God at the office. As she stared at her new friends, God felt close. He hadn't abandoned her. Instead, he'd sent these women at Val's request to minister to her. Her vision blurred as she sipped her pop. *Thank you, Father, for looking after me even when I was so mad at you. I'm sorry.*

Janey held out a piece of pizza to her.

"Thank you." Lauren smiled, thankful for more than just the food.

Chapter Thirty

After Janey and Isobel left, Lauren dumped the box of winter clothes she hadn't unpacked since moving to Ottawa on Val's couch. Tunes blared from the speaker as she searched.

Her hands rummaged through her sweaters, jeans, and jackets. No plastic bag of personal items. She was glad to have something to do so she wouldn't focus on what Sol had done. He had changed so much over the last few years. Despite being a little cocky, his heart had been good at first. At one time, he'd truly desired to shepherd his flock.

Aaron's voice filled the living room. She raised her head from her chore. He wasn't there. She was losing it. He was in Almonte, singing at a concert. The lyrics from one of The Light's biggest hits filled the air around her.

> *Love whispers in my ear,*
> *Love whispers to my heart,*
> *Am I willing to hear*
> *You calling me home?*

Her first impulse was to steel herself against the emotion rising up. As a pastor's wife, she never allowed herself to show emotion because she worried people would think something was wrong. Sol had reinforced that view with his "appearances are everything" approach to life. She'd been wrong. Being vulnerable didn't make you weak. Faking it made you weak because you could never let anyone in. Today she'd needed Val, Janey, and Isobel. Lauren was happy she'd been able to bare her heart to them. Their friendship made Lauren stronger, gave her a better perspective of her life and the events in it. Lauren Grace did not have it all together and she needed people. Isobel and Janey liked her, wanted to be friends. Val had known her for years and hadn't run away.

"Yes, Lord, I'm willing to listen." She spoke the words softly as tears fell. She sniffed as Val came into the room.

"You okay?"

"Yeah, just having a moment." She blew her nose into a tissue. "Thanks for sending Isobel and Janey over."

"No problem. I'm sorry I couldn't get away. One of the new colourists had botched a colour job, and I was the only one left to fix it. Plus, another stylist called in sick." Val stared at the mess on the couch. "By the looks of things, you haven't found it. Would you have tucked it away? Maybe thrown it out?"

"The last time I remember seeing the USB stick, it was in the bag of Sol's personal effects." Lauren plopped on her clothing. "I can't believe Sol did this. I'm not sure I even knew him at the end."

Val rubbed circles on Lauren's back. "Is Lily looking in the stuff you left at her place?"

"Yes. Either way, I've got to go to Toronto. If she finds it, I need to get it or else I need to search every nook and cranny of her apartment until I do find it."

Val picked up a pair of jeans and neatly folded them. Moving onto a sweater, she made her way through the pile. Lauren sat and stared at the wall, retracing her steps after the accident and funeral. Most of that time was a blur. She could have done anything with it and not remember.

Her phone buzzed in her jeans pocket. Her sister's face came up on the screen. Val stopped folding.

> **Lily: Can't find it.** ☹

> **Lauren: Did you check all the boxes?**

> **Lily: Yes. What now?**

> **Lauren: I'll be home tomorrow at lunch. I got time off work.**

> **Lily: See U. we'll find it.**

> **Lauren: <thumbs up emoji>**

"By the look on your face, I take it she didn't have good news." Val set the pile of folded clothes on the coffee table.

"Nope." Lauren tossed the phone on the couch. "What happens if I can't find it?"

Val squeezed her knee. "We'll worry about it only after we've searched under every rock and in every crevice."

The "we" in Val's sentence didn't go unnoticed. It wasn't Val's problem, but her friend was all in. Lauren wasn't alone. "Thanks, Val. You're a good friend." Lauren hugged her.

After throwing in the rest of the clothes and ignoring the protest from Val for not folding them, Lauren sealed the box. "I should pack."

"How long will you be gone?"

"I asked for a week off work."

Val lifted the box from Lauren's hands. "You're coming back?"

"You can't get rid of me that easily."

Val didn't need to worry. Ottawa, the community centre, and her new friends were her life now. She'd found her second chance, and she wasn't going to give it up without a fight. And maybe Aaron could be a part of it, too.

Lauren stared at the ceiling of the living room. It was after 11:00 PM and sleep was elusive. Her phone bounced on the coffee table. Aaron. "Hello."

"Hi. I'm sorry to call so late... I was thinking of you and thought I'd call and say hello."

He'd been thinking of her. She smiled despite the day she'd had. "Did you just finish a show?"

"Yeah. I was called back for the encore. So, this is a little later than I'm usually done."

"It was nice you were included in the encore. Are things going well?"

"They are. It's been kinda fun."

"That's great."

"Is everything okay? You sound kinda down."

Lauren didn't want to sour his mood. She hesitated.

"Spill it. I can hear it in your voice. What's wrong?"

She gave in and filled him in on her day.

"Wow. I'm so sorry, Lauren."

"Actually, as I was listening to music, one of your old hits came on. It got me thinking."

"I'm intrigued."

"Maybe I've been wrong about a few things. God hasn't abandoned me. And maybe I was wrong about you, too. I'm sorry I judged you."

"I appreciate the apology. I understand where you're coming from." His deep voice warmed. "I'm so glad you've seen the light."

"That's a really corny joke." But she couldn't stop the smile.

"So many have told it to me, I couldn't resist."

"I'm heading to Toronto tomorrow."

"I'll pray you find it. It's going to be okay."

He said goodbye, and she stared once again at the ceiling in the silence. She needed to trust that God was in control. Whatever the outcome. She closed her eyes and let the night close in around her. For the first time in a long time, Lauren felt calm.

LILY'S ARMS TIGHTENED AROUND Lauren as she tried to wiggle out of her sister's grip.

"Hey," Lauren mumbled into her sister's sweater, "you're suffocating me. I've only been away a few months."

Lily finally let go and they walked into her sister's semi-detached house arm-in-arm. The space opened up into a welcoming living room—blanket draped over the loveseat, magazines on the coffee table. Lily's house was comfortable and cozy, even though she wasn't home much. Lauren had missed her sister.

"Ready to get to work?" Lily asked. "I've grabbed the boxes from the basement." She pointed to a stack in the corner.

Lauren sighed. "Yeah. Is that all there is?"

At Lily's nod, Lauren surveyed the stack. "Okay, let's get going." She pulled a box down.

For the next few hours, they sorted through the boxes but came up empty. Lauren sat back on her heels and studied the room. Lily had gone in search of supper.

Lauren went through her memories of the days after the crash for what felt like the thousandth time. She wouldn't have trashed the bag because it had a Rolex in it. Sol had said it was a gift from a board member. Questions welled up in Lauren. She forced them away. What was done was done.

She remembered she hadn't taken anything out of the bag. At the time, she'd been too exhausted and grief-stricken to do so.

Only one box remained. She'd purposely left it to last. It was a small decorated box she kept mementos and old letters in. It wouldn't be in there. Before she could stop herself, she tugged it toward herself. Opening it, she rummaged around. No USB. Her fingers landed on a single page of notebook paper.

Lauren's List of Rules for Pastors' Wives.

   1. *Never fidget.*

   2. *Don't criticize the sermon.*

   3. *Appearances are everything.*

   4. *Never admit your weaknesses.*

   5. *Dancing isn't allowed.*

   6. *Don't complain.*

She crumpled the paper. The day she'd written the list had been awful. She'd been compiling the items in her head since she'd become a pastor's wife, but that day she'd felt like an utter failure.

The board chair's wife had sat her down for a "friendly" chat. The talk had proceeded to list everything Lauren was doing wrong. Humiliated, Lauren had sworn to herself that she'd never be in that position again.

"I ordered Chinese." Lily interrupted Lauren's memory. "What's that?"

Lauren shoved the paper into her back pocket. "Nothing. Garbage." It was past history—one Lauren wanted to forget.

LAUREN STRODE THROUGH YORKDALE Mall like she was on a mission. Lily huffed beside her. "Slow down. This isn't a race."

"Sorry. My brain is going a mile a minute and I guess my feet are trying to keep up." She had reluctantly agreed to a quick break to go shopping with Lily.

"What are you thinking? Are you worrying you won't find the stick?" Lily motioned to a bench and plopped down.

Lauren sat, although she wanted to keep moving. She pulled the list out of her back pocket and dropped it in Lily's lap. "I found this while I was searching for the USB."

Lily read the items on the list. "I've always been curious why you married him. I could never figure it out. You, of all people, had these big dreams of travelling and earning a degree, and you ditched them when Sol appeared."

"Why didn't you say anything?"

Lily laid her hand over Lauren's. "Would you have listened?"

"Probably not." What if Lily had spoken up? Lauren's life might have been totally different. She shoved the thought away. The what ifs would kill you. She couldn't play that game with herself.

"You would have been mad at me. I was afraid to lose you more than I already had."

"You didn't lose me." Yet Lauren had dropped everything for Sol.

"Why did you give up your dreams?"

"I didn't realize I was giving them up. I naively thought we'd pursue them together. In the end, we only followed Sol's dreams."

"You never saw…the manipulation?"

"I justified it, telling myself I desired what he did. He wooed me and told me he wanted me to himself. I was flattered. He made me feel seen in those early days. I wasn't just the pastor's wife."

Lily lifted an eyebrow. "That's ironic."

Lauren didn't need to be reminded. After Sol became a mega church pastor, she was only seen as his wife.

"Hey, maybe now's your second chance—to follow your dreams, meet a guy."

Aaron flashed through Lauren's mind. Stop. She shut down the thought.

Lily narrowed her eyes, zoning in on Lauren. "You met someone. Who is it?"

"No, it's not like that." Heat crawled up her neck, pooling in her cheeks. Maybe because her face was a traitor. "It's nothing."

"Is it the judge from the competition? Aaron Miles Scott? Val thinks there are sparks between you two." Lily leaned in, examining Lauren's face. "Ooo. It is."

Val. Lauren might have to have a talk with her friend. "There's nothing going on. He's a nice guy. End of story." Even as she spoke, her cheek tingled where Aaron had kissed it.

"He's gorgeous and talented. Val said he's super nice. Why *isn't* something going on?"

"Because the last time I got mixed up with a man who came across as charming, was a rockstar—in the pastoral sense—and claimed to follow Jesus, I lost myself. You just said so."

"No. Sol was different. He was always full of himself. Maybe he was different at first, but if you look at his life at the end, there was no fruit. He kept you down. You were his ornamental wife. That's wrong on so many levels. Aaron doesn't sound like that if what I hear is true." Lily nudged her with her elbow. "Rumour has it that he even got you up singing. You never would have done that a year ago." Lauren fiddled with the handle of a shopping bag. "It doesn't matter."

Lily eyed her. "You've had it tough. Don't give up. Aaron might surprise you."

"Maybe." Truth be told, Aaron had already surprised her. Still, Lauren didn't want to get her hopes up. She stood. "Let's get that baby shower gift. I need to get back and look for that stick."

Lily's words bounced around Lauren's head the rest of the time they were at the mall. Maybe Aaron was different than Sol, but Lauren wasn't sure she could risk her heart again even if she wanted to.

Chapter Thirty-One

THE WORSHIP TEAM HAD just finished practicing when Aaron spotted Ryan walking into the sanctuary. Aaron groaned softly. He was back for the weekend to lead worship. Saturday was practice and Aaron wanted to get home and crash. It was a grueling schedule: doing concerts Thursday and Friday, then driving back to Ottawa for worship on the weekends. He'd only been doing it for a few weeks and he was already tired.

And now he had to deal with Ryan. The guy had been ignoring Aaron's texts. Not so nice words ran through his mind. *Stop. Help me to be kind, Lord, because I'm not feeling it right now.*

Aaron waved goodbye to the other team members. A few stopped to talk to Ryan. Others left by another door. Were they avoiding him?

"Ryan."

"You called; I came. Obedient enough for you?" Ryan scowled.

Ignoring the jibe, Aaron pointed toward his office. Ryan was in a mood.

"Another command. I will obey like a good little soldier." Sarcasm dripped from the words.

Aaron clamped his jaw tight. Maybe he needed reinforcements? "Wait. Let me send a quick text." He pulled out his phone. He knew Will was in the building setting up for a youth event in the evening.

Aaron finished the text before waving Ryan forward. They sat as Will entered.

"Thanks for joining us, Will." Their eyes met and Will nodded.

Ryan's brows furrowed. "What are you doing here?"

Will popped a peanut in his mouth from a package he held and took the seat next to Ryan. "I was invited." That was the only explanation Will gave. Will's easygoing vibe often hid his shrewd wisdom.

"Ryan, I—we—wanted to talk to you about returning to the worship team." Aaron leaned back in the chair across from the two, trying to appear nonchalant and not give away the fact he felt like throwing up.

Ryan leaned forward. "You're going to let me return." He finger-quoted "let me."

"First, I want to clear up a few things. Did you spread rumours about me?" Aaron relayed what he'd heard at the community centre and in the parking lot.

Ryan shifted slightly. "I can't control what people say about you, especially if it's factual."

Will raised a brow. "It sounds like you're undermining Aaron's authority."

"Sounds like his inexperience as a leader is what people are talking about. That and his reputation from his band days." Ryan lifted a shoulder and dropped it.

His casual attitude irked Aaron. He ground his teeth as Will subtly shook his head. It wasn't worth losing his temper.

"What I'm hearing is that even though there's gossip going around, and your name's attached to it, you don't know anything?" Will clarified. Thank God he'd asked the man to sit in.

"Shouldn't believe everything you hear." Ryan stood. "Are we done? Email me the new schedule."

Aaron rose too, his nostrils flaring. He breathed deeply. "Yeah, we're done. Unfortunately, you're finished with the worship team for now."

The cockiness dropped from Ryan's face, which turned to granite. "What did you say?"

"You're off worship, Ryan. This time off hasn't changed your attitude or perspective one iota. You're defiant, rude, and I can't use you on the team because you're not a team player. You haven't even come to church."

"Are you checking up on me?" Ryan's voice rose.

"Worship is spending time with God. In your weeks off, I saw online you went to the beach, you partied at a friend's house, and you attended a Rough Rider's game. Not once did you set foot in here unless you had to meet with me. Not one week in four was it a priority for you to worship with other believers. I'm not saying you have to come to church every time the building is open. However,

God does ask us to meet with his people regularly. Your absence speaks louder than anything you can say."

"What I'm hearing is that you're spying on me. You're jealous of anyone who threatens you." Ryan smiled smugly. "I'm not the one done here. You, washed-up boy band has-been... You're the one who's done." He stormed out of the office.

"That went extremely well." Will scrubbed his hands over his face. "Kudos to you for doing what nobody else has had the courage to do, tell Ryan no, hold him accountable."

"Lot of good it's done. He's distancing himself from God."

"No. It's eventually going to make him take a look at his heart."

"That's a very Pollyanna view."

"I'm serious. It's tough love. Everyone is intimidated by him. Except Ed and me of course. And now you. The exception is that you're in a position to do something. And you did. Bravo!"

"I might not be in that position after Ed finds out." Aaron ran his hand over his head. What a mess. "Boss-man wanted us to work it out. When Ryan lied, I couldn't do it. Working with a liar doesn't work. Plus, he's self-centred and selfish. I need to see a lot more maturity there before he leads again." Aaron picked up a guitar pick and rubbed it, the smoothness soothing. "That kid is divisive and he'll tear the worship teams apart if he's given the opportunity. I'm not going to let that happen."

"Good for you. I'm impressed, and you know, *that's* what counts." Will clapped Aaron's shoulder. "Thanks for the invite. Entertaining as always, 'Mr. Washed-Up Boy Band Has-Been'." Will's grin widened. "Could he use any more compound words?"

"Thanks for having my back."

"Anytime." He slipped out the door.

Aaron stared at the window. Although Will might have his back, Aaron wasn't confident of Ed's reaction. His boss seemed to have a soft spot for Ryan. Guess there was only one way to find out. Aaron headed to Ed's office, the acid from the little tea he'd drank burning his throat.

Chapter Thirty-Two

LAUREN STARED AT THE ceiling, lying corpse-like across the bed in Lily's guestroom. How could a plastic bag disappear? Poof. It had vanished into thin air. In a last desperate attempt, they'd asked Penny to look around at the church. The woman had covertly searched the washrooms, the lost and found, and anywhere else a small bag could fall. Nothing.

Lauren swung her legs over the side of the bed, shivering in the cold air. Fall had descended on Toronto. She opened the closet, hoping to find the extra housecoat she'd seen earlier. Soft terry cloth met her fingers and she tugged it off the hangar. After slipping it on, she wrapped it snuggly around her. Her hand slipped into the big pockets only to find one pocket full. She pulled out the plastic bag containing Sol's wallet, his watch, and the USB stick.

Lauren stared at the items in the bag. She held it up to the light and turned it around, her heart beating erratically.

Thank you, Jesus. Eyes burning, Lauren sank to her knees. Yet another example of God's kindness.

I've been right here all this time. If you could feel truth, Lauren felt it, all the way to her soul.

"Good morning. Do you want to go out for breakfast... Lauren?"

Lauren whirled to see her sister standing in the doorway.

"Is that...?" Lily's eyes widened as she pointed at what Lauren held.

"The USB stick," Lauren whispered, afraid if she spoke too loudly, it would disappear.

"Where did you find it?" Lily's voice squeaked.

"In the pocket of this housecoat." Lauren rubbed at the now empty pocket. "I remember now. The police dropped it off here when I was dressing for the funeral, and I stuffed it in the pocket. After overhearing the cheating stories at the funeral, I was completely flustered."

"Overhearing cheating stories can do that to you."

"Today I was cold and remembered the housecoat."

"Thank you, Jesus." Lily lifted her hands and her face to the ceiling.

Lauren fingered the items through the plastic. Unbidden, doubt replaced the relief. "What was the point of losing it in the first place?" She hated that she even asked the question. "I want to understand and lately everything is confusing."

"You've been through a lot and this was brutal. Maybe it was God's way of showing his faithfulness. That you aren't lost to him."

That made sense. God had been revealing his hand at work in her life through all of this. "You're right."

"And Sol?"

"What about Sol?"

"I don't think you can move forward without first dealing with what he did and what you've gone through. It's been a traumatic year."

That she could agree on with her sister. "I'm trying to forgive him. It's hard." She forced a smile and shook the bag. "Right now, I just want to celebrate that I found it. I'm calling Hulk at the CRA right now."

"Hulk?"

Lauren chuckled. "It's the nickname I've given the one cop. He's massive."

Lily stared at her.

Lauren smiled sheepishly as she picked up her phone from the bedside table. "You have to have seen him."

Glad for the change of topic, Lauren dialed the officer's number. She knew she'd have to deal with forgiving Sol and herself, but not today.

Chapter Thirty-Three

Aaron paced the waiting area at the local TV news station while keeping his eyes glued to the entryway. Lauren was back from Toronto and scheduled to do this follow-up interview about the competition. He wiped his sweaty palms on his faded jeans. What was wrong with him? It hadn't been that long since since he'd last seen her.

He halted his pacing as voices drew near, recognizing one voice in particular. Lauren walked in, looking rested and peaceful. "Hey, you're back." His lips curved up as his heart did a drumroll in his chest at the sight of her. Before he thought better of it, he pulled her into a hug, then let her go far quicker than he wanted.

Face flushed, she swiped her hair behind her shoulders. "I got in last night and passed out shortly after."

"It had to have been a pretty stressful week."

Lauren shed her light jacket. "Maybe now I can move forward with my life."

"I'm sorry you had to go through that. I can't imagine how difficult it must be to be betrayed on so many levels by the person you were married to."

She bit her bottom lip. "There are days I doubt I really knew Sol." Shaking her head, her hair swaying, she said, "I want to forget it."

"Sorry, I'm not trying to bring up bad memories. If you want to talk to someone, there's a good therapist on staff at the church." Even as the words left his mouth, Aaron cringed inwardly. *Hypocrite.*

Lauren stared at a stack of magazines sitting on a circular table. "Maybe."

The intern poked her head in the door, interrupting the awkward silence. "Five minutes."

"Have you ever been to a therapist?" Lauren pulled sheets from her large tote bag.

"When my cousin died, I was messed up. I saw a grief therapist for a year. He helped me deal with my feelings and take one day at a time." Aaron never spoke about this with anyone. While his therapist had helped him move forward, Aaron hadn't been able to let go of the guilt. He probably should have stuck it out longer.

"How did your cousin die?"

The words hit him like a sucker punch, the air whooshing out of his body. He sucked in a long breath. "He overdosed," he rasped. Aaron closed his eyes. What had possessed him to blurt that out?

Lauren covered her mouth with her hand then dropped it. "Oh, my goodness. That's awful."

That was an understatement. He wondered what she'd say if she knew the part he played in it all.

She waited a beat. When he didn't add to the conversation, she spoke. "When do you finish with the fair tour? Honestly, I'm surprised you're here today."

"Only a few more weeks left. This week we're in Tweed. So, I was able to come home for a few days. This is worse than touring with The Light," he half-joked. Maybe he was just getting old. And he'd missed Lauren. It had been a priority to be here today, mainly so he could see her. His heart was in so much trouble.

"Did you miss performing?"

"I love engaging with an audience—listening to them sing and worship. Now I get to do that every Sunday, although it's different. However, it's been hard to leave. I was just starting to get the hang of things, and then I had to tear myself away. Not that I'm not grateful for this opportunity." To complicate matters, Ryan was an issue. Thought of the trouble the kid could cause while Aaron was away kept him awake at night. "I'm sorry I wasn't around to help you with the search for the USB stick."

"No worries. You couldn't have done anything."

Maybe. Still, he wanted to be there for her. Her late husband had let her down so many times. Lauren didn't deserve that. Aaron wanted to be a better man for her.

Chapter Thirty-Four

LAUREN CLUTCHED HER HANDBAG as she weaved through the waves of people entering Cartwright Community Church. She regretted her earlier idea to come with Val for Sunday service. It was different being here on a Sunday than for the competition. Lauren slowed her steps.

Val turned back. "Are you okay? You look as if you're going to pass out."

"I'm fine. Let's find a seat." She could do this.

They found seats near the back and Lauren settled in. Familiarity washed over her as she stared at the stage, with its piano, drum kit, and guitars sitting there, waiting for the musicians. Her shoulders eased down an inch. After her conversations with Lily and Aaron about dealing with her past, Lauren decided to take action and attend church. Maybe she could find answers here. It wasn't a bad place to start.

Curiosity influenced her decision as well. Pastor Ed was different than Sol. Lauren wanted to see him in action on a Sunday because she had a suspicion that the Ed she saw through the week was the same on Sunday. There were no pretenses. Even Will didn't have the ego she'd seen in many pastors through the years. No, these men from Cartwright cared for their people, reminding her of her dad. Pastor Ed's kindness had hooked her, reeling her in. And Isobel was becoming a friend.

Chatter filled the air as people greeted one another with handshakes and hugs. Sol had put a lot of stock in attendance numbers and being the best church. His competitiveness had stressed Lauren out. Nothing had been good enough for him. Church had become one more thing to achieve. God had seemed far off and silent. Lauren was looking for something different.

A girl's squeal of delight woke Lauren from her thoughts. She lifted her eyes in time to see the little girl jump into an older man's arms. She giggled—definitely a "poppa" from the sounds of it. Lauren smiled at the tender scene.

The worship band entered. This was Aaron's last Sunday until he returned from the tour. Taking his place at the centre mic, his guitar strapped over a navy T-shirt, and wearing dark jeans, he looked like a rocker. However, his genuine smile wasn't cocky, and a sense of humility came off him as he nodded to his band members. This was a much different Aaron Scott than the one who led The Light. Her heart sped up.

A woman stepped to the mic, welcoming everyone. The worship drew Lauren in, and she soon forgot about Aaron and concentrated on the lyrics of the songs and the music. All too soon, Pastor Ed took the stage, and the worship team left.

"Today, I want to start with a story about a prisoner. And that prisoner was me. Now, before anyone has a conniption, I wasn't in jail for a crime. I was a prisoner in my own mind. A friend, a brother in Christ, had done me wrong, and I justified in being angry. The world would say I had a right not to forgive. That's not true. Instead of being free of my anger and bitterness, I was caught up in ruminations of putting the person in his place. I imagined getting revenge. I was angry and bitter and complained to my wife ad nauseum. I was in my own private hell."

Lauren slouched a little lower in her seat. *Could you be more obvious, Lord?*

Sol's sins against her were wrong; yet she wasn't innocent either. It was exhausting being angry with him. She was miserable. All the good times they'd had had been buried under all the hurt, anger, and unforgiveness. Lauren didn't want that. There had been a time when she and Sol were deeply in love and anticipating the adventure of ministry.

If she didn't forgive Sol, how was she going to move on with her life? God had forgiven her when she didn't deserve it. Wasn't she called to do the same with Sol?

Val reached over and squeezed her hand. Gratefulness for her friend washed over her.

When Pastor Ed completed his message, he led the congregation in prayer. Lauren bowed her head. *Lord, help me to want to forgive Sol. And even though I don't feel like it, help me to do it with your power.*

Peace enveloped Lauren. She hadn't felt that in a long time, even before Sol's death. It wasn't going to happen overnight, but at least she felt like she'd made a positive step forward.

Lauren hurried out to Val's car, practicing yoga breathing techniques. The after-church conversations and crowds had always stressed her out. So, she'd abandoned Val, who chatted with a friend, for the fresh air. She wanted to think about what had transpired that morning at church. Sagging against the car, Lauren exhaled a long breath.

"Does it work?"

Lauren's eyes flew open at the familiar voice. "Wh—what?"

"Does that kind of breathing work?" Aaron imitated her.

"Um, yeah." Her laugh was breathless. Good grief. His presence did things to her.

"Church makes you that uncomfortable that you have to resort to breathing exercises and hiding out in the parking lot?" His light tone belied concern, not judgement. He leaned his forearms against the hood of the car. "You weren't exaggerating when you said you had issues with church."

Lauren hugged her arms around her midsection. "A little PTSD. I get triggered here on a Sunday morning. The sermon was a hard one to hear. Pastor Ed doesn't pull any punches."

"He's a straight shooter. Forgiveness sounds nice and we think it should be easy. However, it's not. We can't do it on our own. That's my experience at least." He stared across the parking lot, his focus elsewhere.

Lauren wished he'd open up about his own struggles. He'd let a little slip about his parents only being interested in his success.

And his cousin. Aaron had seemed broken up about that. Fame seemed to bring out the worst in people.

"It's a hard journey. I'm going to try though—to forgive Sol. Honestly, I didn't want to. I wanted to hold onto my anger."

He glanced down at her, sympathy lining his features. "That's totally understandable—and why we ask God for help. I can pray for you, if you're comfortable with that."

Lauren hesitated. Praying with another person was an intimate act. She hadn't prayed with Sol over the last few years. She hadn't been willing to let him see her heart. Swallowing hard, Lauren nodded. "I'd like that."

"Yeah?" He took her hand, his fingers entwining with hers, and bowed his head. As he prayed over her and for her, Lauren's racing mind and heart calmed. Worry over what people thought as they walked by left her. All too soon, Aaron finished. "Amen."

He held her hand a few seconds longer before letting it go, much to her disappointment. Had he felt it, too? The bond that wove around them as they prayed?

"Got lunch plans?" he asked.

"Peanut butter, lettuce, and mayo sandwich with potato chips."

Aaron grimaced. "What is that?"

"It's a sandwich. My mother always made them. It's very tasty."

Aaron faked a gag. "I'll take your word for it, but I think I can do better than that horror. A few of the worship team members are going to The Pit Stop. Do you want to join us? Val, too."

"Sounds fun." Lauren agreed as Val hurried toward them.

Aaron jangled his keys. "We'll meet you there."

Lauren opened the door to Val's car. Aaron wasn't the man who she'd imagined he was. He was kind, compassionate, and humble. The rockstar persona was completely gone—if it was ever there in the first place. She'd probably projected her own ideas onto him. People were late for things all the time. Yet she'd been unforgiving in that, too. Assumed the worst. Her own attitude and heart needed work.

However, her first priority was to sort through her feelings toward Sol before she ever could consider another relationship. Overwhelmed, she closed her eyes. *Help me.* Maybe the single life was best. Her infatuation with Aaron was just that, an infatuation. He was good-looking but also kind and made her feel seen, something Sol hadn't done in a long time. She'd get over her feelings. Right?

Chapter Thirty-Five

They picnicked in a nearby park, enjoying the golden sunshine on the mild fall day. Eleven girls and guys from the worship team and their partners, as well as Will and his family, sat around picnic tables, pulled together to form a long table. Aaron slipped on sunglasses and bit into his chicken pita wrap, enjoying the spice and garlic. Lauren, next to Val, sat across the table from him, the sun's rays reflecting off her hair. She'd done away with the pink tips. Thankful for his shades, Aaron couldn't look away from her. The woman was gorgeous no matter how she dressed or styled her hair.

Laughter erupted at the end of the table. Aaron focused on the rest of the group. Will stared back, a smirk on his face, suggesting Aaron's gawking hadn't gone unnoticed by his friend. Great. He ignored Will, only to find himself again watching Lauren laugh along with Val and the others. Her smile lit up her face and the world around her. Too bad she didn't do it more often. He wanted to be the guy who made her laugh. Taking a bite of his sandwich, he tried to think about something other than Lauren. Man, he was in so much trouble.

"What do you think, Aaron?" Will's voice cut through Aaron's reverie, bringing him to a skidding halt.

"Uh, sorry? Zoned out there." His ears prickled as they heated up. "What were you saying?"

Will laid out a few fish crackers for Matty, who sat on his lap. "Any embarrassing moments the frontman of The Light would like to share with us ordinary folk?"

"Too many to count." He licked sauce from his thumb.

"What? God's gift to music embarrassed himself?" The voice raised the hairs on Aaron's neck. Ryan stood at the end of the picnic table. Kelsey, another member of the worship team, stood beside him, holding bags of food. The muscles in Aaron's shoulders and neck pulled tight. Quiet settled as the air around the table charged. A few people glanced between Aaron and Ryan. Ed's suggestion to work it out blared like a foghorn in Aaron's head. "Care to join us? There's lots of room." He forced the words to sound light.

"Wouldn't want to crowd you, Band Boy."

Will set his soda on the table with a sharp thud. "That's enough, Ryan. What's your problem?"

Ryan's stepped away, palms up and facing out. "No problem." He and Kelsey walked to the far side of the park.

"What's with him?" Val asked.

Aaron twirled the straw in his soda. "Nothing. A disagreement is all." He stared at Ryan, the warning bells that had been going off in his head now pealing loud and clear. As he picked up his half-eaten sandwich, Aaron met Will's gaze. It reflected Aaron's own concern, which knotted his insides. Nothing good was going to come of this.

Honeysuckle wafted under Aaron's nose. His glanced up from the bed of his truck, where he'd been returning the blanket, they'd used as a tablecloth. It had provided a good excuse to avoid talking about Ryan. Lauren stood two feet away, her hands in her back pockets.

"What's up with Ryan?"

He secured the back of the truck. Guess he wasn't going to avoid the topic after all. "Worship stuff. Difference of opinions."

She toed the asphalt. "It sounded personal to me."

Aaron ran his hand over his mouth. "It's not. At least not on my end. He's not happy with me." He clamped his lips shut, having said too much.

"I understand you can't talk about it with everyone. I don't go to Cartwright and I understand ministry. So, if you need a friend to talk to, I'm here." She laid her hand on his forearm, sending a jolt of electricity up his arm. A small smile creased her lips. "Thanks for inviting me today. I had fun and enjoyed meeting everyone."

As she removed her hand, he grabbed it back, twining his fingers around hers. "You're welcome anytime. There are a few good people here." *Smooth, Scott.* He gave her fingers a squeeze before letting go.

"You might be right."

What looked like surprise crossed her face. Aaron wanted to say more, but he was at a loss for words, the feel of her hand in his warming his insides.

"When do you join up with the fair tour this week?"

"On Thursday."

"Good luck. I hope it goes well."

"Thanks." Although the thought of being away was less appealing than it once was. One of the reasons was standing in front of her. However, he couldn't tell her that.

She waved as she headed across the parking lot to where Val was parked.

"Wow. You're quite the ladies' man." Will strolled over to the truck.

"Were you eavesdropping?"

"Nope. I just happened upon the conversation. I mean, I thought you had game." Will patted the door to the passenger side. "Can you give me lift back to the church? Janey and I came in two separate vehicles."

"I'm not sure I should after that last comment," Aaron joked. "Also, you were misinformed."

"Obviously. Seriously, there's no denying the major chemistry between you two. You could set off fireworks with the heat you two have going."

"That's remarkable, since nothing is going on. Considering who her husband was, Lauren has issues to work through. Besides, I don't need the complication of a relationship right now, with Ryan, the album, and the fair tour."

"Lauren came to church this morning. That's gotta count for something."

Aaron pulled out of his parking spot. "Maybe." He didn't want to admit how his hopes had jumped at seeing Lauren there during the service.

"You think? She seemed into the worship…or maybe it was the leader."

Aaron tightened his grip on the steering wheel. "I don't want her to focus on me when she's at church. I want her to worship God."

"Who says she wasn't? If she isn't into church anymore, maybe she needs other reinforcements."

"Like me?"

Will lifted a hand. "Just saying."

"You're ridiculous. I never want to be the replacement for God in any relationship. It will never work." He sighed. "I don't want to be like her late husband or an idol for anyone. I've had enough of that. She needs to figure it out and if…" He held up his finger. "If anything was to happen between us, it would only be after that."

"Smart." Will held up his finger. "You two are good together. Mark my words."

His friend's words echoed in his mind. Aaron smiled to himself. He'd like it if he and Lauren were to end up together. Was that part of God's plan? That he didn't have an answer to.

Will jabbed at the radio button. "Ryan is a problem. I couldn't believe his hostility today in front of everyone. This could get ugly.

I don't trust the guy. This fair tour of yours can't be over soon enough."

Aaron swallowed. "I know. Only a few weeks to go." He would have to trust that God was in control of the situation and that Will and Ed had his back. Because it wasn't a question of *could*. It *would* get ugly.

Chapter Thirty-Six

Two Weeks Later

THE AJAX FAIRGROUNDS WERE like every other Aaron had been to. The aroma of popcorn and sugar tantalized his nose and tastebuds. He didn't dare eat that junk before a performance, although his stomach grumbled a protest. He'd arrived early for the sound check, and now he was putting in time before the show. It was the last week of the fair tour. By this time the following week, he'd be back in Ottawa, the tour only a memory.

The fall fair circuit had been enjoyable. It had been a long time since he'd done it with the band in their early days. Until their first album became a global hit. Although he should feel like a failure being back on the tour at almost thirty, Aaron didn't. Perhaps it was because he was over the big stadiums and arenas, where the people blended into a blob even if you could see past the lights. He was enjoying the more intimate concerts these venues provided. It had felt like church. As an added bonus, he had time to speak with fans, old and new, after the shows.

Unlike in his youth, Aaron knew that an album or tour was not what mattered. Being faithful with the gifts God had given was important, however his own success diminished. Witnessing kids use the church pantry to get food for their families was a wake-up call. Aaron's priorities had changed. It made him sick when kids and families didn't know where their next meal was coming from.

Aaron strode to the grandstand, where his sound check was happening. One of the roadies handed him the mic. Memories of Wade flooded him. He shook his head, hoping to shake away the thoughts. No time for that. Ignoring the buzzing of his phone in his pocket, he sang a chorus of an old rock tune. Picturing himself in front of the audience always calmed his nerves. If he could imagine it, he could do it. Whoever was on the phone could wait.

After the sound crew and roadies were done, Aaron headed to the trailer that was used for "the talent." The half-ton trailer hardly fit a band, but Aaron wasn't going to complain. It was air-conditioned and had a small bathroom. He sank into the small seat by the window and let the cold air cool him off. The mild fall had been a bonus to attendance at the concerts.

Although Jeremy had been right, Aaron wouldn't admit it to the man. The fall fair circuit had been great for Aaron. Miracle of miracles, he had felt at home on the stage. That hadn't happened since before Wade died. Leading worship at church was different than a concert. Unlike Lauren, who got triggered in church, Aaron had been okay on the church stage. It was on the concert stage with roaring crowds that had made him sick after Wade overdosed. Closing his eyes, he let himself imagine Lauren singing with him and then drifted off. A knock sounded, waking him from the short nap. "Half hour, Mr. Scott." One of the PAs for the 'talent' from the show called through the door. He wasn't considered that person any longer and Aaron didn't mind. Not one bit. He'd trade all the fame for peace and love.

"Thanks, Maisy." Aaron stretched, refreshed after his nap. He'd get dressed, tune his guitar, and be ready to go.

Jeremy intercepted Aaron on his way to the stage.

"Aaron, my man. Or should I say Superstar?"

"Jeremy, your use of hyperbole is outrageous as usual."

"I'm not exaggerating. The place is sold out tonight."

"That might have to do with a little band called The Douglas Family. They have the fastest climbing album in the country. Plus, they're from the area."

Jeremy wasn't fazed. "You're helping each other. The latest sales of your album have jumped too."

That was good news. "Thanks for coming. I gotta get on stage."

"We'll talk after. Good luck." Jeremy gave him a thumbs up.

Sound crew guys surrounded Aaron once he was in the wings of the grandstand. Fans screamed as the emcee introduced Aaron. He raised his brows at the noise as the mic guy fiddled with several knobs on Aaron's pack. Maybe Jeremy wasn't wrong.

The stage lights blinded Aaron as he walked onto the stage. He strummed his guitar as he welcomed the audience to the show. Finding his groove, he enjoyed engaging with the people and singing a number of old favourites.

Forty minutes later, perspiration streamed down Aaron's back. He didn't care. "For this last song, can we turn down the lights? I want to see everyone's face."

The crowd cheered. He strummed the melody of the Light's song "Hero." Singing the chorus, his eyes landed on a middle-aged couple near the front. His heart stuttered as he sang from muscle memory. His eyes trailed back to the couple—Wade's parents—his aunt and uncle. He couldn't end the song soon enough.

"Thanks, everyone. It's been great being here." Aaron hustled off the stage, tearing the mic off as soon as he got backstage. The tech helped with the wires as Aaron fidgeted with his guitar. It was a coincidence they were here. They didn't live that far away. Scurrying down the stairs, Aaron practically ran to the trailer to grab his bags and guitar case. He had to get out of there.

"Aaron."

Too late. Closing his eyes, he prayed for God to make him disappear. Too ashamed to face his aunt and uncle, Aaron hadn't spoken to them since Wade's funeral. Afraid of the fallout of his cousin's death.

Hearing their footsteps behind him, Aaron turned, forcing his lips into a smile. "This is a surprise."

"I'm glad we caught you." His aunt grabbed him in a bear hug and didn't let go, despite Aaron's tense shoulders. Eventually, he relaxed in her arms and managed to swing his free arm around her waist.

After his aunt released him, it was his uncle's turn to smother him.

"What are you doing here?" he rasped past the lump forcing its way up his throat.

"To see you of course." His aunt's smile lit up her face. "It's been so long, and when we saw an advertisement that you were playing, we had to come."

What?

"You should have called us... Did you think we didn't want to see you?" His aunt pulled her sweater closer as the breeze picked up.

Yes. Yes, he did.

"You should have called us...like four years ago. We've missed your ugly mug around the place." His uncle never beat around the bush.

Aaron hung his head. "I... I'm so sorry. After Wade died, I couldn't face you. I thought you'd be angry with me."

"Why would we be angry with you? We've missed you so much." His aunt squeezed his hand. "I'm sorry we didn't seek you out before this."

"We don't blame you, Aaron. We never have. Wade struggled with his mental health even before he went to work on the crew." His uncle motioned to a picnic table off to the side of the path. Aaron sat, his guitar resting against his leg. He couldn't wrap his mind around the words coming out of his aunt's and uncle's mouths.

"I had no idea." He and Wade had been tight. He'd thought they'd shared everything.

"Wade didn't want you to know. You were busy with the band and he didn't want anything to interfere with that. He asked us not to tell you. He had been seeing a therapist to help with the depression. However, it didn't stop him from experimenting with drugs and alcohol. Short-term, those things proved a quicker fix than therapy. He could be impatient. We didn't know how much pain he was in." Aunt Ella leaned her arms on the tabletop, her hands clasped tightly. "By the time he joined the crew, he seemed to be in a better spot. We didn't realize the addictions had taken hold."

"I promised to look out for him. I knew life on the road was hard. I shoulda—"

"Shoulda, coulda. You'll drive yourself nuts thinking that way. We know, because it took up the first year after Wade died. You weren't responsible for Wade. The only person you're responsible for is yourself. And Wade was responsible for Wade. Once we accepted that, it got a little easier. We could breathe again, but a parent never fully recovers from the death of a child." Uncle Daniel ran his hand through his dark beard.

"I wasn't a great role model. It may not have been my fault, but I didn't help matters."

"You were a kid yourself. You can't live like that. Don't you think Daniel and I have gone through every conversation and action wondering what we could have done differently?"

Aaron stared at the peeling paint on the picnic table. His aunt and uncle shared his struggles. They had coped and dealt with their loss while Aaron had hidden. Will was right.

"Let yourself off the hook, son. God created you to give music to the world. It gave us so much joy to see you sing tonight. We'd love to see you continue to live out your purpose. Wade would want that, too." Uncle Daniel tapped the table.

Aaron stared at his uncle. Wade had been a mini–Uncle Daniel in looks and in his easygoing personality. Apparently, Wade hadn't been as carefree as Aaron believed. The truth of his uncle's words seeped into his soul. Wade would want him to live.

"Do you have time to catch up? We'd love to grab a bite to eat with you and find out what's happening in your life." Aunt Ella smiled. "Are there any girls?"

His uncle rolled his eyes. "Ella, that's none of our business."

Aaron smiled, his mind on Lauren. He wished there was a girl. One in particular. "Sure, I have time. I'd love to grab a burger with you."

As he followed his uncle to the food area, Aaron sifted through their conversation. He had work to do. One thing was clear: Aaron needed to come clean with Ed about Wade as soon as he got back to Ottawa.

Cars lined the two lanes in front of the church offices, indicating a full house for the board meeting. As far as Aaron knew, there were no other scheduled events that Monday night. He'd taken the weekend off after arriving home from Ajax. He'd needed a few days to rest and process the visit with his aunt and uncle. However, the board meetings were mandatory for staff, at least the first half. Slowly opening his door, he stared at the building, ignoring that his whole body wanted to get back in his truck and drive away.

Will drove into a spot nearby and hopped out. "Hey, man. Good to see you. How was the tour?"

They fist bumped. "Great. I enjoyed it, but I'm glad I'm back to work full-time."

Will peered around the parking lot. "A lot of people here for a board meeting. What don't I know?"

"I've been away. So, don't ask me." Aaron fisted his fingers, then flexed them. Sweat popped out on his brow. "I have a bad feeling," Aaron muttered.

They strode in to find tense silence filling the boardroom. Aaron's breath whooshed out as his eyes locked with Ryan's, who sat off to the side along with his parents. The smug grin on the kid's face only made Aaron feel sicker. Will sucked in a breath beside Aaron.

Gwen greeted them, as did several board members and staff. Aaron found a seat at the opposite end of the room from where Ryan sat. Will sat in the chair beside him in a kind of "I've got your back" statement.

Aaron's phone dinged. A text from Ed.

> **Ed: Come to my office. Now.**

"I'll be right back," he whispered to Will.

He jogged to Ed's office, tamping down the rising panic. The man stood behind his desk, staring at the framed photos sitting on it. Aaron knocked before walking in. "What's up?" Sweat rolled down Aaron's spine

"Ryan showed up with his parents, and they wanted a tete-a-tete. We finished a few minutes ago. They don't think you gave Ryan a chance and are questioning your leadership. They believe your ego is blinding you to Ryan's musical and leadership ability. They think your celebrity status is a problem." He ran his hand over his head. "I told them I was aware of disagreements between you two. Ryan is demanding time with the board."

"Can they just show up and ask to talk to the board?"

"Yes. It's policy. It's not my favourite way to deal with issues, but it happens occasionally."

"I've gone out of my way to meet with Ryan and explain why he's been benched. He won't listen and the chip on his shoulder is a mile wide."

"I wanted to give you a heads-up along with a few minutes to collect your thoughts. You'll have the opportunity to tell your side."

"Was there anything else?" Aaron barely got the words out.

Ed raised an eyebrow. "We ran out of time." Ed picked up his Day-Timer and Aaron followed his boss to the boardroom. Will glanced at him and Aaron shook his head once.

Ed brought the meeting to order. After opening in prayer, he gave the floor to the young man. "Ryan has asked to address the board. As part of our policy, it is allowable. Ryan, you have five minutes." He glanced at his watch. The chance of Ed letting Ryan go beyond his few minutes was slim.

Ryan stood and glared at Aaron. "It's important that our leaders be upfront and honest. It's come to my attention that Aaron Scott lied about his past."

Aaron's phone dinged. As did several others in the room.

"I've had Christa text you photos we found, showing the kind of fraudster you hired as director of worship."

The photo staring at Aaron made his stomach roil. He hunched slightly as he gaped at the shots. Where did Ryan find these? Even Aaron had never seen them before. He squeezed the device, wishing he could make the image of him drinking and playing beer pong with Wade disappear. All eyes in the room bored into him. Before Aaron could respond, Ed interceded.

"Ryan, we're aware of Aaron's past mistakes. He told us in his interview. It's not a secret and it did make the news at the time."

Aaron let out a breath. *Thank you, Ed.*

Ryan nodded, the smirk never leaving his lips. "Did he mention his cousin Wade, the guy Aaron's partying with in these pictures?"

Aaron's heart stuttered. The skeleton he'd buried was being dragged out from the closet, bone by bone. "How—?"

Ed's brow furrowed. "I'm sorry. Who's Wade?"

Ryan jerked his head to Aaron. "His dead cousin. Ask him."

Ed lifted an eyebrow.

"How..." Aaron cleared his throat "Where did you get this information?"

"A buddy of mine has an older cousin, Dwayne, who knew Wade from college. They texted once in a while. Recently I met up with them both, and we got talking music and bands, and The Light came up. Let's say I was 'enlightened'."

Aaron fisted his hands. Dwayne—the reporter. He was sure it was the same guy.

Ed held up his hand. "Aaron, would you mind explaining?"

Tell the truth.

Aaron picked up the phone. Wade's slitted eyes and sloppy smile piercing his heart. An equally drunk Aaron was hanging off his cousin, red cup raised. He had no recollection of this party. Laying his phone face down, Aaron didn't raise his eyes to meet those he knew were staring at him. "My cousin Wade worked on the road crew for the band. As you know, a few news headlines broke that The Light partied. A lot. As I told the hiring committee, I was a part of that. What I didn't mention was that my cousin was also involved. In fact, we were often party buddies. Recently I found out he suffered from depression and was addicted to drugs and alcohol. He hid it from me. Frankly I was too preoccupied with my own life to notice his behaviour. Wade was drunk and high often—and not only at parties." Aaron swiped a hand over his mouth. "I saw the signs and ignored them because I was selfish. I cared more about my reputation than my cousin. The night Wade overdosed we were at a music producer's house. We had been in talks with a secular label, hoping we could widen our audience.

"I had been writing all day and didn't want to go to the party, but the guys convinced me to go. I grabbed Wade on the way. Once there, I realized we were in way over our heads. The mansion we were at was like a pharmacy and liquor store all rolled into one. To fit in, Wade and I did shots. After an hour, I suggested we leave. I was uncomfortable with the surroundings, and I had a tune that I wanted to write down. Wade refused. We had words and I left. I figured he'd take an Uber or get a ride with one of the other band members. I've regretted that decision every single day." Aaron closed his eyes. The phone call he received later was embedded in his memory. "The next thing I knew, the hospital was calling. Wade died alone in a bedroom at that producer's house because I abandoned him at a party we had no business being at. My selfishness… I can't help but wonder what would have happened if I'd dragged him home with me. I couldn't handle the guilt I felt every time I stepped onstage. So, I quit the band. Ryan's right. I'm not a person you want leading others, let alone in a church." His voice caught on the last word.

"I'm sorry I didn't say anything at the interview. I was scared and ashamed. The PR people buried the story. So, it never made the news. If I could redo that day, I would." Aaron met Ed's eyes. "I'm sorry." He picked up his phone and trudged out the door, his eyes focused on the ground. Ryan had won, but that didn't matter as much as disappointing Ed and the rest of the board. If only he'd told his boss sooner.

Aaron headed straight for his truck, not bothering to stop at his office. He'd clear it out later, after everyone had left. Or maybe the board would do it for him. He was done at Cartwright. The board would not keep him on staff. He yanked open the driver's door and hauled himself into his seat. The rumble of the engine got Aaron's attention, and he wheeled out of the parking lot, hoping to run away from not only the people in the boardroom but also his memories as well.

"THIS SEAT RESERVED?" Will stood at the end of the truck bed holding two coffee cups.

"What are you doing here?" Aaron scowled. Aaron had parked in the lot at Mooney's Bay Beach. At the late hour, the lot was empty, as was the beach.

"Could ask you the same question." His friend hauled himself into the bed, his weight bouncing Aaron slightly.

Aaron stared at the water lapping the shore.

Will handed a cup to Aaron. Sighing, he held the cup to his lips, the steam warming his face. "Anyone ever tell you to mind your own business?" He sipped the hot liquid.

Will popped the top on his own drink. "All the time. Still, you need to find a new place to go when you want to think or be alone."

Aaron had always come to the beach when he needed a break. Maybe he'd come here hoping Will would find him. He didn't really want to be alone with his thoughts.

"Why did you run out of there?"

"I hadn't told Ed or the hiring committee about Wade. I chickened out when the opportunity came up. Tonight, I could have told Ed in his office. I knew I should speak up. I figured he'd never hire a person like me... I didn't do my job and look after Wade.

How could anyone trust me to lead a whole worship team when I failed my own cousin?"

"Aaron, you weren't responsible for Wade's death. God has forgiven you. You need to forgive yourself."

"We fought. My last words to him were angry ones." Aaron frowned. "I should have protected him. I failed him in so many ways."

"None of us is perfect. People make mistakes."

"Wade paid for those mistakes."

"He'd hate how you live right now. Let him go. He's gone and punishing yourself will not bring him back. He knew you loved him."

"You don't think I've tried to get on with my life? I wish I—"

"Stop wishing. What's done is done. You can't do anything to change the past. There's only one who can redeem this. God specializes in second chances." Will tossed the dregs of his coffee onto the ground. Aaron stared at his own full cup, afraid he'd throw up if he drank any more. He set it carefully to the side.

"How is he gonna bring good from Wade's *death*?" Doubt filled his voice.

"I don't have that answer. Perhaps this secret coming out will finally help you deal with your shame and guilt so you can start to live. Or not. I don't know. Whatever the answer is, God's moving in your life. Open yourself to what he's asking of you. That's your job. He'll do the rest."

"I have no idea what he's asking me to do."

"Don't you?"

Aaron stared at his clasped hands. Did he?

"I guess I need to talk to Ed. Fill him in on everything."

"I think that's a good place to begin. Bringing Wade out into the light will make a huge difference for you."

Aaron tipped his head and stared at the pinpricks of light in the black velvet backdrop of the sky. Would spilling his feelings make a difference? Would coming clean rip the bandage off the wound that needed light and air to heal? He was going to find out.

Chapter Thirty-Seven

"What can I do for you, Aaron?"

Aaron held out the white envelope to Ed, who glanced at it before turning his attention back to his computer.

"If that's what I think it is, I'm not interested."

"It's for the best. It's only a matter of time before people demand it." Once word got out about his lies of omission and what happened at the meeting—and it would—people would call for it. Ryan wouldn't be wasting any time telling his version of the meeting. He'd probably use a megaphone. Add on the heaping of humiliation that Aaron had run out of the meeting like a little kid in trouble. A shudder coursed through his body at the memory.

"Have a seat." Not a request.

Aaron slumped into a chair. A tap sounded on the door.

Paul, a member of the board, walked in along with Will. Aaron's eyes narrowed. What was going on?

"Put that away, Aaron." Ed turned to the men who had entered the space. "Welcome, Paul. Thanks for coming in. Will, I know you're busy. I appreciate you making the time."

Ed gestured to the corner of the room, where four comfy chairs sat around a square table. They all sat.

"I figured you'd try to resign. So, I asked Paul to come in as well as Will since you guys are close. I'm not interested in your letter. What about you, Paul?"

"Nope. But that doesn't mean we can't talk about what happened."

Ed nodded. "Will, do the rest of the staff have a problem with Aaron?"

"Not that I know of."

"Good. We'll address it at staff meeting just in case."

"Aaron, why do you think resigning is the answer?" Paul leaned forward in his seat.

Aaron blew out an annoyed breath. "This isn't going to work. I lied. How can you even want me on staff? This will be a huge headache for you."

"We all make mistakes, son. Every one of us is on the wrong side of God. However, because of Jesus, we belong. We're his children. Keeping mum about Wade was not a wise choice, but we're all guilty of making poor decisions from time to time."

"I can see why you have troubles trusting people, Aaron. Still, you can trust the board and Ed." Paul folded his hands in his lap. "We're family—with all the good and the bad."

"I think you've punished yourself for what you did. So, there's no disciplinary action needed. There will be talk. What would you like to do about that, Aaron?"

Aaron stared at his boss. "I'd like to address it publicly. I want to save as much of the headache as possible for you."

"I appreciate that. Would you want to address the congregation on a Sunday morning or at a town hall?"

Aaron glanced at Will, who leaned forward. "Can I make a suggestion? For privacy, I think it should be a Sunday morning. Chances of alerting the press about a regular service are slim."

"I like that idea." Aaron could always count on his friend to have his back.

Ed wrote in his notebook. "Okay, sounds good. The other reason for Paul being here is to talk about setting up a mentorship group for the younger staff. Paul has set up a great group at his business, which has had a lot of success."

Aaron listened as Paul talked about ways to support each other and build in mentoring opportunities for the staff alongside the board. "We want to build strong, godly leaders." Paul finished.

"That sounds like an excellent idea. I'm in." Will nodded enthusiastically.

Aaron agreed.

Paul smiled before turning to Aaron. "Why don't you write music anymore?"

Aaron blinked at the topic change. "I'm washed up. I think I either had beginner's luck or my muse took a hike." His joke fell flat. "The song I wrote for the teen competition was a fluke."

"You know it's not luck. The muse you speak of is not a muse at all. It's the Holy Spirit." Ed poured four glasses of water and passed them around.

"He's punishing me for my selfishness and pride." The words were out before Aaron knew what he was saying. Relief washed over him as the burden of carrying around that worry and guilt lifted.

"Is he?" Paul lifted a brow.

It seemed obvious to Aaron—there hadn't been any new music or albums.

"Here's how I see it. You can't forgive yourself. Until you work that out, you're not writing any new music. The block is going to continue, but not because God is punishing you. He's waiting for you to accept his forgiveness and love. And for you to forgive yourself. Can you trust him with your life, with your past and your future? Trust him with your gifts? Why is it so important that you write music?"

Aaron stared at Paul. "It's what I do."

"Or is it who you think you are? Are you less in your mind's eye because you don't write music anymore?"

Yes. "I thought writing was a way I could make it up to God for letting Wade down. Letting my friends, my bandmates down." Aaron's nose burned and he sniffed.

"You can't make it up to God. Your past is gone in his eyes. You need to let it stop defining you. You aren't a musician first. You are a son of God. If he wants you to use his gifts, it's not transactional. Why don't we pray about this? And if you need to talk to me about it or you want to speak to the counsellor, I'd be happy to help." Ed bowed his head and led the group in prayer.

Warmth rushed through Aaron and his eyes stung. Other than Will's friendship, he'd never had this kind of care and love poured over him before. Gratitude welled up in his heart for this family that God had brought him to.

Afterward, they stood and shook hands. As Ed walked Aaron to his door, he said, "The board stayed late and we talked through Ryan's accusations. I relayed how you tried repeatedly to speak to him, but he wouldn't listen. You did as we asked concerning Ryan. His actions have consequences, too. I will be meeting with him and his parents. I'll try to provide extra support and friendship to the kid." He laid a hand on Aaron's shoulder.

"Those photos... I thought I was invincible back then."

"And now?" Ed asked

"No." Aaron shoved his hands into his jean pockets.

"I think your pride has been dealt with. Give me a call if you want to talk."

Aaron beelined to the staff exit. Ed's words echoed in his mind and through his heart. He truly had been given a second chance and he wasn't about to waste it.

Chapter Thirty-Eight

Lauren hummed as she mixed the chocolate chip cookie dough. She stopped the beaters and swung them away from the bowl. Maybe she'd take the cookies to work for the rest of the staff.

Val strolled into the kitchen. "Smells yummy in here." She swiped a finger along the side of the bowl, licking off the dough.

"Ew! You can get food poisoning from eating raw cookie dough, you know?" Lauren grimaced.

"Twenty plus years and still not sick." As she reached for the bowl a second time, Lauren yanked it away.

Val wiped her hand on the dishcloth before folding it neatly and laying it by the sink. "I asked Tony out."

Lauren forgot about the cookies. "I want details."

Val leaned her elbows on the counter. "I have tickets to the minor league hockey game against the Peterborough Petes. Tony is a big hockey fan. I decided instead of pining away, hoping he'd ask me, I'd take the bull by the horns as they say."

"And?" Lauren set down the wooden spoon.

"He said *yes*." Val's smile was a mile wide.

Lauren clapped her hands. "Yay. Good for you."

"I'm not sure he likes me that way, but we're friends and I'm actually okay with that. Will I be disappointed if nothing more happens? Maybe. But I'll deal with that if or when it happens. Right now, I'm just glad to spend some one-on-one time with him."

"You go, girl." Lauren wished she had half of Val's courage. Aaron scared her to death, or rather, the thought of a relationship did.

"Hey, the local business Chamber of Commerce is looking for items for their silent auction and gala in November. I belong to the group. Do you want to help me gather the items we've already got and brainstorm about more? I'm going around to the businesses that have already donated."

Lauren scooped a spoonful of dough onto a cookie sheet. "Sure. What kinds of things are they donating?"

"Services. Products. I donated a free haircut and style as well as a basket of products. The bookstore is giving a gift card. That sort of thing. Do you think Aaron would consider donating any Light memorabilia?"

"I have no idea, but it doesn't hurt to ask." She slipped the sheet into the oven.

"I'm glad you feel that way because I think you should ask him."

"Me? Why me? This is your idea."

"You have more powers of persuasion with the man." Val lifted her brows suggestively. "And I know he's given his time for the teen talent competition. So, it's a lot to ask him for this, except it could bring in serious cash for the charity."

Lauren pursed her lips. "It is a lot to ask, although he may not mind doing it for a good cause." Because Aaron was a great guy who wanted to help people whenever he could. "For the record, I don't have any more powers of persuasion with him than you do."

"Keep telling yourself that. Please ask him?" Val clasped her hands in front of her chest.

"Okay. I'll do it."

"Perfect. Thank you. Now I have to figure out what to wear on my date."

"Sweater and jeans. You'll be in an arena."

"Doesn't mean I can't be cute."

The timer dinged, signalling the cookies were done. Lauren pulled them from the oven, the sweet aroma filling the room. Gingerly grabbing two hot cookies off the tray, she quickly put them on a plate and followed Val to her room to help her chose an outfit for the game. Did she have pull over Aaron? Lauren wasn't sure if it was a good thing or if she should run away as fast as she could.

Chapter Thirty-Nine

Lauren poured herself a glass of milk and set another two cookies on a plate. Val had left for her date and Lauren was praying it would go well between her and Tony. She noticed a voicemail notification on her phone. She hit Play.

"Hi, it's Isobel. I wondered if you would be willing to help me decorate for a ladies' meeting at the church? I'm not that good at this kind of thing, and I could use some help. Plus, Ed is out and I'm lonely. Are you game?"

Isobel was lonely? How many nights had Lauren sat alone, waiting for Sol to return home from a meeting? Why would it be any different for Ed's wife? The woman had been honest about life not being perfect. Yet Lauren had put her in a box with the label *Perfect* on it. That wasn't fair. She hit the Call button.

"Hello." Isobel's cheery voice filled the air.

"Hi, um, it's Lauren."

"Hi Lauren. How are you? Did you receive my message?"

"I'd love to help." Lauren smiled even though Isobel couldn't see it. Suddenly she did want to help the woman.

"Wonderful. Can you come right away?"

"See you in ten minutes." Lauren shoved the phone into her purse. After grabbing a sweater, she hurried out the door. Maybe tonight she could help a lonely pastor's wife be less alone.

Isobel met Lauren at the front door. "I'm so happy you could come." Isobel's features were warm and welcoming. "The meeting is in the multipurpose room, and I got tasked with decorating with a fall theme." Isobel gestured to a heap of fall decorations sitting on a table. "I'm no good at centrepieces."

Lauren nodded. "I'm not sure I'm that great either, but between the two of us, surely, we can come up with something presentable."

Isobel chuckled. "I like the way you think."

They sorted through the items. Strings of leaves and sunflowers were put off to the side. Lauren collected all the vases that were on the tables. The sunflowers and greenery could be the main part of the centrepieces.

"Is Ed away a lot? Sol was out at least three or four nights a week." Lauren sucked in a breath as the truth dawned that not all those nights had been for work. She jabbed a stalk of wheat into the vase.

If Isobel noticed Lauren's aggressive arranging, she didn't let on. "Ed's gone a couple of nights a week. When the kids were young, we found it necessary to establish boundaries because he could have been out every night. We've kept those boundaries in place because our relationship is important, too."

"Smart." Lauren twisted twine around the vase.

"You look like I feel tonight—a little lost. Is everything okay?"

Lauren lifted a shoulder and let it drop. "Yeah, I guess... I don't know. I don't understand my life right now. Moving to Ottawa was supposed to be my second chance at life. It feels like I just brought the mess with me. And I don't know where God is or what I'm supposed to do." Lauren clamped her mouth shut. She hadn't meant to say all that.

"I can see why you'd think that. Because by the world's standards, it appears God's not close. We need to remember we stand on truth, not our feelings. And the truth is that God told us he wouldn't leave us. That's where faith comes in. We believe it's true even though everything is screaming that it's a lie. Feelings are nasty little devils. They make us believe they are the truth. But you know what gives them away? Feelings are fickle. The truth is solid. It doesn't waiver."

Lauren tapped her temple. "I know this in here. Yet it's hard to live out."

"Faith is challenging. It's hard to stand firm on what you know when you don't feel it. As I age, I'm realizing seasons change quicker than we think they will. Something good might be right around the corner."

Lauren eyed the woman. "And if not? There's no guarantee."

"You've lived this." Isobel straightened the tablecloth. "You're not alone. When we go through the hard stuff, God is right beside us even if we can't see him or won't acknowledge him." The older woman laid her hand over Lauren's. "If you'll let me, I'll walk beside you, too."

"It would be nice to have a friend who understands." Lauren's eyes filled with tears.

"Now, what is it you don't know what to do about?"

"Oh, it's nothing." Heat prickled Lauren's cheeks.

"It wouldn't happen to have anything to do with a handsome musician, would it?"

Lauren's eyes widened.

"It was hard to miss your chemistry when you sang that duet at the competition."

"Oh." Right, the duet. "I'm confused. And scared."

"Because of your late husband?"

"Yes. I'm afraid it will turn out the same. Maybe I'm a fool who gets sucked in by these successful men."

"Was Sol a success when you met?"

"No, but he had the same charisma as Aaron."

"Did he?"

Maybe? No, he didn't. Aaron wasn't self-serving. "No, I guess not."

Lauren bit her lip. Isobel seemed so at ease in her own skin. Lauren envied her that. "Do you worry Ed will ever...you know, have an affair?"

"No." Isobel's eyes met Lauren's. "We're accountable. We have access to each other's devices. It's more than checking over each other's shoulders. We've invested in and worked on our relationship. I enjoy hanging out with Ed and he doesn't mind my company either. We're friends. And he's a good kisser." Isobel winked.

Lauren laughed, more out of surprise that Isobel was so forthcoming. "It helps." Her smile faded as she remembered her marriage. They hadn't gone on dates because Sol was always busy with the board or members of the congregation. Or so she'd thought.

"Lauren?"

"Uh, sorry. You were saying?"

"Are you okay?"

If she wanted a friend, maybe Lauren needed to be truthful. "For Solomon, church came first. From what you're saying, Ed's different."

"It's learned behaviour. Ed unlearned it."

"Sol and I—our relationship was a business partnership built around God. At least near the end. He didn't have time for dates *with me*. And if I'm honest, I didn't want to put in the effort either."

"Neglect and rejection are big wounds. I'm sorry you had to go through that."

"It's jaded my thoughts on who God is—and the church." There, she'd admitted it out loud.

"That's totally understandable. Have you gone to counselling or spoken to a friend?"

"No. Part of me wants to move on, forget the past. I don't want to talk about it."

"If you ever do decide you want to speak to someone, I can recommend a great therapist."

Maybe she needed to talk to a person who would listen and have an unbiased approach. She didn't want to be alone. Yet fear wouldn't let her be vulnerable with others. With Aaron. She sucked in a small breath. She wanted to try with Aaron.

Isobel surveyed their work. "It looks awesome in here if I do say so myself. All the credit goes to you, my dear." Isobel swung her arm around Lauren's shoulder and gave her a squeeze. A warmth surged through Lauren and she smiled.

Lauren's phone buzzed and she pulled it out of her back pocket. Aaron.

"Hello."

"Hi, Lauren."

"Hey. Are you okay?"

"Yeah, I was hoping we could meet tomorrow?"

"Of course." Her heart flipped at the thought of seeing him again. "Would breakfast work?"

"I'll pick you up at 8:00. We can try that new diner in the neighbourhood."

"I'll see you in the morning." She smiled as she tucked her phone back into her pocket.

"Your young man?"

Lauren nodded.

Isobel didn't fish for any information on Aaron. The woman put her money where her mouth was. She didn't gossip. How refreshing to see people live out their beliefs. A small shard of Lauren's cynicism broke away.

Chapter Forty

Aaron spotted Lauren outside Val's apartment as he pulled into a spot right in front.

Lauren opened the passenger door. "That's service."

"Service with a smile." He pasted a cheesy grin on his face. She giggled. A warmth spread through his chest and he wanted to make her laugh repeatedly.

She buckled herself in before twisting slightly to face him, her eyebrows raised. "So…"

Okay. She was going there. "You want to know about Ryan's accusations," he guessed.

"I want to hear your side of the story."

Aaron told her everything.

"I'm sorry, Aaron. How awful."

Aaron stared out at the asphalt ahead of him as he drove, avoiding looking at her. "I've lived with the guilt of 'what if' for years. My life was a mess, too. I knew I wasn't living out what I was proclaiming from the stage. It was a problem. At the time, I didn't want to admit my own guilt in the mess I'd made of my life. I didn't want to be caught up in Wade's drama. We'd had a few scandals earlier with the band over drinking. I didn't need another mark against me, especially when we'd just won a Dove." Fame was messed up. "After he died, none of that mattered."

Aaron turned left into the diner's parking lot, pulling into a space at the back of the crowded lot. He dropped his hands into his lap. "My aunt and uncle showed up at the Ajax Fair one night I was performing." He told her about their visit. "It got me thinking, but when I got back for the board meeting, it all hit the fan. I ran. I was afraid that even if I did forgive myself, there would always be somebody there to fling it in my face, someone like Ryan. I thought, 'What's the point?' I'm always going to be guilty in someone's eyes." He stared out the front window at nothing in particular. "After speaking with Ed and praying, I feel like I've taken a major step forward. It's going to take time, but I'm moving in the right direction."

"I'm happy for you. I'm glad you got some closure." She scratched the side of her nose. "You could have told me about Wade."

He ran his palms over the leather steering wheel. "I know that now." He puffed out a breath. "We got off to such a rough start. I didn't want to add to my list of my perceived faults. I thought you saw me as another rockstar punk. I'm sorry I didn't trust you."

She ran a finger over the stitching of her sweatshirt's hem. "It kinda hurts that you didn't. I mean we did have a truce." She gave him a weak smile.

What was she getting at? "I'm not Solomon. I made a mistake, which I'm owning."

Aaron angled his body in the tight space to face her. He couldn't make her trust him, but he wished he could.

She nodded. "I'm hungry. Let's eat." Her hand on the door, she turned back to him. "Oh, I forgot. I was supposed to ask you if you would consider donating any memorabilia for the city's Chamber of Commerce Gala and Silent Auction."

"Oh. Uh, sure. I think I can do that."

"Great. I'll let Val know."

Aaron stared at her a minute longer, unsure where he stood. "Sure." They headed inside. The meal was awkward and he could feel Lauren distancing herself. Oh, she was friendly and that disappointed him because it wasn't what he was hoping for. He wanted a chance with this woman. He sighed after dropping her off at the community centre. The one thing he'd tried to avoid had happened. He'd fallen for a girl and his past had chased her away.

Chapter Forty-One

Lauren collected the music sheets off the piano as the young boy jumped up from the bench.

"Jerome, we're not finished. Please sit back down."

"Aw, Ms. Grace, I wanna play basketball."

Lauren glanced at her watch. Ten minutes left. "I'll make you a deal. Play the rhapsody piece without making more than three mistakes and I'll let you out early."

The kid's smile made his dimples show. "No sweat." He opened the book to the music. Lauren was sure the kid was a musical genius. He was already playing a couple of years ahead of his age. Jerome's fingers raced across the keys.

Lauren held up her hand. "Too fast. It's not a race."

Jerome sighed loudly before playing at the correct speed. He finished the piece with only two mistakes.

"Excellent, Jerome. You may go."

The kid grabbed his stuff and shot out of the room. Lauren laughed. She gathered her bag full of music and headed to her office to drop it off before heading home.

As she passed the basketball court, she cheered as Jerome made a basket. "Way to go, Jerome."

Will jogged over to her. "Hey, Lauren."

Lauren grinned. "I see you have your work cut out for you."

"This kid has so much energy." Will rolled his eyes. "Want to help?"

"Sorry, I'm done. I just spent an hour reigning that energy into piano lessons. What are you doing here?"

"Meeting Tony." He bounced the ball a couple of times. "Would you want to help out with the youth group at church?"

Lauren stole the ball away from Will. "I'm not sure I have anything to offer."

"If you play ball like that, that's all you need." He grabbed at the ball and missed as Lauren deked away. She shot and hooked it. All net.

"Yay, Ms. Grace!" Jerome fisted the air. She laughed.

"You're embarrassing me." Will laughed. "Volleyball was my game."

Lauren threw him the ball. He caught it and bounced it twice. "Think about it okay?"

"Maybe."

"And stop showing off." Will fake scowled.

She turned to leave.

"Aaron met with Ed and he's given the thumbs up for Aaron to return to work. Aaron may have made mistakes, but he's got a good heart. He's a good man. I thought you should know." He eyed her a moment before he sauntered over to the kids.

She hurried to the bus stop. Aaron had a great heart, but could she trust him? The doubt nagged her. To complicate matters further, there was that little fact that he worked at a church. She'd been there, done that. She didn't want to repeat her mistakes, and her mind told her that Aaron Miles Scott would be a big mistake.

Aaron stared at his phone, his fingers hovering over the keys. He had written at least five texts to Lauren and deleted every one. He hadn't seen or heard from her since their breakfast "date." He'd wanted to reach out but got the distinct impression he needed to give her space.

The feeling was no different now. Groaning, he put his phone on the coffee table. He had the items for the silent auction ready. He could use that as an excuse to see her.

No.

He ran his hands through his hair. Okay, Lord. Whatever you say.

Immediately the frustration and restlessness waned. He picked up his guitar, admiring the wood before setting it back down. What was the point? He'd just make his newfound peace vapourize. Despite his inner protests, Aaron picked it back up and strummed the strings. The vibrations resonated through him.

Yeah, maybe he just needed to do the deed. He sat on the couch, picking out an old hymn. He sang and played different worship songs and choruses. A few bars of a chorus came to him, and he played it a few times, adding to it. He grabbed his pen and notebook, scribbling down the notes. Soon several pages were filled with notes and a few lyrics. He laughed out loud. Thank you, Lord.

He played the song again. Even if it never saw the light of day, it was for him and God, and that was all that mattered.

Chapter Forty-Two

Lauren fingered the soft wool of the sky-blue sweater. Too bad she couldn't afford a new outfit on her limited budget. The women's department of the store was busy with Saturday shoppers. A faint floral scent wafted around her, the remnants of the perfume tester's spritz. A head of white-blonde hair in the next aisle caught Lauren's attention. She peeked around a rack of skirts. *No, it couldn't be.* She edged around another rack, removing the distance between them. *What was she doing here?* Focused on the woman perusing a rack of blouses, Lauren didn't see the low-lying table of pants. Instead of stealth, Lauren fell into a rack of jackets, several falling, their hangers clattering on the hardwood floor. The woman turned, then froze.

Lauren righted herself. "Hello, Brittany."

The woman, who'd had an affair with her husband, stepped back, her eyes wide. "Lauren." Her hand flew to her throat. "What are you doing here?"

"I live here now. What brings you to Ottawa?"

"Business trip." Brittany glanced around. Perhaps looking for an escape.

Lauren stood for a moment, not sure what to do or say. "I forgive you." The words spilled from her mouth.

Brittany looked like she'd been slapped. "What are you talking about?"

"I know Sol had an affair with you. It's not okay, but I forgive you."

The woman's face was the colour of a beet. "I don't need your forgiveness. Maybe if you had been a better wife, Sol wouldn't have been looking elsewhere." She shoved the blouse back on the rack before hurrying away.

Lauren stood mute. Val walked up to her, arms full of dresses to try on for the gala. "Why do you have that look on your face?"

"I just told the woman who Sol had an affair with that I forgive her."

"What? And?"

"She threw it back in my face. But you know what? I feel lighter having said it. If I don't forgive her and Sol, then I'm the one who'll suffer with bitterness and misery. I don't want that."

Val freed one arm and slung it around Lauren's shoulders. "Way to go. I'm so proud of you, girl."

The simple words had a lump forming in Lauren's throat.

"Let's go try these on, shall we?" Val turned toward the change rooms.

"I'm not sure I'm going to the gala. I don't have a date?"

Val spun to face her. "Only because you haven't asked." Val handed her a dress. "Try this one."

"It was weird between us when I saw him last."

"Make it unweird. You just need to communicate with him."

"I know." Lauren ran her fingers over the chiffon. "Maybe I'll go stag like you."

"I'm not taking a date because I'm on the committee and I'll be too busy."

"That's a lame excuse." Lauren headed to the dressing room, ending the conversation.

After dropping off Val at the salon, Lauren, feeling restless, drove out of the city until she came to a rest stop. An aged picnic table worn smooth from use sat in the middle of a small clearing. Dropping onto the bench, she leaned her head on her forearms, grateful for the solitude. An old pickup rumbled by, a large object rattling in its bed. Lauren tracked it until it disappeared. A light breeze whiffled through her hair. A sob rose up her throat. She tried to suppress it. Her eyes burned. Maybe if she let it out, she'd feel better. Tears flowed and she let them. For the first time in a long time, Lauren cried. She cried for the loss of her dreams—the children she'd never have with Sol and their non-existent future together. She cried for Sol because she didn't understand what had happened to him, and now, she never would. She cried for herself—what she'd lost and her bitterness and unforgiveness. And she cried because she was disappointed with God. This wasn't the life she'd planned.

After what could have been minutes or an hour, Lauren wasn't sure, she lifted her head. Fumbling in her pocket, Lauren's fingers latched onto a soft tissue. After blowing her nose, she wandered to the trash can near where she'd parked the car. A gust of wind blew her tissue out of her hand. As Lauren plucked the tissue off the ground, a smudge of pink amongst the beige stones caught her attention. Her fingers dug out the small trinket, a heart-shaped plastic charm from a kid's bracelet. *I love you* was written across it. Squeezing it in her palm, Lauren felt it imprint itself into her skin. Didn't the Bible mention that God had engraved his people into the palms of his hands? *God, do you see me?*

She opened her fingers and stared at the heart. A memory came of her mother drawing a heart into her small hand, telling her that even when Lauren was big and lived far away, her heart would still be close to her. She smiled at the thought. The imagined heart-prints turned into holes from the nails that kept Jesus on the cross because he loved her.

Isobel was right. Feelings were finicky, while truth held firm. God's feelings about her never wavered no matter what.

Her thoughts drifted to her conversation with Aaron. Like Wade, Sol's decisions were his own and in the past. She had to leave all the unknowns in God's hands or else she'd drive herself crazy.

Forgive him. She blew out a shaky breath. If she wanted to move forward and get her second chance, she needed to forgive Sol. Eyes burning, Lauren whispered, "I forgive you. God help me to forgive him." Another chunk of the stone heart she'd put in place fell away. Calm washed over her. She walked back to the picnic table and sank down on its seat.

The old truck that had been by before, passed by going in the opposite direction. It stopped on the side of the road. An older gentleman got out, swiping the ballcap off his head. His hobbled gait slowed him as he made his way over to her.

"Are you okay, Miss?" He gestured to his truck. "I saw you on my way to make my delivery. It was over an hour ago. Now, here I am again, and you're still here. Has your car broken down?"

Kindness emanated from his watery blue eyes. She smiled. "No, my car works perfectly. I'm enjoying some peace and quiet. Thank you though."

The man nodded slowly. "Alright. You enjoy the peace and I'll be on my way."

"Thank you for stopping." Lauren stood. "To make sure I was okay. I appreciate it."

"No trouble, Miss. We're supposed to take care of each other. Even strangers. Isn't that what it says in the Good Book?"

Lauren's smile split her face. "Indeed, it does."

He settled his cap on his head and walked to his truck. As he drove away, Lauren chuckled softly, her thumb rubbing the small trinket she held. Of all the bobbles she'd been given over the years, none were of more value than this little heart.

Thank you.

Dropping the heart into her pocket, Lauren walked to her car. The list of rules needed to go. She imagined tearing them up before setting fire to the scraps. Fresh starts called for new guidelines, not rules.

Guidelines for a Good Life #1: You are loved.

Chapter Forty-Three

A WEEK LATER, AARON stood at the sanctuary doors, shaking hands, greeting friends and strangers as they entered for the Sunday service. The family of five, all tall, enthusiastically shook his hand and thanked him for his transparency the previous weekend.

"I was a huge fan," admitted the mom, her cheeks turning a rosy colour. "We hope you feel welcome here at Cartwright. We're blessed to have you."

"Thank you. People have been kind." Aaron smiled. They walked away, leaving in their wake a brown-haired former pastor's wife.

"Lauren." Her name was a breath on his lips.

Her full pink lips lifted, mesmerizing him briefly. He forced his eyes up.

"Hi. I wasn't expecting to see you here… I mean, greeting at the door." She tucked a piece of hair behind her ear.

"My assignment this morning. Ellie's leading worship." He wiped his sweaty palms on his jeans, hoping Lauren wouldn't notice. Either way, she didn't offer her hand. He cleared his throat. "I'm glad you're here."

"Me too." Her eyes darted around the room, and she ran her hand up and down the length of her purse strap.

The desire to pull her near swamped him like a rogue wave. Instead, he jammed his hands into his back pockets, words fleeing, leaving him standing there like an idiot. Another family waited behind her. Lauren stepped aside, hesitating. If she stayed, he wanted to sit with her.

The request was on the tip of his tongue, but a check in his spirit held him back. Before he could change his mind, she gave a small wave, disappearing like a puff of smoke into the throng of people entering the sanctuary.

Aaron turned to the group of people waiting to greet him, tamping down the disappointment. He shook their hands, focusing on the mom and dad instead of the woman who had walked away. Resisting the urge to run after her, he welcomed the family. His intuition told him to leave Lauren be. Despite their shared chemistry, today Aaron would listen to that small voice. He was learning that ignoring it wasn't a good idea. After casting one last glance at the spot he'd last seen her, Aaron turned to shake hands with the elderly woman who stood in front of him.

TAP, TAP.

Aaron jogged to his front door, hoping that maybe Lauren stood on the other side. He flung it open. It wasn't Lauren.

"Hey, Val." He tried to keep the disappointment from his voice. "I'll get those items for you for the auction." He couldn't help glancing behind her, hoping her roommate was hiding in the hallway.

"No, she's not with me. Sorry." Val made a face.

He shook his head, not bothering to deny it. He grabbed the drumsticks and signed vinyl album. "Here you go."

She stared at the items. "Are those Tye's?" she whispered.

He chuckled. "Yup." He handed them to her. "You could bid on them."

She clutched them to her chest. "Maybe. Thank you so much for these." She seemed to shake herself out of her daze. "We really appreciate it."

"My pleasure." He hesitated. "He's single you know."

"Who?"

Aaron raised a brow. "Tye."

Val laughed. "Yeah, right." She headed to the door. "Don't tempt my daydreams."

"What happened to Tony?"

Her cheeks flamed. "Oh, you knew?"

"It was kinda obvious." He wasn't going to throw Lauren under the bus.

"We're better off as friends. We went out and it just didn't have the spark of romance."

"I'm sorry."

Val shrugged. "You win some; you lose some." She lifted the items. "Thanks again."

"You bet." He closed the door behind her and leaned against it. He sincerely hoped that Lauren wasn't one of his "lose some."

Chapter Forty-Four

Six Weeks Later

AARON STRUMMED HIS GUITAR, the melody of the new song filling the empty practice room at the church. He played the first verse again, adding the lyrics he'd written. He needed another line to complete the verse.

"Sounds good. New music?" Will strode into the room, a steaming coffee cup in his hand.

"Hey." Aaron leaned the guitar against his chair. "Yes."

"That's awesome, man. I can't wait to hear about it."

Aaron pointed to the cup of coffee. "Gwen made it fresh?"

"Yep. Better hurry before it's gone." He sipped loudly. "By the way, I have a couple new recruits for worship. Remember Jordan's friend Mike? He's a talented musician and he's been coming to church. He'd like to get involved."

"Great. Send him my way. I've been talking to Paul about mentoring new worship team members, especially the young ones. Mike would be perfect." Aaron hesitated. "He's the kid who came to use the pantry a while back, right?"

"Yeah. The whole family has started to come to church because of that. A few people have hired his dad to do work for them to help supplement his income until he gets a full-time job."

"That's amazing." Aaron headed out to the staff room with Will. "It never gets old." He wished Lauren could know about this. It might change her perspective on church. God was working through his people, at least at Cartwright.

He left Will at the youth room and followed the smell of fresh brewed coffee down the hall. Aaron hummed the tune he'd been working on. In the kitchenette, he poured himself a large mug and checked out the plate of cookies sitting on the counter.

Voices in the hall caught his attention. His heart leaped as he recognized Lauren's. He hadn't seen her much in the past month and a half, giving her space that he knew she needed.

Isobel accompanied her and both waved at him. He saluted with two fingers, drinking in the sight of Lauren. Gone were the dark circles under her eyes, and her skin glowed as if she'd just washed her face. Magnetism pulled between them, drawing him in. He stepped away, the opposite of what he wanted to do. Instead, he focused on the cookies and plucked two from the plate before heading to his office by a different route, avoiding the two women. Rounding the corner, he stopped short, his coffee sloshing over the edge. Lauren stood at his office door.

"Hey." He wiped at the drips of coffee.

She smiled. "Oh, hey."

Encouraged, he motioned to his office. "Want to come in?"

She nodded, and he followed her in, setting the dripping mug on his desk. "Have a seat." He wiped his fingers on a tissue and sat in his desk chair. She pointed to his guitar. "Were you practicing? I can come another time."

"It's okay. I was going over some new music."

"New music? As in you're writing?"

He smiled.

Her eyes widened. "Aaron, that's terrific!"

"It's been great actually. The truth is freeing." He smiled.

"I know. I've been seeing the counsellor here at Isobel's suggestion."

Right. Ed had mentioned the two were becoming friends. "How's that going?"

"Really well. It's helping me process the last couple of years...Uh, I have a favour to ask."

"What can I do for you?" He'd do anything for her.

"I wondered if you'd be interested in being a guest in one of my music classes at the community centre. I wanted to do a class on songwriting and thought maybe you could help me out." She pointed to the guitar. "Especially if you're writing again."

He pressed his lips together. Not what he'd been hoping for but better than not seeing her. "Let me know the date and I'll check my calendar."

A shadow flickered across her face and disappeared as quickly. Probably his imagination. "Sure, I'll check when I'm back in the office." She ran her hand along the handle of her tote. "And...

I wondered... I know it's late notice... But would you go to the Chamber of Commerce Gala and Silent Auction with me?"

Wait. What?

A rosy hue pooled in her cheeks. "If you're busy or not interested, don't worry about it."

He shot out a hand. "No. It's not that. I, uh, I'm definitely interested. I got the impression you needed your space. Maybe I needed time, too."

She nodded slowly. "And now?"

Aaron paused, calming his thoughts. He felt peaceful. A grin spread across his face. "It would be my pleasure to go with you." *Play it cool.* Who was he kidding? He'd lost that battle long ago.

Her full lips lifted. She was gorgeous when she smiled. Her countenance appeared brighter, too, like a shadow had passed by and now she stood fully in the light. "Excellent. It's Saturday."

"That's fine. I'm not busy." The words rushed from his lips.

She stood and motioned to the door. "Good. I should let you get back to work."

"Can I pick you up?"

Lauren smiled. "That would be nice."

"I'm looking forward to it. And let me know the date of the class."

Lauren waved as she headed down the hall and disappeared around the corner, leaving Aaron staring at an empty space. Lauren Grace had asked him out. Who would have guessed that would ever happen? Warmth exploded through him, and he pumped his fist. Inspired, he picked up his guitar and began strumming the melody he'd been playing before and added to it.

Chapter Forty-Five

Val draped a sheer shawl over Lauren's shoulders and pinned it together with a large round brooch. "Perfect. You're going to knock him out."

Lauren stared at her image in the mirror. Little black dress, heels, and hair swooped up in a loose bun, curly tendrils framing her face.

"Breathe. I'll answer the door." Val's voice trailed behind her as she hurried out of Lauren's room.

One last check in the mirror before she snapped up her clutch from the bed and headed out of the room. Aaron, dressed in dark pants, a blue button-down shirt, and a sports coat, stood chatting with Val. When Lauren entered, his attention reverted to her, his eyes widening. "You look amazing."

Lauren's heart leaped in her chest. Her cheeks warmed. "Thank you."

Aaron held out his elbow. "Ready?"

She nodded and tucked her hand in the crook of his elbow, relishing the heat emanating off his body.

"Have fun, kids." Val chuckled. "I'll see you there."

Lauren rolled her eyes. Aaron had parked right in front of her building. The gala was downtown and the traffic was light. He pulled into the lot and parked. He got out, opened her door, and helped her down. He didn't let go of her hand as they strolled to the foyer of the centre where it was being held. The feel of his hand against hers sent an electric jolt up her arm.

The hall was decorated nicely and they wandered through the silent auction items. Lauren noticed that the vinyl of The Light had a nice total going already.

She went to pick up a pen to bid on a pretty watercolour at the same time Aaron did. Their fingers brushed, and her eyes locked on his. She stared a minute too long.

"Do I have something on my face?" He rubbed his clean-shaven jaw, something Lauren's own fingers itched to do.

She cleared her throat, her eyes quickly darting to the stage. "No, you're good." So good. "Are you bidding?" She held out the pen to him.

"No, it's okay."

He took the pen from her and set it down. Lacing his fingers through hers, they wandered through the room. It was going to be a good night.

A JAZZ BAND PLAYED in the corner while servers went around with hors d'oeuvres and drinks. Lauren sighed contentedly.

"I've never really listened to much jazz. The band is incredible." Aaron sipped his drink.

"Doesn't it inspire you? I want to wring the music out of the kids at the community centre."

He grinned. "Do you now?"

Lauren smoothed her skirt. "Yes, I do." Her words came out breathy.

He leaned closer. "It does inspire me." He moved closer until his lips were so close she could feel his warm breath on her own.

"Oh?" she breathed the word.

His lips gently brushed hers. It lasted a second, but he managed to jolt her whole body into overdrive in that brief moment.

He leaned back, his eyes navy. "Wanna dance?" He set his drink on the tall bar table they stood beside and held out his hand. She slipped hers into his warm one and followed him to the dance floor. He brought her in close. "You aren't going to leave me standing here, are you?"

She laughed. "No. I'm sorry about that."

He chuckled against her ear. "As long as it doesn't happen tonight." His hand ran up and down her back, sending tingles along her spine. Maybe they could stay right here like this for the rest of the night. They danced for a long time, enjoying the music. Afterward, they chatted with Val before she had to run off to help a patron who'd lost their purse.

Aaron glanced around the ballroom. He slipped his arm around her. "There's a great little gelato place a couple of blocks from here. Feel like a sweet treat?" He leaned down and kissed her softly.

She nodded, her lips not obeying her mind. Sheesh. One little kiss and she was a mess. Aaron's smile had a tinge of a smirk. Did he know what his closeness did to her?

The evening was mild for October, and they took advantage of it, eating their ice cream as they strolled along the Rideau Canal. Lauren scooped the tart lemon gelato from her cup into her mouth. "So good."

Aaron wiped the corner of her mouth and licked the creamy sweetness from his thumb. "Mmm." He smiled mischievously. "You had a little dab."

She hid her smile behind her spoon. He didn't need any boosts to his ego, but the man was seriously making her swoon.

He pulled her over to a bench, and they sat, the dark night cocooning them in their own world.

"How do you feel about volunteering at the youth group?"

Lauren had taken Will up on his offer, after praying about it. "It's okay. Better than I thought. The kids are great and Will is incredible with them. Makes the youth leaders' jobs easier."

"Pretty sure you're good with them, too." He smiled. "No PTSD being back in a church setting?"

She set her empty cup beside her. "Going to therapy has really helped. Maybe we can both move forward now that we've dealt with our past. What do you think?"

He slipped his arm across the back of the bench, drawing her to him. "You want to get involved with a has-been rockstar and God guy? I believe you told me once—or maybe it was twice—that was off the table."

"I changed my mind." She leaned in an inch.

"You couldn't resist my charm?" He grinned.

"Yeah, that was it." She leaned in another inch.

Aaron gently caressed her jawline with his thumb, sending sparks over her skin. His fingers wove through her hair and cupped the back of her head, his breath a whisper against her lips. His mouth covered hers, and tingles ripped down her body to her toes. His other hand went around her waist, holding her close. Lauren slipped her arms up around his neck as she pressed into his chest. Time slipped away until Aaron eased back, his forehead touching hers. "I've waited a long time for this to happen."

Lauren smiled. "You've been thinking about kissing me? For how long?"

"Since you stared daggers at me at the radio station when we first met." His fingers skimmed along her neck.

"That made you want to kiss me?"

"Yup. Because you weren't fawning all over me. You didn't want anything to do with me. It was refreshing and I like a challenge." He ran his thumb over her bottom lip.

She ran her fingers up the back of his neck, into his hair. A shudder went through his body. She whispered against his ear. "I'm not sold yet. Perhaps you could be a little more persistent."

The corners of his eyes crinkled, and she felt his smile against her lips as he obediently embraced the challenge to convince her, thoroughly kissing her until her head spun.

"Did it work?"

"Absolutely." The word was more breath than anything else. She needed oxygen.

"Good." He fingered her necklace. "I wanted to ask you a question."

They sat in the green room behind the sanctuary. She hoped her face wasn't as green as the colour of the walls.

"Lauren." Aaron's voice brought her to the present and away from the rollercoaster her stomach had jumped on. "Ready?"

She swallowed hard. *You can do this, girl.* "My fingers are so sweaty they'll slip off the keys."

"The other musicians' instruments will cover if they do." He cupped her cheeks, gazing into her eyes. "Look at me. You've got this. I'll be right beside you."

As the musicians opened the door leading to the sanctuary, Will's voice filtered in. "Sign up at the...."

Aaron's blue eyes captured hers, giving her a boost of confidence to put one foot in front of the other. The lights blinded her as she sat at the grand piano. He stood near, his guitar slung across his torso. He spoke into the mic.

"As Pastor Ed said earlier, God wants nothing more than for us to come running home to him. He is a God of second chances. He's our champion. I wrote a song about it, and Lauren Grace and I are going to sing it for you."

Strumming the first strains of the song, he faced the congregation. Lauren set her fingers on the cool ivory keys, the guitar chords reverberating through her chest. Her fingers danced on the keys as her voice joined his, the lyrics coming from memory. Opening her eyes, Lauren couldn't see much beyond the lights. Instead, she focused on Aaron. Their voices mingled, harmonized, and a delicious tingle ran up her spine. Aaron's lyrics drew her to the throne of God. Everything stopped except the music. She pictured herself sitting at the feet of God while he stroked her hair. Another chunk of stone fell away from her heart. She slowed her fingers as Aaron sang the last verse. When he stopped strumming, she lifted her fingers off the keys. Their voices lifted, praising the God she'd thought had abandoned her. Yet he'd been beside her on each step of the journey. A father whose speciality was second chances. Redemption. It was the grandest love story of her life.

Acknowledgements

This book has taken four years to get into your hands. It has been written and rewritten, and rewritten. Many people helped to get it to its present form.

Thank you to my first reader, Trina Jones. Your honest feedback always make my stories better.

Thank you to my beta readers, Nicole and Marguerite. You've read so many versions of this book, you must be tired of it. Yet, I know if I asked you to read it again, you would cheerfully do so. Thank you.

Abigail Lance, Kristin Stringer and Pam Reeder, thank you for also beta reading this book from the pastors' wives point of view. Your insight was invaluable.

Thank you to Karin Beery for your critique that changed this book for the better.

Thank you to Sara Davison for your insight and encouragement.

Thank you to Stephanie Nickel for your editing prowess. You made this book so much better. It was a joy to work with you.

Thank you to Alison Christiansen for lending your expertise about fraud investigations. Any mistakes are my own.

Thank you to Yummy Book Covers for this fabulous cover. It thrills me every time I see it. You've captured Lauren and Aaron perfectly.

Thank you to Ian and Ben who always inspire me. You are both amazing men.

Thank you to Mark for reading a romance.

Thank you to my readers. There would be no book if not for you. Thank you for sharing my books, and talking about them with your friends and on socials. I appreciate each and every one of you.

About the Author

Jennifer lives in Ontario, Canada with her husband, two sons, and pet rabbit. She loves hearing from readers and talking about books to anyone who will listen. She is the author of the YA series, Wolf Kingdom, a retelling of Little Red Riding Hood and the award-winning Exit Stage Right. Keep in touch with Jennifer by visiting her website and to sign up for her newsletter for updates and book news at https://jenniferwillcock.com/

bookbub.com/profile/jennifer-willcock-87459ffd-509a-4658-b612-b244dca066ae

instagram.com/jenniferwillcock

g
goodreads.com/author/show/16322364.Jennifer_Willcock

Also By Jennifer

Read the first book Into the Forest: A Retelling of Little Red Riding Hood

What if the Wolf fell in love with Red Riding Hood?

Prince Teowulf, Crown Prince of Wolf Kingdom, believes the lessons of superiority he's learned from childhood until a chance encounter with a despised Forester, Jenna "Rider" Hood. Rider is the daughter of Dr. Hood, the premiere pharmacist of Wolf Kingdom, and she turns Prince Teo's world upside down, making him question everything he's ever believed about the Foresters. When sickness strikes the Wolf clan, Rider and Prince Teo must work together to save lives. But can they get past their own hate and prejudice to help others? Will the sparks between Rider and Teo fizzle or burst into flame?

Be sure to visit Jennifer's website to sign up for her newsletter (get a free story) and check out her other YA novels. Sign up at https://jenniferwillcock.com/

Made in the USA
Columbia, SC
13 February 2025